Definitions of Indefinable Things

Definitions of Indefinable Things

WHITNEY TAYLOR

Houghton Mifflin Harcourt

Boston New York

hmhco.com

The text was set in Adobe Caslon Pro.

The Library of Congress has cataloged the hardcover edition as follows:
Names: Taylor, Whitney, author.
Title: Definitions of indefinable things / Whitney Taylor.
Description: Boston ; New York : Houghton Mifflin Harcourt, 2017. | Summary: "Follows three teens in a small town whose lives intersect in ways they never expected, teaching them that there are no one-size-fits-all definitions of depression, friendship, and love."
—Provided by publisher.
Identifiers: LCCN 2016001796
Subjects: | CYAC: Depression, Mental—Fiction. | Friendship—Fiction. | Love—Fiction. | Youths' writings.
Classification: LCC PZ7.1.T395 De 2017 | DDC [Fic]—dc23
LC record available at https://lccn.loc.gov/2016001796

ISBN: 978-0-544-80504-0 hardcover
ISBN: 978-1-328-49801-4 paperback

Printed in the United States of America
DOC 10 9 8 7 6 5 4 3 2 1
4500746360

For Jamie, Haley, and Kasey—
Thanks for walking this tightrope with me.

CHAPTER one

NOTHING MADE ME WANT TO GET hit by a bus more than Tuesday night <u>happy pill</u> (see: Zoloft) runs. After a lengthy car ride with my mother, who spent all ten minutes singing a God-awful Christian melody and praying for the state of my wayward soul, I'd have to physically restrain my hands to keep myself from shoving the door open and rolling out onto the highway. Sometimes I prayed, too. That a piano would fall from the sky and crush my miserable, suburban existence. Or that God would set CVS on fire to spare me from having to choose between Mickey Mouse and Flintstones gummy vitamins. Since I was, quite unfortunately, still alive, I took it that God couldn't hear me over my mother's off-key rendition of "Amazing Grace." Or maybe he just didn't bother noticing the pitiful lives of Flashburn inhabitants at all.

Once we made it inside CVS, my mother always played this super annoying game of Find the Most Lame Thing and Force It on Reggie. She used to do this to my brother, Frankie, when she took him clothes shopping. Which probably explains why he turned out to be a sweater-vest-wearing, pleated-pants-enthusiast youth pastor five hundred miles away.

"Regina, look at this little notebook," she exclaimed right on cue, lifting up a composition journal with a cartoon duck on the front. "This would be perfect for you to journal in."

I rolled my eyes. "Great idea, Karen. I'll write about how much I hate baby ducks inside a baby duck. It'll be one giant eff you to ducks everywhere."

"Don't call me Karen," she scolded. "You know I don't like that. And don't insinuate curse words."

"Fine. I'll just say it outright next time."

She adjusted her cat-eye glasses and sighed. "I just thought it would be nice for you to have a journal so you can start writing your feelings down like Dr. Rachelle advised."

"What would be nice is if you and Dr. Rachelle stopped forcing activities on me like there's actually a chance in —" She raised both brows in a warning. "*Hades,* that I'll enjoy it."

"We just want you to be happy, sweetheart."

There was a difference between being happy and being

distracted, but I knew Karen wouldn't understand. And picking one of our signature <u>back-and-forths</u> (see: screaming matches) in the middle of the school supplies aisle seemed a bit melodramatic.

Somehow, I was able to break away from Karen with minimal objection. I was halfway through the store before she could call my name from the creams and ointment aisle, but when she did, it was something like, "Reggie, do you still have that pesky rash on your backside?"

I didn't respond. Needless to say, her fascination regarding the condition of my ass went unsatisfied. Set on autopilot, I ended up at the back of the store where the pharmacist was rearranging cases on a shelf. When she saw me, she smiled politely and moved to the counter.

"I'm here for a refill," I recited. "Reggie Mason. Zoloft."

She glanced at a sheet of paper. "Birthdate?"

"January ninth."

"Okay, that will be ready in about eight to ten minutes if you would like to wait around. Sorry for the delay. We've had an influx of orders with it being allergy season."

"That's all right. Thanks."

I'd started scanning for a place to sit when some guy practically shoved me to the side. "Excuse me, prescription refill for Prozac. Last name Eliot," he said to the pharmacist.

She nodded, marking the paper. "Birthdate?"

3

"December twelfth."

"That will be ten minutes if you would like to wait."

He turned and caught a glimpse of my vengeful stare. Brown hair hung loosely in front of his eyes, toppling over his ears. He had this stupid, diamond-shaped tattoo on the left side of his neck that looked like it was done by one of those wannabe tattoo artists who work from their garage and use bum needles that give people bacterial infections. His grungy THE RENEGADE DYSTOPIA band T-shirt crept out from behind his acid-washed jacket.

"That band sucks," I mumbled just as he was about to walk away.

He stopped directly in front of me. "Interesting observation," he responded; his raspy voice sounded like he was recovering from a nasty cold. "I find that their irreverence toward the norms of modern age grunge culture is kind of their appeal."

"Maybe to people who are so desperate to be original that they're actually more banal than everyone else."

He glanced down at the shirt with the stupid band. "You're right," he said, sliding his arms out the jacket.

"What are you doing?"

He lifted the shirt over his head, exposing a white T-shirt underneath it. "The band is shit. I mean, they sing the same lyric eight times in a row and call it a song. It's pathetic."

"Then why were you wearing the shirt?"

"I guess to send a message."

"The message being?"

"I like shit music and need a pretentiously opinionated emo girl leaning against a rack of laxatives to help me with my taste."

Dulcolax (see: terrible first impression) caught my eye the second I dared take a look behind my head. "Your taste in music should be the least of your worries," I said, crossing my arms across my black sweater as if to declare the laxative display my territory. At least it wasn't feminine products. That could have gotten awkward. "Prozac is the worst antidepressant on the market. I couldn't fall asleep for days when I was on it."

"Don't forget the dizziness," he added. "I tripped in the shower and about busted my head on the toilet. They don't show you that on the commercials."

"Nope. Not unless the sun was beaming through your window or you were on a bike."

"Man," he said, snapping his fingers. "The one time I don't ride a bike in the shower."

He was staring at me with a weirdly attractive grin on his face, and I felt like telling him to screw off. But there was a slight anger in his snarled mouth, like he disdained convention and flirty conversations and was only still talking to me because I looked ridiculous with MiraLAX poking up from behind my head.

"So, what are you on?" he asked.

"Zoloft."

"Clinical? Obsessive? Panic?"

"Clinical."

"Me too. Another thing we have in common."

"We suck at life?"

"No. We aren't ignorant."

"That's debatable."

"Not really." He reached into his pocket and whipped out a strand of red licorice. "Twizzler?" I shook my head. "You see, stupid people are happy with knowing nothing. The less they know, the better things seem. But smart people, geniuses, we see everything exactly for what it is. And then we take pills to make us stupid, because stupid is happy. Whatever the hell that is."

"And which do you prefer, stranger?" I asked.

"My name's Snake."

"Snake?"

That was the most obscenely ambitious nickname I'd ever heard.

"Like the reptile. Yours?"

"Reggie."

"That's a dude's name."

"That's a misogynistic assertion."

"Fine." He grinned, narrowing his eyes. "It's unisex. And what do you mean, which do I prefer?"

"Being smart or being happy?"

A muffled voice echoed across the store. "Pickup for Regina Mason."

"Regina?" Snake mocked. "What a prissy little name."

"At least I'm not named after a slimy predator that sucks the life out of everyone it comes in contact with." I pushed past him and snatched the folded bag from the pickup basket. I zipped the medication into my messenger bag and tossed exact change onto the counter.

"Leaving so soon?" Snake asked. Now that he was standing directly under the light, I could see the way his eyes were burrowed deep into his skull. How his full lips had a perfect model pout, like his whole mouth had gotten stuck on the kissy-face setting. His pretty face was too posh for his image.

"As fascinating as this conversation's been, I've got to get home and eat dinner."

"You should invite me over."

"A dude named Snake with a pierced ear, a crap tattoo, and a fixation on violent screamo music? Yeah, not gonna happen."

He shook his head as he ate another Twizzler. "Are you this mean to everyone you meet?"

"Only the special people," I muttered.

As I was preparing to leave, he grabbed my arm. I was one security camera away from clocking him.

"I'll see you around?" he asked, his tone strangely earnest.

I yanked my arm out of his grasp. Even though he was determined and forceful and weird, at least he wasn't annoyingly exuberant. I had to give him brownie points for that.

"I'm not really around," I said as I walked away.

My mother was waiting for me at the front doors with a bag in her hand. "I bought you anti-itch ointment just in case your fanny chafes again." She smiled, proudly holding up a thin white tube. "And I picked you up a journal just in case you change your mind."

"It better not have ducks."

"Duck-free. Promise."

She proceeded to babble on about birthday cards and half-price two-liters and a bunch of other irrelevant things I didn't care about. We got in the minivan and rode away, listening to some girl group singing a ballad about the joy of the Lord.

CHAPTER two

AT LUNCHTIME, I ATE OUTSIDE. Hawkesbury High had a closet-size cafeteria with round tables interspersed between microwave stations. Each table had been claimed from the first day. The table closest to the door was for the <u>boys soccer team</u> (see: assholes), who drank insane amounts of Gatorade and occasionally threw cheese at the table by the condiments rack. That table was reserved for the <u>girls volleyball team</u> (see: skanks in Spanx), who ducked flying cheese while whispering about the table near the exit door. That turf belonged to the <u>cheerleaders</u> (see: blonde brigade), and the one beside it to the <u>drama club</u> (see: future fast food employees of the world), and so on and so forth until every table was accounted for. If you didn't care to sit with the teachers and be subjected to a million jokes you had to be stoned or drunk to find amusing, you sat outside at the picnic tables.

Polka, a Taiwanese exchange kid from my creative writing class, sat across from me. He ate sushi out of a Ziploc container and read a Japanese comic. I didn't mind eating with him because he wasn't in a clique, didn't like to talk, and always brought a dessert he was willing to share.

On days when getting up in the morning felt like a feat, when the air was sticky and humid and the courtyard reeked of moldy cheese, I would let myself remember what it was like freshman year, devouring hamburgers in the cafeteria. What it was like to have a clique, even if it was only with one other person and nobody else knew we were there. But there was no purpose in dwelling on things like that.

Polka looked up from the book he was reading, a shiny one with a picture of a shark on the front, and slid a slice of birthday cake across the table. "You can have whole thing," he said in his broken accent.

"You sure?"

"My guardian make it, but I don't like coconut."

I grabbed the fork and took a bite; the cake melted against my tongue. "This is great, Polka. You should eat it."

He mechanically turned his head from side to side. It was funny whenever he shook his head like that, his eyes expressionless, mouth straight as a ruler. Polka never seemed to get up or down with his emotions. He might not have had any, and that was all the more reason to sit with him rather than inside, where everyone had an opinion on everything and most of them were totally stupid.

"My birthday yesterday," he said as he resumed his reading. "I turn twenty-one."

"You did not turn twenty-one, dude. You're in the eleventh grade."

He flipped the page. "Friend said I turned twenty-one. That's how I take shots."

"You drank shots?" I couldn't see Polka, with his incurious eyes and khaki pants, downing shots with a group of friends. Really, I couldn't see Polka having friends, but he did. He hung out with a few other guys from the exchange program. I couldn't see them taking shots, either. "How'd they taste?"

"Taste like shit," he said.

The way he cursed stuff was awesome. It was just small talk: "How are you?" "The weather's great." "Liquor shots taste like shit." He would say it, I would go on eating his dessert, and that was the extent of our conversations. It always got left at shit, and that's exactly where I wanted it.

He didn't need to be friends beyond the picnic table, and neither did I.

Sometimes I was pathetic. Fine, all the time. But I liked to think I was pathetic in a way that was sort of inspiring, if there was any such brand of patheticism. Especially on the rare occasions I would go the park after school and sit on the swing set by myself.

It wasn't like I went there to be meta about it. Like, *Look at that sad goth chick all alone on the swings. She's probably listening to indie rock through those Skullcandy headphones.* Even though I was a sad goth chick and, fuck the stereotype, listening to indie rock through those Skullcandy headphones. Basking in my own blatant misery, as cliché as it may have been, hurt and felt good at the same time. I didn't like much, but I liked that I felt the pull of gravity even when I was floating. I liked that, even in the air, there was weight.

It was cold that Wednesday. The wind blew my hair into my eyes as I pumped my legs, reaching higher and higher, tilting my head back to peer at the pinkish gray of the sky. My mom hadn't called me yet to ask when I'd be home, and I didn't have to go in to work at Oinky's Ice Cream. I could shut off my phone and not worry about anyone calling me, not worry about anyone looking. I could go anywhere, nowhere, or everywhere, and it wouldn't make a difference.

And that was the good and the hurt. It felt good to be alone, and still hurt that there was an empty swing.

o o o

This number is no longer in service.

The recording sank into my eardrums, beating in slow, lulling motions. Sweat trickled down my jaw from where the phone was pressed between my cheek and the pillow. I was probably crying, but barely recognized the sensation anymore. All I recognized was the phrase *no longer.*

No longer in service.

No longer friends.

No longer here.

Every night I fell asleep to darkness. And the only thing that kept me going was that I didn't always wake up to it.

CHAPTER three

THURSDAY WAS MY LEAST FAVORITE DAY. Not because it followed the hype of hump day or because it was too close to Friday to not be Friday, but because it was a workday. Plus, that particular Thursday was the day my dad mounted the creepy wolf he'd stitched up at work that week. For a beast caught midsnarl, it was a surprisingly tame-looking creature. One that practically begged for a stare-off. Unfortunately, my wandering, curious, and tired eyes were no match for his marble opposition. He won in ten seconds flat. The deer from February was my favorite opponent. He was missing an eye.

"You like that one?" my dad asked. He was reading the newspaper from his corduroy La-Z-Boy recliner, his hanky clawing its way out of the pocket of his bowling shirt. "Got him hoisted up there this morning."

"He looks bored," I said. "Definitely in the right place."

My dad smiled and went on perusing Flashburn's obituaries. I tell you, that man had a fascination with death, an inability to let things reach their inevitable end without trying to preserve some fraction of their legacy. Apparently, a career in taxidermy just wasn't enough to satisfy him. Wherever something died, there he was trying to fix it. Electronics. Kitchen appliances. Cars. He hated when he couldn't do it, when something was gone and he couldn't bring it back. He'd start to mumble to himself when his patience was thinning, and I used to find it funny and slightly pitiful. But most of the time, I just found it sad.

He grunted and adjusted the lever on his seat, keeping his head down to avoid meeting my eyes longer than either of us was comfortable with. The only person who hated serious talks more than me was my dad. "How are you . . . uh . . . how do you feel today?" he asked, glancing out the window at the overgrown hedge.

It didn't bother me when my dad asked me how I was doing. He didn't ask to pry the way Karen did. Dad was a man of few words. He started a conversation only when he really cared about the topic, meaning he spoke only when the topic was dead animals or me.

"Same as always," I said.

"No crippling headaches or anything?"

"Nope. No crippling anything. Well, unless you count breathing."

He kept his eyes on the window and tried not to smile. It wasn't exactly kosher to laugh at the subject of your kid's depression, but my dad could appreciate a bit of morbidity every now and again.

"Don't let your mom hear you say that. You know how she feels about dark jokes."

"As long as my soul is whisked away to heaven at the end, I think she'll be okay."

He craned his neck away from me so I wouldn't see him smile. If my mom knew he was egging me on, he'd be in a lot of trouble. When it came to joking, there were two house rules.

1. Don't joke about Jesus.
2. Don't laugh at anything Reggie says.

My dad was smart to hide his amusement, because my mother bustled in from the kitchen right as he was turning in his chair. She had a frilly apron tied around her waist, her hair pinned on top of her head like a housewife from a retro ad. But instead of a gourmet apple pie, she handed me a burnt sandwich and a juice box. "I made you a grilled ham and cheese to eat before work."

"Thanks, but I have to be there in five minutes." I

bit the sandwich and tasted the cheese and char mixture between my teeth. "I'll eat on the way."

"You can't eat while you drive. I heard this story about a sixteen-year-old girl, precious little thing, who tried to eat a cheeseburger while behind the wheel of her mother's Chrysler and . . ."

She recounted a horror tale she'd read on some *How to Make Your Teen Hate Life* blog for conservative moms. By the time she finished, I was walking across the front lawn toward my chariot (see: minivan). "Reggie!" she called. "At least tie up your hair a little neater, it's all over the place. It's bad enough you insist on dying it that awful black."

I didn't need to glance at my ponytail in the rearview mirror to know that I looked like a dark-haired troll doll. It kind of went along with the whole "screw this" attitude I had going on. "Will do, Karen! Crochet me a noose while I'm gone," I shouted out the window, triggering an immediate gesture on her chest and shoulders for the sign of the cross. She wasn't even Catholic. Just desperate. Poor woman would have prayed to a rock if she thought it would change me.

I drove to work in two minutes. Karen always got on me for taking the van such a short distance when I could walk. She said it wasted gas, and since she quit her job at the daycare and landed a full-time gig as a homemaker/knitter/life ruiner, the extra twenty cents was really digging into her wallet. I promised her I'd make up the difference with my tip money (plot twist: I rarely got tip money).

Once I parked the gas-sucking van, I tossed my royal blue uniform shirt over my tank top. Oinky's Ice Cream Parlor was a doublewide trailer stationed in the parking lot of an abandoned Japanese antique shop. A blowup head of a very questionable pig sat atop the roof and blinked its peering eyes every time a gust of wind blew through. The <u>cherry on top</u> (see: pun) was that not only did we get these badass shirts with a picture of the questionably intentioned pig, but written in swirly lettering reminiscent of a love letter one would find in a twelve-year-old girl's Trapper Keeper were the words *We all oink for ice cream!* I only endured working there because my therapist said it would be a good distraction for me. Distraction? Sure. Good? Hell to the no.

"Reggie! I didn't know if you were going to show up." My wonderfully neurotic boss greeted me as I came through the back door. Her brown hair was soaked in grease, and she had a wrench in hand, which worried me because she'd broken her index finger using the register last month.

"I'm one minute late, Peyton. Literally. It's five-oh-one."

"Ice cream machine's down. Something is wrong with the crank," she said in that panicky, the-sky-is-falling way that she had mastered over years of being a total nutjob. "The new guy hasn't gotten here yet, and there's no one at the window."

"New guy?"

"Mr. Banks is making Carla go on maternity leave."

Mr. Banks, the owner, was this absurdly rich dude who owned a bunch of small businesses and lived by the pond, which was a huge deal in Flashburn, because there was this unwritten law that only elitists were allowed to live by the enchanted swamp of fish piss. His daughter, Carla, had worked at Oinky's since we were in seventh grade. She was this stuck-up pageant queen/Pilates junkie that I'd had the honor of schooling with from kindergarten to junior year at Hawkesbury. Thankfully, we never talked much. But in the rare yet unavoidable conversations we did have, the only logical takeaway was that her favorite objects were ones she could see her reflection in and *ohmigodtotally* was her life's motto. I'd credited it to sweet poetic justice when she got knocked up by some mysterious loser from across town and blew up like a float at the Macy's Thanksgiving Day parade. Listening to her blast Taylor Swift from glittery iPod speakers while I did all the work was taking a hefty toll on my patience.

"I'm going to go look for a bolt in the back room," Peyton said, turning the wrench in what was clearly the wrong direction. "When the new guy gets here, show him how to use the register."

Show him how to touch a button and open a drawer. Got it.

"Okay. Let me know if you need any help."

I sat down in the folding chair beside the window and stared out at the empty parking lot. I was just beginning to admire the weeds growing beside the telephone pole when there was a knock on the back door. The guy actually knocked. Knocked as if he would be interrupting something important. At Oinky's. In Flashburn.

Newbies.

"Come in!" I yelled.

The door stuck a little like it always did. He shoved it with his shoulder and stumbled inside, practically tripping over Peyton's toolbox, which was sprawled out beside the ice cream machine.

It was a virtual impossibility that his unwashed hair and puckered lips could go unrecognized. Not far behind a greater virtual impossibility that, evidenced by his subtle smirk, I was pretty recognizable myself. Once I got a better look at him, I couldn't decide if he looked more or less idiotic in the Oinky's uniform compared to his THE RENEGADE DYSTOPIA T-shirt. It was probably a tie.

"We meet again, reptile," I greeted him, no doubt committing some sort of crime of flirtation by acknowledging him first.

"Chick with the butch name," he replied, leaning against the machine to try to look cool or something that really wasn't working for him. "Shall I call this fate or destiny?"

"You should call this an underpopulated town."

"Fate it is."

I pointed to the chair beside me. "Sit. We're going to be exercising your fingers."

"And here I was thinking this is a family business."

"You obviously haven't met Oinky."

He sat down, crossing his knees one over the other in the daintiest fashion.

I couldn't help myself. "What are you, a woman? Sit like you have something between your legs."

He grinned that same unconcerned grin from the pharmacy. "Don't make me report you for sexual harassment."

"That wouldn't be the worst thing to happen to me today."

"And the worst would be?"

"Waking up."

He looked mildly surprised for a moment, like he didn't know what kind of response I was expecting from him. And then, as if on cue, he erupted with laughter. "I'm starting to think you waking up was the worst thing that happened to *me* today."

"Did you just wish me dead? It usually takes people at least a week to get to that point."

"You must hang around some very patient people."

"Oh, like you're some gem."

"Well, I don't joke about suicide."

"I wasn't joking about suicide, I was joking about death." I grunted. "Whatever. Congratulations on your unshakable moral compass, Mother Teresa."

"My moral compass is far from unshakable," he muttered to himself.

For the next few minutes, we engaged in the kind of stimulating conversation Peyton would have been proud to witness, taking orders and making change. Riveting stuff. After he got the hang of four quarters equals a dollar, he serviced one of our few-and-far-between customers, who had ordered a large dreamsicle cone; Snake had to sell her on a blueberry snow cone after she pitched a fit about an ice cream parlor not selling ice cream. She left cursing about how she was going to warn the masses of this crime against the dessert industry, and then hopped on a hot pink motor scooter and embarked on her mission.

"That's something you don't see every day." Snake laughed. "An ice cream vigilante."

"Reggie!" Peyton shouted from the back. She ran into the room with black gunk smeared on her face and a screwdriver clasped in her palm. "Oh, hi there," she said to Snake. "I would shake your hand, but—"

"You're gross," Snake finished. She looked embarrassed. "I would give you a hand, but mine are burned-out from all this strenuous button pushing."

"Has it been busy?"

"Snake almost got stabbed with a plastic spoon handle."

"What?" she gasped. Peyton lived in a very nonactual actuality where exaggeration and sarcasm were as foreign as the execution of DIY.

"I saw my entire life flash before my eyes," he added. "Which was basically a series of mistakes with an occasional what-the-hell moment."

Peyton eyed him but didn't put much stock in his behavior, considering he was fresh off of spending time with me. She always said that my attitude was a contagious and terminal disease that infected anyone who talked with me for more than five minutes. It had to have at least been ten, so poor Snake was already experiencing symptoms of my dark cloud mentality.

She stuck the chunk of metal inside the machine and pulled a lever, which released a cloud of smoke. She uttered an obscene word. "I'm going to have to call Mr. Banks. I'll be outside if you guys need me."

Snake sat down by the register and drew a Twizzler from his pocket. "Twizzler?"

"Are you serious? What's the deal with the Twizzlers?"

"You don't like Twizzlers?"

"I don't tote them around like loose change, no."

"They help me." He wrapped one around his finger while he balanced another between his lips. "I used to chew."

23

"Tobacco? So you replace nicotine with strawberry artificial flavoring. Natural substitute."

"My moms told me the chemicals would satisfy the craving."

"Your moms? What were you, raised by nuns?"

He shoved two strands in his mouth like a pouty-lipped walrus. "Lesbians, actually. But that was a creative guess. I've never gotten that one before."

I could have imagined my <u>mother</u> (see: drama queen) in this situation, collapsed on the ground after fainting from such a terrible blow. "Well, my mom is religious. Like, super religious. I think even God is embarrassed by how religious she is."

"She sounds lovely. We should get our families together for dinner sometime."

"I'm not trying for *Clash of the Titans: Flashburn Edition*."

He laughed, and it didn't annoy me, mainly because it wasn't overtly showy or desperate to impress. He laughed softly and manically at the same time, which was so appealing and foolish and cool that it almost made up for the T-shirt incident at the pharmacy.

Another customer came by and received the news of the ice cream machine's demise in a far more graceful manner than that of the motor scooter woman. He even wished us luck in fixing the problem, which I personally thought was overkill. Like, you ain't gettin' ice cream, dude. No need to plaster your lips to my ass.

"I bet that guy is a serial killer," I said after he left.

"Why? The creeper van?" Snake asked, licking a Popsicle he was probably supposed to pay for.

"That, and nobody is that nice when they don't get what they want. He was just trying to balance his karma."

"I bet he's a cannibal."

"Why?"

"Because he didn't mind not eating ice cream. What's up with that? It's inhuman, I tell you."

"Ice cream is one of the few things in life that don't royally suck."

"It's a better antidepressant than Prozac, that's for damn sure." He swallowed the last bite of Popsicle, his entire mouth dripping purple. "Do you ever wish that you could stop therapy and pills and just, I don't know, do trivial and pointless things for purposeless reasons with other humans who are as weak and hopeless as you, and for even the slightest instant in time forget how vain it all is and just let yourself enjoy it?"

"You just described friendship. And no, I don't really wish anymore."

"Side effect of Zoloft?"

"Side effect of depression."

He seemed to understand, and it made me feel oddly

at ease. Talking to him was cathartic for me, somehow. I wanted to go so far as to tell him that I hated Oinky's and my old co-worker was obnoxious and our hideous shirts made me want to beat myself to death with one of Peyton's wrenches, but it was still too early to put it all on display.

Minutes passed in silence. He had this tacky silver ring on his finger that he twisted as we waited for the next adventure in the ice cream–less ice cream parlor saga. After a span of inactivity, he studied my face as if he were searching for a pimple.

I kicked his chair. "Is there a frickin' car wreck on my face? What are you staring at?"

"You have a birthmark above your eyebrow," he said, still scrutinizing me.

"Groundbreaking information. Let's alert CNN."

"I've just never seen someone with a birthmark on their face. It's weird."

"You're weird. And your tattoo looks like you drew it on with a dried-up Sharpie."

"I wasn't insulting your birthmark, just pointing out its uniqueness." He opened the register and tossed a dollar in for the Popsicle he stole. "Some people are so touchy."

"I'm not touchy. I just don't give a damn what you think."

He grinned, his lips and teeth bleeding purple. "I'm

starting to believe you don't give a damn what anyone thinks."

"I don't."

"You know, Zoloft is a cure for depression. Not personality."

"Stellar insight," I mumbled. "I'll mull it over while I'm discarding all of your opinions."

I pulled out my phone and brought up my gaming app, hoping it would signal him to shut up. Shooting a pixel creature from a slingshot was more entertaining than anything he could possibly add to a conversation about cannibals and birthmarks. Peyton came back minutes later and tinkered around with the machine. She even had a product manual this time, which would have been great if it wasn't in Chinese.

Time dragged on, and Peyton eventually hopped in her Jeep and sped home. Of course, that was after she drowned in aggravated tears, badgered with guilt at her utter failure to save the ice cream. Basically, she had a total meltdown (see: best pun ever).

Snake and I were left alone to close shop, which meant wiping down untouched counters with cleaning solution, buffing machines that were going to be used the very next day, and cleaning windows that children were going to smear with their grimy fingerprints within the following twenty-four hours. While I was washing the sink, Snake appeared behind me with a cone of vanilla ice cream.

"Who knew I could read Chinese?" he said, tilting the cone toward me. "Take a lick."

"You fixed the machine?" I looked at the gray heap of metal. The top was firmly shut, the levers, bolts, and coils bound in place.

"It wasn't broken. I tightened two bolts, and voilà." He held the cone in his hand like it was a trophy of his not-so-grand accomplishment. "You want it?"

I reached out and he snatched his hand away, my fingers crumpling into his chest. If I had just tucked my thumb a bit, it would have been a full-on punch. Curse my reflexes.

"I would like to make a deal," he said, hanging his head toward me.

"Does it involve me physically assaulting you with either the ice cream or the cone? Because we're heading in that direction."

"Cage the rage, my friend. I would like to offer you this delectable, carved by the gods, explosion for the senses, if you would hang out with the one and only me tomorrow night."

"You want me to go on a date with you? And you're paying for the pleasure of my company in ice cream?"

"This is called hitting rock bottom. A concept not unfamiliar to either of us."

"I'm rock bottom?" I *awwed* sweetly, touching the spot

28

above my heart. "That is the most romantic thing anyone has ever said to me."

"I came up with that gem while you were discarding my opinions. Yes or no?"

I tapped my chin. "Tomorrow night? Nope. Sorry. I'll be busy doing nothing and hating it."

"Well, there's your problem." He smiled. "You're supposed to do that on Saturday. Did you not read *The Guide to Successful Depressive Behavior*? There are pie charts and everything."

"Must have forgotten to pick that one up."

I brushed past him and began spraying the counters with Formula 409. When I finally turned around, he was gone. I checked the back room, but there were only freezers and boxes of inventory. I heard a tap on the order window and found him staring in from the outside, lifting the ice cream cone in his hand like a torch. "Do I want to know what you're doing?" I asked once I slid the glass back.

"That's no way to greet a customer." He reeled. "I'm offended."

"Fine. Welcome to Oinky's. Do I want to know what you're doing?"

"I would like to return this vanilla cone."

"We don't have a return policy on ice cream."

"Then I would like to make an exchange."

"Okay?"

"I will exchange this vanilla cone for the pleasure of your company tomorrow night."

I snatched the cone out of his hand and dumped it in the trash can under the cabinet. "I'm going to say yes so we can get out of here, but I think you're immature and talk too much and are not nearly as cool as you think you are. Are we clear?"

"I heard nothing after yes."

We left at nine. The minivan light stayed off when I opened the door, because it was a 1992 Town & Country and my dad insisted he would be able to fix it without having to take it to a repair shop. Snake had parked his car next to mine. He had a gold Prius with a license plate that said NAMASTE. I assumed it was his moms'.

"That's a chick car," I said as he reached for his keys.

"That's a misogynistic assertion," he returned quickly. Well played. "I'll pick you up at eight."

"Whatever."

"I already put my number in your phone while you were washing the sink."

"That's thoroughly creepy."

"Oh, by the way." He leaned across the top of his car. Towered over it, actually. "My answer is smart."

I had no idea what he was saying, but I figured that he just said a bunch of random stuff all the time to hear himself talk. "Answer for what?" I asked.

"Tuesday, when you asked me if I would rather be smart or happy. I would rather be smart."

"Why?"

"Because intellect can be proven scientifically with machines and litmus tests and IQ evaluations, but happiness is only based on a loose pool of interpretive data drawn from perception and emotion. It's a theory, see? And I'd rather put my faith in something real than something that's inconclusive."

"So, you don't think happiness is real?" It was the first time I'd questioned him and been eager for his response.

"I think it's tolerable pain. Happy people have a really high tolerance, that's all." He tapped the hood of his car. "See you tomorrow."

He drove toward Sun Street with one of his taillights busted, flooring it through a yellow light that blinked red the moment he crossed the threshold. I read the word NAMASTE until the letters disappeared.

CHAPTER four

SYMPTOMS OF A DEPRESSIVE EPISODE ALWAYS came in three major stages—wait, scratch that. Symptoms of a *Reggie* depressive episode always came in three major stages. As I lay on my floor, my knees curled beneath my chin, the most exaggeratedly morbid song moaning into my headphones, I knew that I was in Stage 3: Disconnect.

Stages 1 and 2 were pretty brutal, sure. Lots of sobbing, shaking, sore body parts for no reason whatsoever, walls that did all but swallow me whole, a bunch of upbeat, cheery things like that. But they were nothing compared to Disconnect.

My mom had tried to help when it first started happening. She would suggest taking a walk together whenever the silence got loud. When I wouldn't answer, she'd bake me chocolate chip cookies and leave a note under my door to let me know when they were ready. Eventually, though, she just sat downstairs and ignored me because she said the devil had to release his control before the Lord could do His work. Personally, I wondered if even the devil was Stage-3-caliber mean. Sometimes it felt like it was my mind that was the cruel one. Like it was true what people say about you being your own worst enemy. That, or I was just plain crazy.

Anyway, Disconnect was either the best or the worst stage, depending on how you looked at it. It was numbing. It was staring for half an hour at a spot on the ugly wall Karen insisted on painting yellow to make me <u>stupid</u> (see: happy) while the piano from my earbuds spilled into every bone and vein and fiber. Numb. That was what made it the best stage. It didn't hurt. It was also the worst, because I could feel nothing for only so long.

That's where I was that night. I was in frayed jeans with a coffee stain, a white T-shirt with a cross-patterned scarf, and my black combat boots laced halfway up my shins, lying in a heap of human on the bed. And Snake was supposed to pick me up in less than two minutes.

"A little gold car just pulled into the driveway!" my mother called from the living room. I had hoped he wouldn't pick me up at the door, because one look at his tattoo, and he would be walking out of there with a Gideons Bible tucked into his pants.

It was hard to move during Disconnect, but I picked myself up by the bootstraps (almost literally). When I dragged my wobbly legs into the living room, I saw Snake standing on the welcome mat just inside the door with both hands in his ripped pockets, my dad studying him from his usual spot in the La-Z-Boy, and my mother's wide-eyed, disapproving stare as she took her place on the love seat. He was wearing a T-shirt that said ONLY THE GOOD DIE YOUNG with the word YOUNG marked out by a red X.

He wasn't the least bit uneasy or ashamed or anything close to what I would have expected, given the pretty portrait I'd painted of my mom the night before.

I walked toward him and motioned to my parents. "Snake, this is my mom, Karen, and my dad, Dave. Mom and Dad, this is Snake."

A customary awkward silence ensued, followed by my mother being unable to deny her nature. "Snake can't possibly be your real name, sweetheart. Does your mother approve of that nickname?" she asked.

He grinned his Snake grin. "My mothers prefer it. Self-expression, and all that."

She raised her brows at the mothers part. I nudged Snake so he would know to gear up for battle.

"Your mother and stepmother?" she asked, wringing her hands in her lap.

"No. My mothers. You know, like you and Dave, except neither has a mustache."

"I'm working on a Fu Manchu," my dad added.

"Dave." My mother's face turned redder than the sweater she was knitting. She turned back to Snake, unable to let it go. She never could. "So, two mothers. That's . . . interesting. Is that difficult for you?"

"Really, Mom?"

"It's okay, Reggie." Snake reached into his pocket, and before I even saw it, I knew he was after a Twizzler. "Let's see," he said, tapping the licorice to his chin. "I moved here this past year from Westbrook, just south of Flashburn. I'm sure you know where that is. And I lived in a two-story Victorian. And I had a racecar bed. And we went to Cedar Point every summer. And I got bedtime stories read to me about the Lorax. And they were always still there when I woke up the next morning. So, if that sounds difficult to you, then, yeah. I guess I had it pretty hard." He took a bite.

My mother glared at my dad for reinforcement, but what could he do? Snake had just answered an invasive question the best way he knew how. Couldn't fault him for that. And besides, when it came to fight or flight, my dad was a first-class pilot. He would have been much better off in the basement, stitching the skin of a dead squirrel.

Another uncomfortable silence oozed into the room. I knew if I didn't get out of there fast, Karen would find a way to make the unembarrassable Snake feel embarrassed.

I grabbed his arm and pulled him through the door. As he was stepping onto the porch, he leaned his head back inside and said, "It's Matthew, in case you were wondering."

"What?" my dad asked.

"My birth name is Matthew."

Then he shut the door behind him.

He parked the Prius at the end of a cul-de-sac in a dingy neighborhood downtown. I didn't go downtown much, but I liked it. Everyone walked slowly, like they were dying, and even the sun that was beginning to set over the hills couldn't brighten anyone's day. Misery with no end in sight. These were my people.

"You didn't seem keen on coming out with me tonight," Snake said as he yanked the key out of the ignition.

"Was it the insults or the blatant no that gave you that impression?"

"It might have been the attempted assault. That was pretty telling."

"Would you be keen on going out with you?"

He leaned closer. His dull blue eyes judged me beneath his hair. "I'm going to reverse that question. Would you be keen on going out with you?"

"I wasn't the one who begged for a date. If you think you're doing me some favor, you can do me another and take me home."

He grinned and spun his keys around his finger. "It's not me who's doing the favor." He reached into the back seat and grabbed something, then bumped my face with cardboard as he pulled it to the front. "Sorry." He laughed, touching my forehead. The cardboard was a pizza box. "I know you hate most things, but I'm assuming you like pizza."

"It's all right."

I love pizza.

"Well, this pizza is two days old. And it's cold. And we are going to eat it over there." He pointed to a dump-site beyond a barbed-wire fence, stacked with garbage bags taller than the houses. "You may want to know why, or you don't care. Either way, I want us to dig into a cold pizza and whine about how lonely and depressed we are while sitting on top of a heaping pile of rot. An anti-date. Is that terrible enough for you?"

He opened the car door and popped the trunk, retrieving a bulky black video camera that probably cost more than my house. I wondered how he could afford it.

"What are you doing with that?" I asked as we headed toward the fence.

"I'm a filmmaker. Aspiring filmmaker, actually. I like to document moments so I can watch them back and mourn the sheer uselessness of our condition."

"You just film things for the heck of it?"

"I enter contests on occasion."

"You ever win?"

"Winning is such an abstract term—"

"You've never won."

"Yeah, no." He smiled. "But I've been runner-up. Like, a lot."

I kicked a pebble and it whizzed across the lot. "So what's the subject tonight?"

"Tonight." He shrugged. "I just want to capture *the sheer uselessness of our condition.*"

He led me to the waste site. The fence was conveniently torn where the metal met the dirt, just round enough for us to crawl through. The camera was a challenge, but once Snake scuttled under, he dug a spot in the ground to give it room to slide. We climbed up a ladder on the side of a green disposal bin, me with a pizza box under my arm and Snake with a camera tied around his back. When we reached the top, we were at least fifteen feet in the air, the romantic aroma of spoiled food and dirty diapers stinging our nostrils from below. I sat down beside Snake on the edge of the bin, and he offered me a slice of cold pizza.

"You don't know how pitiful Flashburn is until you see it from above," I said.

"Right? Up here there's a great view of the black hole sucking inhabitants into the void. It's between suburbia and the pond." He unhooked the camera from where he had fastened it like a backpack and flipped a switch that triggered a flashing red button. "Landscape shots," he said, as images of the dilapidated houses reflected in the lens.

"It must be nice to have a talent."

"Not exactly." He turned the camera off and placed it beside him. "It's painful to have a passion. You care so much it hurts." He looked at me. "I'm sure that you've experienced too much caring, or you wouldn't be so depressed."

I hadn't cared much about anything the past few months. My therapist said it was because I overanalyzed simplicities, that life wasn't so complex that I couldn't take the good for what it was and accept it. But that didn't seem like an applicable observation. More like something I could find in a self-help book (see: feel-good bullshit).

"My therapist makes me write," I told him.

"What kind of stuff does she make you write?"

"Journal entries. Self-evaluations. My own eulogy."

His eyes bulged behind his camera. "No way."

"Okay, the last part was a lie. But she might as well. She's basically forcing me to find a passion."

"Well, do you like writing?" he asked.

"Kind of. But it doesn't really matter if I do or don't."

"Why?"

"It just doesn't. We're the smart ones, remember? Caring about life and dreaming that you can change the world in any significant way . . ." I almost laughed at the idea. "It's . . . I don't know . . . it's kind of . . ."

"Like searching for a pebble in the sand?" he finished.

I had never thought if it that way, but it was true. Like digging for a needle in a haystack. "Yeah. Exactly like that."

He grabbed the camera and turned it on himself, the red light flashing in his eyes. "I am but a pebble in the sand," he said into the lens. "I am sitting on a pile of garbage eating pizza that tastes like paper with a girl who hates me almost as much as she hates herself, and I am but a pebble in the sand." He turned the camera off. "Can I tell you a story?"

"No."

"It's about the mouse and the snake," he continued. I tossed my crust into the bin. "There was this baby mouse that got lost in the woods. He found a snake coiled beneath a tree. He asked the snake, 'Can I make my home here?' 'Next to me?' the snake asked. 'If you'll have me,' said the mouse. 'You see, I have nowhere to go, and the forest is too big for a little mouse like me.' The snake raised the mouse for seven days, providing shelter and warmth. On the seventh day, just as the mouse was waking from his sleep, the snake said, 'I'm sorry, mouse. But the forest is too big for a little snake like me.' And he swallowed the baby mouse whole."

My mouth fell open. He had shocked me for the first time. "That sounds like the Edgar Allan Poe version of a nursery rhyme."

"My moms used to tell me that story every day when I came home from school," he said, fiddling with the camera strap. "I was sort of weird and nerdy and didn't have any friends. Hard to believe, I know." He grabbed a Twizzler and wrapped it around his finger. "I used to think it was a story about a poor little mouse and an evil snake. But then I realized what it meant. The snake wasn't evil at all. He was just trying to survive. The world was just too big for him, too big for me."

"That's where you got your nickname."

He turned to me, earnest and eager. "I think it's the same way with caring. Caring about things, no matter how utterly wasted the effort, is just a way to survive. Everything we do is. It's like that old saying."

"What old saying?"

"You're damned if you do and you're damned if you don't." He shrugged. "Might as well do, I guess."

I wiped the pizza sauce from my mouth. "Maybe I should switch to Prozac."

He laughed and ate his Twizzler. We didn't say anything for at least five minutes. I guess we were absorbing, as Snake put it, "the sheer uselessness of our condition." When I finally glanced at him, he was staring at me with that intrusive, pimple-analysis scrutiny I'd seen before.

"Keep staring and I'll punch you in the jaw," I warned.

"I'm guessing you've never had a boyfriend." He smiled. "Guys stare."

"I've had a boyfriend, thank you. He didn't stare."

"Then he wasted his moments. How long did you guys date?"

"A year. He moved to Vermont the winter before last."

"Good," he said. "I'll stare in his absence."

"Fine. Let's see how you like it."

I scooted closer to him, my cold arm pressing against his warm one. His eyes were the dullest kind of gray-blue imaginable, boring and not particularly noteworthy in any sort of way. But they were nice. Beautifully average.

"I want to kiss you," he whispered.

"Pump the brakes, buddy." I leaned away from him. "This is the first time we've really hung out."

"So?"

"So, you don't kiss people on the first date. I'm not even sure I like you."

"I know you don't like me. You don't like anyone. But I think I'm bearable to you, or else you wouldn't be here."

"Bearable doesn't get kissed."

"Did you find your boyfriend more than bearable?" he asked.

"Not really."

"And I'm sure you kissed him . . ."

"Yeah, so what? We'd known each other since kindergarten."

"Well, I've known you since Tuesday, and you already find me bearable. That poor sucker had to wait years for that milestone." He inched closer. "I don't understand this concept of waiting, anyway. You have to wait to kiss. You have to wait to get a job. You have to wait to grow up. You have to wait to live. All this waiting, and they wonder why we're depressed. It's because we're always waiting for the moment that we won't be."

When he put it like that, it did seem pretty ridiculous. If I could get past his deformed tattoo and dumb T-shirts and relentless babble, I could certainly kiss him. And for some reason, he was determined to kiss me.

I reached for his neck and pulled his face to mine. My lips clashed into his in that awkward first-kiss way that everyone hates but endures to get to the slightly less awkward second. He tasted like strawberry Twizzlers. I probably tasted like pizza. He kept it simple, a hand against my back. None of that hit-or-miss groping that was nine times out of ten a miss. He kissed pleasantly, which was bizarre, because I wouldn't have described him as a pleasant person. Compared to my ex, who kissed like a <u>seizing fish</u> (see: terrible kissers), he wasn't so bad.

(Side note: In certain Western European countries, he'd probably be considered skilled. I hear they like weird tongue things there.)

When he pulled away, he looked at me and said, "Tell me that wasn't the best kiss you've ever had."

"Eh." I side-eyed him. "If kissing were an Olympic sport, you'd get, like . . . the silver."

Honestly, it was closer to the gold, but he was too arrogant to properly process the compliment. Plus, my stomach was doing this weird flippy thing, making me sick in the good way. In the I-just-ate-the-world's-sweetest-dessert-and-my-insides-are-going-to-explode way. If I didn't force it down, I might have said something I didn't mean.

"Well, I think it was sheer uselessness." He grinned as the sun finally fell behind the hill. "We should do it again."

CHAPTER five

IF I NEEDED ANOTHER BULLET POINT to add to my extensive list of reasons to hate Flashburn, it manifested itself in Mondays at Hawkesbury. I sat in my advanced creative writing class with Polka, who was as generous with note sharing as he was with packed lunches. Every time we had a homework assignment, we critiqued each other's work the next morning. For a guy whose native tongue was Taiwanese, he sure knew how to harness the English language. Which made no sense, considering he couldn't speak it. He even helped students with their projects after school sometimes, one of them being Carla Banks, whose giant dinosaur baby made it impossible for her to sit upright in the slim desk in front of me. She was facing the aisle, her swollen cankles resting on a metal chair across the row. One of her on-again-off-again besties, Olivia, was making it clear that their friendship was certainly off again, twisting to the side so her back was to Carla and her face was to the blank wall. I might have pitied my former co-worker had her on-again conversations consisted of more than beauty advice and dietary regimes. I might have even sat next to her just for kicks. But the Carla-less silence was too peaceful to wish away with surface pity.

At the front of the classroom, the whiteboard spelled out the same assignment it had since the week before. It was a definition paper due at the time of our final. A definition paper defining anything we wanted. Our own take. Our own words. It sounded easy enough in theory, until I started writing and realized I wasn't as smart as I thought. During one brainstorming session, I tried to define *exercise*. Literally, exercise. I was hitting new lows.

"I think I write about freedom." Polka was thinking out loud, adding ideas to his anime-stickered monstrosity (see: laptop).

"Freedom? That's a good one."

"You write paper yet?"

"Not yet."

"What you write about?"

I rubbed my hand along the desktop. "I don't know."

"I can help you," he said. "I tutor in cafeteria on Wednesday."

"No thanks."

Polka had been offering to help me with the paper for

weeks, but I always shrugged him off. If there was one thing I didn't need, it was anyone's help.

"Keep it in mind," he said.

I nodded, but I'd already stopped listening. I couldn't concentrate that day, for some reason. Every idea and thought and click of Polka's keyboard made me think of uselessness. Uselessness and the guy who'd taught me about it. Uselessness and kisses and dumpsites and cold pizza.

The events of the day got sort of jumbled after that. The three o'clock bell rang through the hall and everyone rushed to afterschool activities. Most were embarrassing exploits, save for a few interesting hobbies that I might have participated in if I hadn't been so determined to do nothing. No one talked to me on my way to the student lot. Shocking. Even more shocking was the sight of Carla Banks waddling across the asphalt, her sonogram clutched between her fingers.

I wondered who she'd been showing it to, what lucky bastard hadn't had the blurry photo shoved up his nose twenty-seven-hundred bazillion times. I mean, she had practically blown it up to size and posted it on the hallway bulletin board. That's not to say that she didn't feel shame in her own Carla way. It's only that she was so incorrigibly vain she would have worshiped a parasite if it grew in her stomach and called itself Banks.

She made her way across the lot to a car parked under

the oak tree near the road. I ducked down by my mother's minivan, crouching with my eyes peeking over the hood in obvious stalker fashion. But I didn't care how creepy I looked when I caught a solid glimpse of the car. A gold Prius. (I don't think it's necessary to note the Hindi word written on the license plate.)

And then I saw him. He was leaning against the driver's door, red licorice dangling from his lips.

Snake.

They were close enough for me to eavesdrop. The conversation went something like:

"The doctor said he's about the size of a squash."

"I hope he's better-looking than one."

"I bet he'll have my red hair."

"A ginger? Let's hope not."

"How was Oinky's? Dad keeps bugging me to ask you."

"Tell him I fixed the machine like a boss."

"Who did you work with?"

"Peyton and some other girl. When's your next appointment? Will your dad let me come next time?"

"April eighteenth. And I wouldn't hold my breath."

"I wish he'd let me around more. I want to be there."

"I know. I'll work on him. In the meantime, I'll keep you updated when anything happens. I promise."

"You better. I want to be in the loop. Especially since we're going to have, like, the coolest kid ever."

"Because I'm so awesome?"

"No, because I am."

They were hugging by the tree when I sped away, fighting back tears and hating myself for it. Next thing I knew, I was sitting on a green couch in my second home (see: therapy) because it was Monday and Dr. Rachelle was convinced I needed to prepare my mindset at the start of the week before life hit me unprepared.

That day I was angry. Furious. My hair stuck to my face, and I had mascara on my shirt, and I wanted to grab the vase of yellow flowers on the table and chuck it against the wall. I was in Stage 1, which I decided upon evaluation was the second worst stage of the cycle. Emotions were cage fighting with their shoes tied together, tumbling and crashing and making my mind spin out of control as if there was ever any control to spin out of. Everything just wanted to be noticed. Everything hurt like hell.

Stage 1: Mania.

"You seem upset today, Reggie," Dr. Rachelle said. She wore a gray pantsuit that hung from her thin frame, bulging in all the places a woman doesn't want to bulge. "What happened?"

"People."

"Will you be specific?"

"I want to be alone. I want to be alone and crawl inside a dark little hole and live inside my dark little hole and die there. Because people are jerks and liars, and I hate it. I hate it." I was crying sort of hysterically. A <u>tissue</u> (see: therapy clichés) ended up in my hand.

"Take a breath," she suggested. "Walk me through the day."

I recapped the events, starting with Tuesday when I met Snake at the pharmacy and ending with the sight of him hugging a pregnant Carla in my rearview mirror. She nodded as I choked through the stories, adding "mmm" or "uh-huh" every few minutes to assure me that she cared. She probably didn't. But she was paid to listen, and as long as we both had to be there, I might as well talk.

When I finished, she propped both elbows on her thighs and leaned forward, her breath close enough to give me a whiff of cinnamon gum. I couldn't get too annoyed at her, considering proximity was something all therapists practiced to convey a sense of intimacy or confidence or whatever. Either way, it was a total invasion of space.

"I want you to close your eyes, Reggie," she whispered. I obeyed, despite the fact that I loathed exercises. My eyelids stung from tears and wet mascara. "I want you to forget for a moment. Forget the anger. Forget the hurt. Forget how betrayed you feel. I want you to think about this boy. Tell me one word that comes to mind when you hear the name Snake."

"Vermin," I spat.

"I don't think you mean that. I know you barely know him, and you feel embarrassed and shamed and maybe even unjustified in having any sort of feelings toward him at all, but think about the boy you went out with on Friday night, and tell me one thing that stood out to you. What was one thing he impressed upon you?"

"He was . . ." I didn't want to think about him, because all I saw was Carla and that damn sonogram. I could hear him calling me just "some other girl." I hated him. "He was . . . presumptuous."

"Presumptuous?"

"Yes," I continued. "He was arrogant. He based everything on assumption. He took me to a waste site because he assumed that I would want the worst date imaginable. He brought cold pizza because he assumed that warm pizza would be too pleasant for my taste. He kissed me because he assumed it would change my mind about him."

"And did you like this about him?"

"It was bearable."

"It's rare for you to feel that way. The last time you felt that way was with—"

"Can we not talk about him please?"

I didn't even want to say my ex's stupid name, because I was over it. I was over reliving how dumb I'd been to believe in him and to think he wouldn't just leave like *she* had. No one who mattered stuck around, and that was just life. Every man for himself.

"Keeping friends has been a long journey for you. I understand that," Dr. Rachelle said. "But like we've talked about before, you'll never get to the places you want to be without opening up. This seems like a great place to start."

"I don't want to start." *No longer in service* turned to ice in my bloodstream. "I want to be alone."

"I don't think you mean that. Have you considered talking to him?"

"No."

"Talk to him. Tell him how you feel. And, I know this is hard for you, but tell him how it hurts."

"I'll pass," I mumbled.

"Reggie." She rolled her chair in front of my knees. Her raspberry perfume settled in the slim space between us. "Our time is almost up, but I can't let you walk out of here without saying this." She always said that. "Don't be afraid to feel emotions. That's human nature. You feel hurt by what he did to you, but you shouldn't fear hurt. Fear is the greatest betrayal we commit against ourselves. Be genuine. And once you've let yourself feel it all, let it go. Don't let every bearable thing in life become unbearable."

I stared at the creases between my fingers, a stupid,

unwarranted tear falling to my wrist. "Why don't you tell me what you really think?"

"And what do I really think?"

"That I'm crazy."

She cocked her head and frowned with both sides of her mouth instead of just one like she usually did. Then she glanced at the clipboard that was resting on the table beside her. "I want to assign you homework, if that's all right."

"Sure," I mumbled.

"I want you to write," she said, not at all to my surprise. She tossed up her hand like she knew I'd object. I always did. "And before you say no, I want you to remember that this is for your benefit. I want you to write one page. That's it. Tell me what *crazy* means to you."

I wiped my eyes, smearing tears on the back of my hand. "Is this what you make all your wackjobs do?"

"No. This is what I make people do when I believe in them." She glanced at the clock. Our time was up. "Will you do this for you?"

It felt like I was doing it more for her, but I nodded anyway because I was shifting from Stage 1 to Stage 2 and wanted to get home before the storm hit.

When I got home, Karen was in the kitchen cooking something that I could only equate to cow dung. I ran upstairs into my ugly yellow room and toppled onto my bed, my ceiling patterned in stripes where the sun filtered through the blinds. I counted the spaces between them. One light. One shadow. Two lights. Two shadows. One mouse. One snake. One dies. One survives.

Stage 2: Emptiness.

I reached to my bedside table, grabbing the bottle of Zoloft. I popped the cap and swallowed a capsule with a swig of water. Laying my head back on the pillow, I mentally chanted *crazy crazy crazy* as I drifted off.

Vibrations were what finally jolted me awake. I opened my eyes to the darkness, the striped narrative of sun and shadow swapped with dimness and beams of moonlight. A single light interrupted the display. My phone glowed on the nightstand.

With pulsating temples, I grabbed the phone and read the screen.

It was only five words. Five presumptuous words.

I want to see you.

I replied in five words. Five presumptuous words.

You can kiss my ass.

CHAPTER six

HE LIVED BY THE POND. SERIOUSLY. That fool lived in a three-story brick house with a rose garden trellis overlooking the enchanted swamp of fish piss. Not only was he a lying sack of crap, he was a rich lying sack of crap. Which made him at least twenty times more unappealing and, frankly, gross. I hadn't seen him since Monday. He called in sick for work on Wednesday on account of food poisoning, a classic excuse that every depressed person knows is code for "I am not a functioning human today."

It came to this. My combat boots squishing the welcome mat beneath my feet. It came to me calling Peyton on Wednesday night with a ridiculous cover story, asking for Snake's address so I could "return his phone." It came to me reaching for the doorbell and making contact with the button before I had time to change my mind.

Footsteps approached, sounding like someone jumping down a flight of stairs. They were weighty and gawky, and I knew who they belonged to. The door swung open and there Snake (see: big, fat, ugly liar) stood, his unkempt brown hair hiding his uninteresting eyes. A white T-shirt doused in mustard stains stuck to his arms. He pushed his hair back and gave me a good once-over. His eyes widened, and I wanted to punch him in his infuriatingly pretty lips.

"Reggie," he said, his voice softer than usual. "What are you doing here?"

"I came to sell you Girl Scout cookies, what do you think?"

He grinned with his mouth closed, his infamous I'm-too-cool-to-even-smile-like-a-normal-person grin.

"Do you want to come in?"

"No, Snake. I thought I'd stay out here and water your moms' flowers."

"You've gotten meaner since the last time I saw you."

"Side effect of Zoloft, I guess."

"It's not supposed to make you mean."

"The label doesn't account for dealing with pathological liars."

He dropped his eyes to the ground with an empty expression, then stepped aside to let me in. His living room was more pristine than a doctor's office, and just about as miserable as a waiting room. There was even a brown leather couch beside the fireplace just like the ones at therapy. I was tempted to search the magazine table for an evaluation clipboard.

He pointed at the staircase. "You want to go to my room?"

"No."

"Okay . . ." He motioned to the other couch, also brown leather. "Does this meet your standards?"

I brushed past him and sat down, hugging my arms and legs against my body. He sat too close to me, and I shifted down. When I saw him flinch, I felt vindicated.

"I got your text," he said, playing with his long fingers. His gray sweats weren't bulging with Twizzlers. He must have been having withdrawals. "I thought you were just hating me in the good way, but then you ignored me for three days, so I'm guessing you hate me in the bad way." I didn't respond. "How did you find out where I live?"

I made him wait an agonizing amount of time for an answer. "I called Peyton. I was going to call Carla Banks, our boss's daughter, but I wasn't sure if you'd met her."

He fiddled with the string of his pants. "Um, maybe. I don't really remember—"

"Perhaps I can jog your memory," I interrupted. He reeled because I said it in the bad way. "She's this preppy, center-of-her-own-imagined-universe daddy's girl with bright red hair and a baby the size of a squash under her dress." I knew I had him at *squash*. He looked at his feet. "Sound familiar?"

He made this weird noise, like an inhale and a groan. "Now I get why you hate me in the bad way."

"I saw you, idiot!" I yelled. I glanced around to see if either of his mothers was home, but my voice echoed as if the house was empty. "After school in the parking lot."

"Oh."

"Oh? I find out that you're dating Carla Banks—I'm sorry, no. Scratch that. *Procreating* with Carla Banks, after you relentlessly tried to impress me for God knows what reason, and all you say is 'Oh'?"

"What am I supposed to say?" He tossed both of his hands up in surrender. "Yeah, I'm dating Carla. Yeah, I got her pregnant. Yeah, that makes me incredibly dumb and careless. And yeah, I really, really, really wanted to impress you. I still do."

"You're doing a bang-up job." I pushed my sweaty hair back. "Why do you want to impress me, anyway? If you're having a ginger squash with Carla, you shouldn't even care what I think."

"I do care, Reggie," he said. I could feel him staring at me. "I don't know why. When I met you, something just . . . I don't know. It sounds ridiculous now."

"Yeah, it does. When did you and Carla start dating?"

"About seven months ago."

"She's seven months pregnant."

"Exactly." His hands shook slightly in his lap, presumably from his Twizzlers withdrawal. I could have used one right about then.

"Well, aren't you a Flashburn gentleman?"

"It's not like I was planning on sleeping with her. We met at some highbrow party for spoiled rich kids, because when your family has money and your therapist says you need to 'be around other kids your age' and 'learn to appreciate the perks of living,' lying in bed and floundering in self-hatred while you listen to a sucky band like the Renegade Dystopia isn't seen as a healthy alternative." He clasped both hands behind his head. "Carla started flirting with me. And at the risk of sounding pathetic, having a girl like Carla notice me wasn't something I was used to. So, yeah. I flirted back. I drank a little bit. She drank some to balance it out. We were upstairs alone. And, well, she was wearing this really short dress—"

"Oh my God, spare me the nitty-gritty."

He closed his eyes to refocus. "Point is, it wasn't supposed to amount to anything."

"Except that it did. And you have to grow some balls and own up to that."

"I'm trying!" he shouted. I hadn't heard him shout before. It was the most impressive thing I'd seen him do, because it was real. He was being sincere for once. "I promised Carla that I'd be there for her, even though her dad hates me and won't let me go to any of her appointments. I took the job he offered me so I can help her when the baby gets here. I've done everything I know to do, but then you come along and ruin everything."

"Me?" I somehow ended up on my feet with a face hotter than Hades in the summer. "I didn't know you'd impregnated the Kate Middleton of Flashburn when you came on to me. How did I ruin everything?"

"You made me want to be hated," he sighed. We stood facing each other. Nothing separated us but a block of sunlight. "Carla is not my type. I'm sorry. I know I should say she is, but she isn't. Don't get me wrong, I care about her. I kind of have to after what we did. But she . . . she . . ." He raked his fingers through his hair. "She is conceited and shallow and bossy and has the worst taste in music I have ever heard."

I could practically hear her screeching to Taylor Swift. "Worse than the Renegade Dystopia?"

"Worse than the Renegade Dystopia during a Prozac seizure." He made an *ugh* noise into his hands. "She drives me insane. And then I meet you, and you drive me possibly even more insane. But it's the kind of insane that makes the Renegade Dystopia during a Prozac seizure seem like one of those perks of living. I want to be around you so I can hate things the way you hate them and endure constant putdowns and near assaults and kiss you on anti-dates." He looked out the window at a young couple fishing by the pond. "But how do you dump a girl who is pregnant with your ginger squash, right?"

Reflections from the window sparkled in his eyes and for a fleeting moment made the gray-blue of them something worth appreciating.

"You should leave me alone," I said.

He stepped closer to me, and the reflections left. His eyes were uninteresting again. "That's Saturday, remember?"

"What?"

"*The Guide to Successful Depressive Behavior.* Being left alone is supposed to happen on Saturday."

"I don't care what this fictitious manual to barely existing says to do. I'm crazy enough as it is. I don't need you coming around and trying to impress me with anti-dates and inspirational speeches about woodland creatures. You're too presumptuous."

"I'm presumptuous?"

"Yes. And I don't need you. I don't need your cold pizza. I don't need to be a front-row observer of the disaster that is your Twizzlers addiction. I don't need your pregnant girlfriend rubbing her sonogram in my face. And I don't need to hate you, because I think you're doing a pretty good job of it without me."

He smirked, that jackass. He enjoyed being told off. He

was so hopelessly presumptuous that he invited rejection at the expense of his own ego. Which was so downright presumptuous that it was really kind of self-deprecating. That's what he was. A self-deprecating egomaniac.

"Easy there," he warned. "Don't want to waste the epic 'I hate you' too soon. It's only been one date, after all."

I knocked his shoulder as I stomped past him. He caught up and tried to hold the door open as if he could still convince me that he was some kind of gentleman. I grabbed it first, purposely jabbing him with my elbow as I stormed out of the house.

As I hopped off the two-step porch, I spun around to feed him one final piece of my mind. But he leaned in the doorway, arms over his chest, hair in his eyes, cool as a lying, cheating cucumber. He was calculating my moves, amused by my anger. Oh, did I have some choice words for him. But I would have to save them for the day I dished out the epic "I hate you," as he said. What a day that would be.

I dug my keys out of my pocket and headed toward the minivan parked at the end of the driveway next to the mailbox. I made a note to knock it over on my way out. I turned around one last time and said, "Next time you decide to stop acting like a pansy and come to work, don't bother talking to me."

I left without hitting the mailbox. Snake was still

grinning in the doorway as I floored the gas, speeding away from the rich kid pond.

When I reached my room, I slammed the door shut. My head hit the pillow, and I knew that meant I was sliding into Stage 2, because the sun was out and my head never hit the pillow before sundown unless I was in Stage 2. But I wasn't in Stage 2, I was just tired. And I wanted to leave my body. And I wanted the sun to be purple instead of orange, because orange was too bright and purple soothed me. And I wanted Carla Banks to not be pregnant. And I wanted Snake to not be her boyfriend. And I wanted people to be there when I called them. And I wanted me to not be me. I wanted too many things for one person.

So I was tired and wanted nothing more than to sleep because it made everything quiet and still and easy. But nothing was ever easy. Not even swallowing my pride long enough to reach under my bed and grab the black composition journal Karen had bought me.

I picked up a pen and opened it up to the first blank page. I wasn't sure I even remembered how to do it, how to put pen to paper and string coherent thoughts together. It had been so long since I tried.

I pressed the pen to the first line and scribbled *What Crazy Means to Me.*

All it took was a bar of sunlight from the window to strike my face, and I had it.

Snake.

That was it. Him. My profound, literary muse. Snake. Fucking. Eliot. The five stupid, arrogant letters of his ridiculous moniker jabbed into my brain, leaving a gaping hole for all of my rage to leak out. I was emitting him from my pores, snarling like a rabid dog. Snake Eliot. I wanted to kick him in his barely there nuts. I wanted to toss out his licorice stash so he'd stop rotting his teeth. I wanted him to leave me alone forever. I wanted to kiss him on his pretty-boy lips.

I pressed the pen down.

What Crazy Means to Me: Hating Snake Eliot so much you really don't hate him at all.

It was no coincidence that *Snake* and *Crazy* were both five letters.

CHAPTER seven

OINKY'S WAS PACKED FOR A SATURDAY night. By packed, I mean there were actually customers the night Snake decided to show up for work again. He knocked on the back door as he made his grand entrance, a trip coupled with a semigraceful recovery. His blue Oinky's shirt was wrinkled in a thousand places, doing his lanky arms no favors. He probably liked how disheveled he looked. He couldn't taint his "Steven Spielberg of indie filmmakers" image with combed hair and an ironed shirt.

Peyton was on vacation, which meant that I was running the show for the night. Looked like Snake was going to have to be my assistant director. The pleasure (see: paralyzing dread) was all mine.

"You look awful," I greeted him ever so politely.

"I was aiming for sexy, but awful works too." He collapsed into a metal chair by the register.

"I wouldn't aim for sexy. It doesn't suit you."

"And blue really isn't your color, but we work with what we've got." He kicked his feet up on the wooden counter. "Any machines need fixing?"

"While you were out playing Where in Flashburn Is Snake Eliot?, Peyton and I successfully tuned every machine and deep cleaned the trailer. Your services aren't needed."

"And yet here I am."

"Yeah, because your future father-in-law is calling the shots."

"He's not my future anything. And he isn't calling the shots."

He said it in a bitter way that was surprisingly becoming to him. I liked it. Bitter was my native language.

"Are you kidding? You're having a baby Banks, which is like having the future president of the Narcissism Guild. You'll be on an exceptionally tight leash for the next eighteen years."

He leaned back in his chair and groaned like he had the last time I brought up Carla and the ginger squash. "Can we not talk about it?"

"And what would you like to talk about instead?"

"Global warming. Nuclear warfare. Relief efforts in Uganda. Literally, anything else."

"You can't just ignore it."

"I know that, Reggie. But I get it twenty-four-seven from Carla and her dad. I'd rather not hear it from you too. Two weeks ago, you didn't even know that about me. Can we just go back to talking about ridiculous and trifling things that are of absolutely no importance to our lives?"

He reached behind him for a vanilla-strawberry swirl I'd made. He grabbed the cone and dug his finger into the center, bringing it out covered in freezing cream. Like the jerk he was, he'd smeared it across my forehead before I had time to smack it out of his hand. "There. That was annoying. You probably think I'm childish. Let's talk about that."

I slapped him across the face. Honestly, it was more of a tap. It was like a love pat without the love. He put his hand to his cheek, shocked for maybe half a second before he grinned. Of course he did.

"You just took our relationship to the next level. We're, like . . . engaged now."

"No, we're not. And there is no relationship." I grabbed a washcloth that was dangling from my chair and wiped my face. "You're a douchebag."

"And you're a bitter old maid. Face it. We're meant for each other."

"You want to know what you're meant for? Blowing through people's lives and wrecking everything. Carla. Me. Lord knows who else."

"You were wrecked way before you met me," he countered, not even slightly offended. On the contrary, he seemed encouraged. What a weird, twisted little soul he was. "It suits you, though."

"What does?"

"Depression. It isn't a good look for everyone, kind of like sexy is apparently not a good look for me. But, man" —he shook his head and pulled a Twizzler from his jeans —"you should patent it."

He watched me with his lips curled up, eyes never leaving mine. Smug. It was even less becoming than his attempts at sexy. I ignored him for the next half hour as customers came and went, each one more stocked with complaints than the next. Flashburn's entitlement issue was getting out of hand with the installment of three additional soft serves on Langley, Mills, and Bayer with prices half that of Oinky's. With all the rate competition, I was tempted to spin a sign out front with an arrow pointing toward Mills so everyone would take their business elsewhere. At least that way I wouldn't have to hear "Five dollars for a small?" gasped every ten seconds.

Snake dialed the portable radio to a classic big band station after the crowds died down. He was leaning back in his chair, swaying side to side with the jazzy beat. Reaching under the counter, he retrieved his hulking video camera that he had taken on our anti-date nearly two weeks ago.

Why he brought it to work and how I missed him trying to squeeze it through the tiny doorway were the two currently unsolved mysteries of the evening.

"Snake . . ."

"Shhh." The red light flashed on. The woman on the radio sang the most sappy, he-loves-me-he-loves-me-not song my ears had ever had the misfortune of hearing. "I'm capturing."

"Quit pointing that thing at me, you freak," I said, shoving my hand over the lens.

He grabbed my wrist and moved my hand away. "This is my favorite song of all time."

"Seriously? This?"

The heartbroken woman yammered on about her ill-fated love story. It was the kind of song I would undoubtedly skip if my music app ever despised me enough to play it.

"It's from the soundtrack of *The Onslaught*."

"That sounds like a mosh pit band."

"It's a movie. You've never seen *The Onslaught*?"

"I've never had the pleasure." The ready light flickered like a candle, the red tint blinding me as I stared into the screen and glimpsed my ungodly reflection. My black hair was clawing its way out of my ponytail holder, eyeliner smeared and smudged beneath my eyes. I couldn't have been more <u>attractive</u> (see: vision-damaging) if I tried.

"The camera really doesn't like you."

"I'm sorry. I didn't realize I was going to be the star of your low-budget indie film documenting the pitfalls of our basic human incompetence. Forgot to notify my hair and makeup team."

"Perfect," he whispered into the camera. He switched a button, and the red light ceased to harass me. "That was cinema magic."

"You're a loser."

"You've really never seen *The Onslaught*?" He tucked the camera into the corner where the wooden leg of the countertop touched the wall. "Margaret? Maks? The best doomed-from-the-start circus romance thriller of all time?"

I blinked at him, going so far as to fake a yawn to convey my disinterest.

He placed his hand over his chest and declared, *"I don't need you to love me, Maks. I need you to look at me and see decay. And temporariness. And death. Because that is the essence of who we are. All these fantasies, they're uselessness. Sheer uselessness, that's our condition."*

I recognized his bleak, and apparently stolen, life motto from our anti-date. "Sheer uselessness? You based your entire life around a lame circus movie? Plagiarizer."

"Not a plagiarizer, a pupil. Margaret shaped the way I see the world. *The Onslaught* inspired the film I'm making, which you're in, by the way."

"What's it about?"

"Loss. Love. Fear. Life as a theoretical tightrope into the bleak nothingness of oblivion."

"I was talking about your movie."

"So was I."

He studied me with a self-satisfied gleam in his eye, awaiting a response that would match my folded arms and vacant stare. It would have been easy and predictable for me to mock his undoubtedly shitty movie. The problem was, I was sort of intrigued, as stupid as it may have been. I wanted to know how big a role I played. I wanted to know if the movie would hold up just as well without me.

I decided to stick with the expected. "Using a person's likeness without their consent is illegal, you know."

"Well, do you consent?"

"Of course not."

"I guess you'll just have to sue me, then." He grinned with triumph. "Because there's no way that I can make a film about tragic mediocrity and not have Reggie Mason in a starring role."

"I thought the camera didn't like me."

"I can fix you up in post. Besides, if you looked good, it would take away from your terrible personality. And I can't have anything outshining your mean-spirited glow."

He had a way of complimenting that was like an insult

reversed to sound pleasant. Afterward, he waited with an expectant smirk, hoping I would get super angry and tell him off, or that he could slowly break me down.

The song on the radio had shifted to a saxophone band with intermittent trumpet sounds. It was worse than the movie soundtrack lady, if that was possible. Snake sprang out of his chair, belting the words to the tune in such an uninhibited and embarrassing display that I lost whatever respect I had for him in a shorter time than it took him to air trumpet.

"I don't think I can love her no more!" he squawked. "She's got her hand in mine, sweet kiss to my ear, time's passing by, and I'm still standing here. I shout it to the sky, and it echoes back clear. No! No! No! I don't think I can love her no more!"

Being exposed to his singing voice was pain of an exponential variety. It was worse than the time Karen had forced me to attend a junior knitters camp in the church basement and I spun a lime green sweater that I had to model at the Sunday school picnic. That was pain. This was agony.

"If you don't shut up in the next ten seconds, so help me God—"

I was on my feet. Not only was I on my feet, but I was in Snake's arms. His sharp, bony, in-desperate-need-of-muscle-toning, semirelaxing arms. He had grabbed me right out of the chair, right above the waist, and just kind of held me in front of him. And stared. It wasn't a pimple stare so much as an I-can-see-the-depth-of-your-soul stare. Peculiarly unsettling, yet coincidentally charming. Yes, Snake Eliot was capable of being charming sometimes. A fact that was similarly proven when I went to yank out of his grip but stopped when his nose crinkled in a goofy, boyish way as my hand grazed his. He smiled when he realized that this wasn't going to turn into one of those near-assault encounters.

"Sing," he pleaded.

"Let go."

"May I propose an exchange?"

"Don't you always?"

"I'll let go if you sing."

The saxophones jived on. "I don't know this song."

"I'll help you." He waited for the chorus to make its way back around. Then he looked at me, though I could barely see his eyes beneath his curls. "I don't think I can love her no more," he whispered. The lyrics weren't being screeched or yelped. They weren't especially unpleasant, either. He was just talking. Murmuring. "She's got her hand in mine . . ."

"Sweet kiss to my ear?" I continued uncertainly.

"Time's passing by, and I'm still standing here. I shout

it to the sky, and it echoes back clear." He paused, waiting for the real singers to catch up. "With me now, belt it."

"I don't think I can love her no more!" we both <u>shouted</u> (see: indulging). His voice wasn't such an eardrum murderer with my slightly less agonizing voice there to mask it. The trumpet blared its final solo as the song streamed out, the station transitioning to a Taco Bell commercial.

Snake didn't let loose of my hips. "We really should watch a sneak peek of my movie together soon. It's nowhere near finished, but I could use some input."

"My mom probably doesn't want me hanging out at your house."

"Why?"

"If her snide comments weren't clear to you, she thinks your family is an abomination."

He beamed, most likely at the insinuation that he was a topic of conversation in my house. Positive or negative, it was the ultimate compliment. "On behalf of my family, we're flattered."

I wrapped both hands around his wrists. "I sang."

He let me go, lightly touching the skin where my shirt had ridden up because he thought that move was slick. It wasn't.

"Cut," he said. I eyed him to explain. "If I were directing our lives, I would cut this scene right here. Tension. Angst. Buildup. It doesn't get much better."

"Some girl," I said quietly. He tilted his head. "When you were telling Carla who you worked with, you said just some girl."

He stared at his muddy shoes and felt guilt. That was exactly what he felt. It was probably written on his forehead; it was just invisible behind his hair. The audience in my head cheered in victory.

"Cut," I said.

A knock on the door interrupted us. I looked to the doorway, and Snake mirrored my movements.

And there she was, karma manifested in the prissy and ever-pregnant form of Carla, both hands folded over her bulging stomach. Snake took a step back, thanking his unlucky stars that she hadn't caught him touching me. Her ruby red hair whirled down her back, her golden eyes like shimmering treasure. She was <u>feminine beauty incarnate</u> (see: mega exaggeration) (also see: worst kinds of people). She blinked shyly as she absorbed the scene.

"Hey, Reggie," she said.

I half nodded in response.

"Hey, babe," Snake whispered. "What are you doing here?"

Babe?

Babe?

BABE!

Was he effing serious? I wasn't sure whether to punch

him in the stomach, groin, or face. Too many attack options. The way he talked to her was infuriating. It was like she was a fragile shard of very broken and expensive china, and he was some kind of master craftsman. He sickened me.

"Can I talk to you?" she asked, her voice trembling slightly. "Alone?"

Translation: I'm about to either A) drop-kick you to Waikiki and don't want any witnesses. Or B) burst into tears about something entirely absurd and don't want any witnesses.

Snake glanced at me. By the way he shrugged his shoulders, you would have thought that we had a secret code of body language, and shoulder shrugging fell under "I'm totally whipped." He followed Carla out the trailer door and into the parking lot.

Babe.

Ugh. I dwelled on that sweet and disgusting expression as I worked through the closing-time checklist. As I swept the floor, I could feel a familiar viciousness budding inside like a weed emerging from the pit of me.

Anger. The trigger emotion. The bully. The menace. With anger came panic. It victimized my thoughts and scraped them through a giant shredder of unrelenting emotion that was a lot like getting multiple tetanus shots at once. Sting. Ache. All the throbbing imaginable. My mind was hazy again. Every thought was louder than the last.

Thought 1: I lived in a deadbeat town I would never escape.

Thought 2: I was surrounded by ordinary and boring people who were stupid enough to enjoy their ordinary and boring lives.

Thought 3: There would always be something standing in the way of me becoming one of those stupid and ordinary people (see: happiness).

Thought 4: I was too intelligent and self-respecting and, frankly, good for a wannabe liar like Snake, who was willing to cheat on his pregnant girlfriend just so he could hate and be hated at his whimsy.

Thought 5: I wanted to be the one Snake Eliot called babe.

Thought 6: Thought 5 made me exceptionally pathetic.

The shredder went a little something like that. And coincidentally, so did Stage 1. I realized I was kind of beating the floor with the broom at that point. I knew I had to get home before I cried in front of Carla Banks, or before Snake could see me cry and realize I wasn't exactly made of steel. Floors dusted, sinks washed, countertops disinfected, and machines down, I strutted toward my car to face the music.

They were huddled next to Snake's chick-magnet ladykiller (see: Prius). He held her body as close as her belly would allow, rubbing her lower back with his hands like those sappy boyfriends from vomit-inducing romance movies. She was crying against his chest, her mascara tears staining his Oinky's shirt.

Aw, he wiped a tear. Wasn't he the sweetest thing? Wasn't she lucky to have him? Watching him hold her like that, no one would ever know he was the kind of guy that hooked up with a girl five minutes after he met her or kissed another girl while five-minute girl was toting his baby squash under her dress. He glanced in my direction, and I shot him a very crude hand gesture that I don't feel the need to elaborate on, given the circumstance. (Side note: I also called him six different curse words in my head, which wasn't nearly as satisfying as it should have been.)

When I side-jumped into the minivan and turned the key, my mother's spiritual guide station shot on, blaring high-pitched, delicate harmonies that made me so irrationally furious I wanted to break the system. I opted for a less dramatic response and flipped to a head-banging rock station that was so anger-cliché it was just cliché enough to work for me.

As I drove by high school's sorriest example of soon-to-be parents, I rolled down my window and called, "Hey, you want to know what I would do if I were directing the movie?" Snake glared at me like he was afraid I would say something that would get Carla's designer panties in a bunch. She peeked up from his chest, batting her wet lashes. "I would switch the male lead. That guy is a dick. The odds of him getting the girl are slim to none."

I glanced at Carla, a sour smile sketched on my lips, a display of scorn that only depression and Snake Eliot could yank out of me. "And you. I get it. Pregnancy sucks. But look at it this way, it's not like it's the first time you've had a boy under your dress."

I sped away before I could bask in what I was sure was her appalled reaction, depicted with gunky black tears and a pouty-lipped plea to Snake for reinforcement. The mini-van bumped along Sun Street, hitting every pothole in its path. The stoplight was red, but I floored it through the intersection anyway without glancing back.

All these theories exist concerning why depressed people do the shit they do. Stuff like, *Depression hijacks the logic center of the brain, thus resulting in intensified levels of emotion that can lead to disastrous outcomes* and blah blah blah. They're usually coupled with these genius "philosophies" about depressed people's carelessness being biologically instilled and likewise untreatable. Ludicrous theories, if you ask me. Psychological white noise.

I didn't speed through the red light because I was

biologically instilled to be careless. I sped through the red light because there was no one there to tell me not to. Unfortunately for science, my untreatable carelessness didn't kill me. It wasn't until I made it home that I realized Snake's shirt wasn't the only one with tearstains.

CHAPTER eight

ONCE A MONTH, I GOT THURSDAY off work. And on that rare and glorious day, pork chops sizzling in the frying pan was proof of that fact. Karen called it Chop Thursday. I called it Just Put a Bullet Through My Head and Be Done with It.

I reclined on the bench behind the kitchen table, relaxing on my one of my mother's infamous puke green sweaters that still had the knitting needle poking through the fabric. I stared at the needle. And heard sizzles. And stared.

Clearly, I was having issues. If it wasn't Snake leaving ten voicemails on my phone begging me to call him back so he could do one more thing to make me want to drown him in the rich kid pond, it was my therapist encouraging me to "face life head-on" and "live with abandon." Were therapists even supposed to use the word *abandon*? I was almost positive that was rule number 1 in what *not* to tell your depressed and emotionally unstable juvenile client. Monday's session had gone something to the effect of:

"Did you complete the homework I assigned?"

"No."

"Why?"

"Because I don't want to write. I don't want to do anything."

"Because . . . ?"

"I hate everything."

"Have you considered that maybe you're projecting?"

"Yes. I'm projecting hatred onto Snake because I hate him."

"Maybe it's not him you hate. Maybe you hate that he is confronting issues within yourself that you've been trying to avoid."

"I hate that he likes that I hate him. And I hate that I like that he likes that I hate him."

"Take the word *hate* out of the equation. Replace it with something entirely different. What is the word you would use to describe him now?"

"Bearable."

"You used that word last time."

"What can I say? He's so incredibly bearable that it's impossible not to hate him."

"How so?"

"Because he's the unattainable kind of bearable."

"Unattainable because of this Carla you mentioned earlier?"

"Unattainable because he needs too much."

After that came the usual Dr. Rachelle version of divine enlightenment. She told me to confront issues within myself to have a fulfilling experience, to understand the responsibility that was born out of getting too close to someone like Snake, the reward that could be produced from conquering such a feat, and then the big "live with abandon" portion that was so uncannily out of therapist mold I all but disregarded it. She even encouraged me to write again too, which we both knew wasn't going to happen.

I decided that I wasn't going to be one of those obnoxious teenage girls who wasted eighty dollars a session griping about my *Romeo and Juliet* meets *Rosemary's Baby* drama over a box of tissues and hard candies. Snake wasn't worth eighty dollars a week. He was barely worth the minimum wage compensation to put up with him every few days.

Babe.

Kill me.

"Reggie, sweetheart, could you chop some tomatoes for the salad?" Karen called over the noisy stove.

"I wouldn't trust me with the knives right now, Mom," I said. "I'm on a revenge binge."

"Revenge over what?"

I sat up and could feel my tangled hair bird-nesting

itself on my head. "I want to blacken the eyes of whoever came up with the concept of dating. Like, you meet a guy who is slightly more bearable than the other available idiots, and you say to yourself, 'Hey, this one's not so bad. He's goofy-looking and thinks he's God's gift to women, but I can get past it.' Then he turns out to be the worst of the idiots, and you're all alone again until another available idiot shows his face and swings the whole process back into motion." I sighed loudly, because I wanted her to hear me for once. Hear me for real, not in her dismissive Karen way.

She glanced at me over her shoulder before turning back to the plate of undercooked meat. "Don't tell me this is about that boy with the scary name."

"Oh, of course not. The core of the earth would incinerate us entirely if one of my chosen available idiots was a guy who used the word *vagina* more than once to describe his parents' relationship."

"Don't start with me tonight," she warned, sprinkling spices on the pork chops. "Start chopping the tomatoes. Dinner will be ready soon."

I chopped, vertical slices first, then cutting through horizontally for perfect squares.

"Don't forget your brother is coming to town in two weeks. He's bringing baby Killian."

Wonderful. Frankie the chosen one and his Stepford wife would be coming down from New York to grace us with their presence. I didn't know what I was more looking forward to, Frankie's baritone solo in our <u>annual car-ride sing-alongs</u> (see: side thorn) or my mother anointing my nephew, Killian, while the theme song to *The Lion King* played.

"When does the parade commence?"

"Don't go showing yourself now. Frankie loves you."

"Frankie loves everyone. Frankie thinks he's the messiah."

"Stop it," she said, setting the table with only two plates.

"What about Dad?"

"He's at a doctor's appointment," she replied, twisting the knobs on the stovetop.

I took a seat at the table, eating a chunk of tomato from the salad bowl. She rubbed her eyes beneath her glasses as she sat down.

"Have you gotten to use your journal yet?" she asked, taking a bite of salad.

"Nope."

"Why not?"

"Because I'm not going to let you and Dr. Rachelle force a hobby on me."

"You've written some great stuff in your creative writing class."

"When have you ever read anything I've written?"

She glanced up from her plate briefly, watching me with

a hint of longing. "Well, if you would share your work with me . . ."

I wanted to bang my head on the table. Instead, I decided to humor her. "Fine. Last week, I wrote a story with a dog in it."

"Oh, a dog. That's nice."

"It froze to death."

"Reggie." The flame of hope went out in her eyes. "You're such a sadistic girl."

"Don't worry, the owner lived," I assured her. She lifted a brow skeptically. "But then he contracted syphilis."

She sighed. "We can be done sharing now."

I watched her take a sloppy bite of her salad, her mouth dripping with ranch dressing. She motioned toward my peas, and I knew I had to take a bite before she got on my case. They were about as disgusting as I'd anticipated. Karen's cooking hadn't improved with her stay-at-home schedule. Most of her time was spent knitting, annoying me, and pretending she didn't miss her job at the daycare. She'd worked there since I was in diapers, and when she'd ended her stint sixth months prior, her Jesus-fused joy was more for appearance's sake than the genuine kind. Even Dad knew she missed it. One day he suggested she go back, and all she did was shrug him off, mumble something about paying her dues, and continue her knitting. Dad might have known why she quit, but he never told me. I was beginning to think that she didn't have a reason.

"That's a hideous sweater," I said, motioning to the work in progress on the bench.

She frowned and smiled at the same time. "That's for little Joshua. He's graduating kindergarten this year."

"Does he go to the daycare?"

She nodded. "His parents don't have much. When he was a baby, his mom would bring him in the same ratty jacket every day, even in the freezing temperatures. Louise said his wardrobe hasn't changed a whole lot since I've been gone."

I rolled my eyes. "Well, you could at least do the kid a solid and knit Spider-Man onto it or something. And, really, is that a turtleneck?"

"He's a little boy, Regina. He doesn't care what he looks like."

There was a length of time when all she did was look at the sweater, forcing joy into her face like it was medicine she was pumping through a tube. She missed Joshua, and I'd have bet she missed all of them. I couldn't imagine why. Personally, I hated children. The farther away from children I could get, the better. But Karen never saw it that way. She'd always been obsessed with kids (see: covered-in-snot mini-humans).

"Why did you quit your job?" I asked.

She opened her eyes bigger, then bowed her head and took a bite of her gross peas. "I got tired of working."

"But you loved working."

"At the time."

"Why? What changed?"

She took her glasses off and pinched her nose. "I'm getting older, sweetheart. Okay? I didn't have the strength anymore. Let's leave it at that." She put her glasses back on and gestured to my plate. "Eat your food."

I would have pressed her the way she always pressed me, but when I did that, I usually ended up grounded, and her answer might not have been interesting enough to be worth it. We ate in silence for the remainder of the meal.

Silence. Now, that was a perk of living. Granted, it never lasted. Just as we were settling into the quiet we both urgently needed, my phone vibrated loudly on the table. I grabbed it and read the text that was spread across the screen.

COME OVER TONIGHT.
PLEASE. I'LL RESPECT YOUR
DEPRESSION AND LET YOU
SULK IN MISERY UNTIL YOU
GROW OLD IN UNHAPPINESS
AND DIE ALONE IF YOU WILL

JUST COME OVER TONIGHT.
AND YOU'RE PRETTY. I THINK
I'M SUPPOSED TO SAY THAT.
COME OVER.

Another all-caps text from Snake begging for my company. That didn't reek of desperation or anything. His focus on me was bordering on obsession. Then again, my hatred for him was bordering on maniac. Something had to be done about our mutual insanities.

"Who's that?" Karen asked, standing to her feet to clear the table.

I tossed my dishes into the sink. "Just Polka asking about our final paper." I took a step aside in case a bolt of lightning tried to strike me.

I didn't want to see him. I wanted to see him. I didn't want to think about him. He was all I thought about. He and I were a contradiction in ourselves, so alike we were entirely different. Grounded or not, consumed by hatred or not, I knew I had to face him eventually. Why not tonight? How could seeing his dumb, pretty face one more time make any of this worse? He would probably try to make me hate him because it was just another thing he needed. But hating him was something I needed too.

I ran upstairs while my mother was distracted with cleaning the dishes, and tossed a gray sweater over my shirt, then laced up my combat boots. When I finally made it downstairs, Karen was wiping the kitchen table with a wet washcloth.

"Where are you going?" she called.

"On a walk."

"It's getting late."

"It'll clear my head, help me get ideas for the paper."

"Fine. You can walk, but be back inside before it gets dark. I read this story about a girl who—"

I was in the minivan before she finished the sentence.

CHAPTER nine

THE ELIOTS HAD THE STRANGEST WELCOME mat. It had dog bones bordering the word *Welcome,* which implied that the family living inside the house had a dog. Except that Snake didn't have a dog. So clearly, he wasn't the only member of his family who did things for the heck of it and made decisions that required absolutely no thought or common sense whatsoever. Jeez. His family had to be a real class act (see: band of tasteless jerks).

I rang the doorbell. One of those fancy doorbells that echoed for ten seconds so that the people outside would think that the people inside needed that long a warning in order to set aside their important lives. Footsteps neared, but they weren't loud and clunky and awkward. I knew they couldn't belong to Snake.

The woman who opened the door was one of Snake's

moms, presumably. She was Latina and petite and gorgeous, the natural gorgeous, not the face-painted-on kind. She'd been working out, so her purple exercise shirt was stained with sweat, and even her sweat was flawless. She smiled a Colgate commercial smile when she saw me.

"Are you Reggie?" she asked.

That wasn't good. She knew me. That meant Snake talked about me. That also meant she knew Snake was a cheating scumbag. Which would have implied that I was the lover of her son the cheating scumbag. Which would lead her to the conclusion that I, myself, was a skanky cheating scumbag. I blamed Snake.

"Hi," I said in a really girly way that was super unlike me.

"Come in," she replied.

I stepped into their sterile living room with the therapy couches and swanky magazine tables.

"Would you like a drink?" she asked.

"No, thank you. Is Snake here?"

I knew Snake was there. The Namaste Prius was parked in the driveway. Asking was my attempt at polite. Unlike depression, it wasn't my best look.

"He's upstairs in his room." She smiled. Perfectly, of course. "He's told us a lot about you."

"All good things, I hope."

"Great things. He's lucky to have you."

That infuriated me beyond reason. I rolled my eyes. So much for polite. "He doesn't have me. He has a girlfriend."

"Carla. Yes, we know."

She fiddled with the string on her pants and didn't say much else. I could tell she was a talker, just by the brightness of her smile and her warm welcome. But saying Carla's name made her visibly uncomfortable. It didn't make sense, considering parents usually loved Carla, even the pregnant version.

"You know, Snake called me a hundred times last night. You should really monitor his cell phone usage."

She smiled. "We're sorry if Snake has caused you any trouble. He's a very sweet kid, and he means well. It's just that his efforts have a tendency to be a tad misguided sometimes."

"Ha," I huffed. "No kidding." I knew I shouldn't have been so abrasive. It wasn't making the best impression. But if Carla couldn't get her approval, I didn't stand a chance. "Permission to speak boldly?"

She let out a soft laugh. "I think you will no matter what I say. So yes."

"I know men aren't really your specialty, but I think the concept of douchelord isn't completely foreign to you. And no offense, but your son is acting like the douchiest of douchelords in the kingdom of Doucheshire, and I just need someone besides me and a pregnant girl I'm not even friends with to understand that."

Her Colgate smile was back. She was amused. Oh no, not another self-deprecating egomaniac. What was it with this family and their fondness for self-directed abuses?

"Permission to speak boldly?" she asked. I nodded. "Snake's never been the best at relationships of any kind. He never tries to get to know people, and he never pursues anyone. Ever. Which tells me that whatever he has or doesn't have with you matters a lot to him. If he's bothering you, then let him go. But I would suggest getting to know him better. He's not just the douchelord of Doucheshire, I promise."

In all fairness, she had to say that. It was coded in her DNA to think highly of her own kid. By the same token, though, Snake really wasn't all that bad in the moments I wasn't dwelling on his stupidity. It wasn't like I was a sunny stroll through the unicorn fields myself. It was a tough decision: hate him for his bad qualities or like him for his good ones. Either way, it didn't look like letting him go would be an option.

"I'll keep it in mind," I said. "Thanks for listening . . ."

"Jeanine." She pointed to the staircase. "Snake's door is the first on the right."

I followed the direction of her finger up a wooden

staircase. Across the hallway at the top of the steps was a square picture frame nailed to the wall. It was the stereotypical, all-American family pose in white shirts and khakis on the beach. Jeanine sat next to a blond woman with curly hair, both of their hands resting on a prepubescent Snake's shoulders. I wouldn't have recognized him if it wasn't for his dull blue eyes that caught my attention. They weren't hidden behind shaggy brown hair for once. Instead, he had a spiked cut and no deformed diamond tattoo on his neck. He looked like the biggest dork I'd ever seen. I needed a photocopy immediately.

"Reggie?" a familiar, raspy voice asked from behind.

When I turned around, Snake was leaning in his doorway, wearing black sweatpants and a white T-shirt that was ripped on the shoulder.

"Don't get all dressed up on my account."

"Pardon me." He grinned his signature, half-bitter, half-unconcerned Snake grin. "If I had known you would respond to one of my texts, I would have tossed on a suit and hired a violinist."

I walked toward him. "You gonna invite me in, or do I have to stand out here and think of ways to get my hands on your best attempt at sexy?" I pointed to the picture.

"I was twelve. I bet when you were twelve you were even more unkempt than you are now."

"My inner confidence radiates. I don't need the add-ons. Not all of us are as insecure as Carla."

He fidgeted awkwardly, looking down at his bare feet. "Yeah, about the other night . . ."

"Don't worry about it. Pregnant girlfriends can be a real buzzkill. Don't stress yourself out, *babe*." I smiled with victory.

He made an exaggerated frown. "I lament that expression, but it keeps Carla happy. A happy Carla makes for a less miserable me."

"And it's all about you."

"That's not fair."

It was incredibly fair, and the insinuation that it wasn't made my eyes roll. "You told your moms about me?"

He rubbed the back of his neck and looked down. "I kind of felt like I needed to explain why I've been hanging out with a girl who isn't Carla."

"Stalking," I corrected. "Stalking a girl who isn't Carla."

He laughed. "Again, not fair."

I bumped past him into the bedroom. It was precisely what I'd expected. Clothes scattered on a carpeted floor. A double bed littered with candy wrappers and popcorn kernels. A computer desk with his expensive video camera hooked up to the monitor by wires. A thousand-dollar television mounted on the wall. A poster of some indie movie no one had ever seen on the opposite wall. It was one of those alternative rich-boy rooms that try so hard to be grunge they border on narcissistic. It was so Snake it was unbelievable.

"This room is a joke."

"Thanks. I wrecked it myself." He moved to the computer desk to grab something and quickly hid it behind his back. "You must be wondering why I was so urgent in my text. Guess why."

"Because you're full of shit."

"That. And . . ." He thrust his arm out, revealing an unmarked DVD case. "Sneak peek at *The Snake Project,* director's cut."

"That's your grand gesture? Asking me to watch an unfinished movie that you unlawfully inserted me into?"

"Still waiting on my court papers." He walked to the TV and pressed the button on the DVD player. He stuck the disc inside and plopped down on his bed, because he was such an irredeemable narcissist that he once again made the assumption I wanted to watch his crappy movie. The truth was, I did. But his assuming nature almost made me walk right back into the hallway, take a picture of his ugly picture, and bail.

"Well?" he grinned. It was a smug grin this time. Smug. A lot like sexy. The *S*'s were not his best. He patted the space beside him on the bed. "Are you ready to bask in the creative interpretation of our tragic state?"

"Talk dirty to me," I muttered.

Notes from a piano piece blared loudly through the speakers on the TV, playing a really depressing song that was the music version of what my brain did during a Zoloft-induced blackout in Stage 3. Snake reached over to his computer desk and turned off the lamp, so that the only remaining light in the room came from the colorful film pixelating on the screen. I sat down next to him on the bed, but made sure to keep a very healthy and considerable distance. If any part of his body touched any part of mine, he was going to lose that limb.

He didn't try anything.

The film opened to faded sunlight filtering through the trees from the vantage point of a car speeding down the highway. The WELCOME TO FLASHBURN sign popped into the frame, then faded to black.

It was an ideal segue into the next shot. A waiting room at a doctor's office. The scene was melancholy, evidenced in the sad, forlorn, and pitiful faces of the patients. From elderly to moms to children, sick and dying, and everything in between. After that was a hodgepodge of random scenes involving pill bottles and prescriptions and a thunderstorm that didn't seem to have much of a purpose. Then, Carla. Lots and lots of Carla. Smiling, radiant Carla. A shot of Snake and Carla kissing down at the pond. Carla, grinning somewhat unhappily, holding up her first ultrasound picture. The sad music played on, a woman's voice muffled in the noise.

There's a wretched brilliance in tightropes, Maks. If one walks it with her eyes closed, she can pretend that it never ends. But if one chooses to tread with caution, to study her moves before she makes them, she's brutally aware that the rope doesn't last forever. Just imagine how miserable a fate it is to be to be a woman unable to close her eyes.

The screen went abruptly black. I thought it was over until a slow pan downward revealed the derelict houses from our anti-date. The beautiful, almost transcendent way in which Snake captured the dripping orange sunset behind them. My own side profile, messy and disheveled, shadowed in the frame. Snake's declaration of being "but a pebble in the sand," with a girl who hated him (see: me) almost as much as she hated herself. Another scene of my dark blue eyes glaring into the lens at Oinky's, expressing my hatred for being on camera. Followed by a slowed-down version of my annoyed frown with another voice-over. This time, a man.

You know, Margaret? I don't think even God himself knows why we all ended up in the same circus, feeding the same horses, walking the same goddamn tightrope every goddamn night. But I'll tell you one thing. I'd consider all of our misfortune worth it if from time to time, you'd glance my way and smile that smile you don't need to force with Vaseline, and wink like I'm the only one who knows the mysteries of our reality. Like I'm the only one who knows that our tightropes are meant to be right next to each other.

The screen went black for good.

Snake sat motionless and silent, two behaviors I hadn't realized he was capable of. I could feel him watching me from the corner of his eye, anxious for my approval or condemnation. Honestly, my response could have gone either way.

Some of the shots were stunning, like the opening sunlight and anti-date, while others had a fuzzy, home video quality that a judge in basically any contest would subtract points for. But I knew Snake wasn't making this film for a contest. He was making this film to stay alive.

I elbowed him. "You need a better title than *The Snake Project.*"

It was all I could say without giving him too much credit.

He smirked. "I was thinking *The Sheer Uselessness of Our Condition.*"

"You said Margaret inspired the outlook? The way you see the world?" I asked. He nodded. "Well, any good director allows a Q&A after the first screening, so I guess my question is, where does sheer uselessness fit into your life?"

It was a solid question. Even if I did sound like Dr. Rachelle.

My putting him on the spot had him all stressed out, seeing as how he needed to shove two Twizzlers between his lips to concentrate. "I make idiotic mistakes," he replied, his gaze fixed on the screen. "I do idiotic things and try to fix them by doing more idiotic things. And, I don't know, sometimes I feel more or less human than most people. I feel less human because I can't be what everyone expects, and I feel more human because I don't want to be. It's uselessness, though . . . being human. Maybe that doesn't make any sense."

"It's actually kind of genius," I admitted. "Please tell me those are your own thoughts and not something you read or watched, because I'm honestly super impressed."

He grabbed the remote and shut off the movie. "My own thoughts. Swear."

"Let me ask you something," I said. He turned to me completely. I could see my reflection inside his eyes. "Do you think Carla was a mistake?"

If there was one thing I couldn't do, it was surprise him. He had a Reggie radar, homed in on directness. He was bold all of a sudden, staring at me in the nonpimple way. "It's hard to say. I wanted to feel, and she helped with that. But now I want to feel long-term. Preferably without Prozac. If I had done things right, it would never have been with her."

Blue eyes. Dull, boring, cheating blue eyes that lied and

hurt and took. That's what Snake was. He was what was in his eyes. But for the first time, they were honest. And genuine. And raw. They were the tangible equivalent of how *The Snake Project* made me feel.

He wanted the world to stop, I think. If only for him, if only for the split second he touched my face with his sticky fingertip. When he let his hand fall to the bed, his earth spun again — wildly, brashly, beyond what he could handle. At least, I wanted to believe that it did. I didn't want to be the only one whose world wouldn't stand still, the only one who took pills to slow it down.

"Why was she crying the other day?" I asked.

"Her aunt Henrietta died. They were pretty close."

"I remember. She came to all of Carla's birthday parties when we were kids."

"Her wake was tonight. I wasn't invited, no shocker there."

"I'm sure her family members aren't big fans of the loser who knocked up their precious debutante."

"I'm sick of everyone blaming me," he said, raking his hand through his messy hair. "Her dad despises me on unnatural levels. She won't stand up to him. I get caught in the middle. It's a whole lot of drama that I never signed up for."

"Slow your roll, Mr. Ego." I pulled a Twizzler from the plastic bag. "Mr. Banks has always been a jerk. Seriously, kids at school used to warn each other about Sir Jerkwad whenever he came for career day. You're not the only one he has it in for. Trust me. And Carla has always been his little princess, sweet pea, sugarplum. Standing up to him isn't even a concept in her world."

The DVD screensaver logo bumped from corner to corner of the screen. "I don't want to live in her world," he whispered.

"It's too late for that."

"I know, but—" He leaned forward. I could tell he wanted to make some grand confession of harbored feelings that I really couldn't hear, because I wasn't sure how much I hated him. And if I didn't hate him enough, I would let myself listen. He watched me with eyes that were slowly becoming more and more . . . interesting. "If I wasn't in this situation with Carla, and all you knew of me was that I listened to the Renegade Dystopia and liked anti-dates and filmmaking, would you maybe hate me in the good way?"

It wasn't a confession, but it provoked one. That time, it was me who was on the spot. "There may have been a microscopic possibility that you would have gotten a second anti-date."

He chewed the end of his Twizzler, watching me like he knew he couldn't wish for more. "I guess we'll never know, will we?"

"I guess not."

After it got dark, I went downstairs. Snake promised he would show me the end of the movie when it was ready, but I doubted I would come back again. Something felt off about being near him. Maybe because I knew he wanted too much, and I wanted too much, and we were too damn stubborn to admit it to ourselves, much less each other.

He stopped at the doorway and stared like he wanted to ask me to stay. I knew he wouldn't.

"I'm glad you came over." He stepped closer, breathing his strawberry Twizzler breath all over my face. The space between us was cloudy and thick and frightening. "Sorry I'm not original or remarkable enough to earn your respect."

"Eh, you managed to impress me once. You'll get there."

I clenched my sweaty hands down at my sides, and felt the need to peek at my driver's license or dig out my birth certificate or look in a mirror to make sure I was still me, because whatever Snake was doing to me had never happened before. It honestly was remarkable.

"I'm going to kiss you," he announced, his eyes gauging my reaction.

"No, you're not."

"Yes, I am."

"I'll tell Carla."

"No, you won't."

"Yes, I will."

"Ugh, fine. It was worth a shot." He placed his hand

on the doorknob and shot me a pleading look that was all kinds of attractive and obnoxious. "We wouldn't be any worse off for it, you know."

"Open the door, Fabio."

He obeyed with a smile, and I walked outside onto the dog bone mat with Snake trailing behind me. I heard him make a sort of gasping sound that was one octave away from being the most embarrassing sound a teenage boy ever uttered. And that was when I saw the porch light reflecting off her long red hair.

Karma (see: Carla Banks).

There she sat, her back against the porch steps, wearing the ugliest purple sundress any hand had ever sewn. She was staring across Snake's lawn where the moon and clouds drew gloomy pictures on the surface of the pond. When she heard the door open, she spun around. Her shaken reaction to seeing me signaled that I was not a welcome intruder. Her eyes were familiar because they were my Stage 2 eyes. Puffy. Drained. All cried out.

Snake brushed past me down the short steps, kneeling to her level. Even with his arm around her, she was still looking at me. "Babe," he whispered in what I dubbed the Official Carla Voice, a composition of whiny, affectionate, and other stereotypical boyfriend sounds. "Is everything okay? Is the baby all right?"

"He's fine," she snapped. "Help me up."

Angry Carla. I didn't mind her. She was way more tolerable than Preppy Carla or Little Miss Flashburn Carla or *Ohmigodtotally* Carla. Snake gripped both of her arms and struggled to pull her to her feet. After a little effort and a lot of emasculation on Snake's part, she was up with her hands on her belly and her teeth biting the blood out of her glossy lips.

"I didn't know you would be here, Reggie," she said through gritted teeth. I could tell she was trying to keep from crying again.

"I didn't either." I glanced at Snake, who was pleading with his eyes again. A different plea this time. "Snake, uh, left his wallet at work. I was returning it."

"He had his wallet last night when we went to dinner."

I glared at him in a way that wasn't exactly a glare, but enough to make him squirm. He knew what he had done. He had been texting me last night. Where was Jeanine when you needed to prove to her that her son really was the douchelord of Doucheshire?

"Why aren't you at the wake?" Snake asked, to change the subject.

"Everyone left an hour ago."

"Did you drive here? I don't see your car."

"My dad dropped me off." She glanced down the street. "He's waiting at the dead end."

"Why didn't you ring the doorbell?"

"I was giving myself time to think."

"About what?"

She didn't answer.

I tried to stop myself from staring at her pretty face, but there I was . . . staring at her pretty face. Again. And, much to my misfortune, she did have a very pretty face. She was dainty and full-lipped and more superficially beautiful than the rest of us suburbia girls. When we were growing up, her looks were one of the main things I had always secretly resented about her. But that night, she didn't look so pretty. Her caramel-brown eyes were droopy, and her pink cheeks were bloated, and she was tired and angry and lonely. She had Snake on her arm and a baby in her stomach and her dad waiting at the end of the street, and she was lonely.

"I better get home," I said, reaching for my keys. "Don't want Karen to send out an AMBER Alert."

Snake didn't look at me. He never looked at me when Carla was around. When he did, it was just his puppy dog eyes begging for me to lie so that he could have his cake and eat it too. Carla looked at me, but I couldn't tell what she was looking for. Maybe a sign that I was hiding something. Maybe a flash of honesty in my eyes that could back up my story. Or maybe she was just afraid of being fooled, and opening her eyes to any possibility was better than being blind to it.

I walked past them down the sidewalk that was all stone

and decorative bead liner. I was almost to my car when I heard Carla yell, "Reggie! Wait!"

She hadn't moved from her spot beside Snake. His back was turned. The coward wouldn't even tell me goodbye.

"I just wanted to say thank you," she called.

"For what?"

She shrugged. "Just . . . thank you."

I was in the minivan before I could press her for an explanation, backing out of the driveway onto the street. Her hair flamed under the porch light. Snake had a hand on her face, whispering something against her skin. I wondered if she liked the way he smelled of strawberry. I wondered if she appreciated his dull, honest eyes. I wondered if she had ever seen *The Snake Project*. I wondered if she knew the right way to hate him.

He led her inside as I drove away, and all I could think of was Margaret and that damn tightrope.

Just imagine how miserable a fate it is to be to be a woman unable to close her eyes.

CHAPTER ten

"YOU VERY MUCH SUCK RIGHT NOW."

"That's a little harsh for a tutor."

"I can say what I want. You don't pay me."

Polka and I had been working on a writing assignment for forty-five minutes, and he was clearly fed up with my shit. Admittedly, he was justified in ripping my first draft to shreds, but hitting me with his notebook felt a tad excessive. I'd finally given in to his begging after I got a C on last week's character study. I'd stated the hero's motivation as "Becoming the biggest mansplainer in history," which, apparently, was a hindrance to the cause.

"You still not write your final paper yet," he accused. He jumped up and slung his backpack over a studded jean jacket, straightening the checkered bow tie around his neck. His style—'80s pop star meets cocktail waiter—was incongruent with his personality.

"I'm getting to it," I said, zipping my bag.

"Getting to it mean waiting to night before."

"I'm not going to wait until the night before."

He focused his black eyes on me. "Because I come to your house and help you."

"Polka—"

"It settled." He said it the same way he cursed, matter-of-factly and nothing to it. "I come to your house and help with paper. When good time?"

"I don't know . . . sometime," I groaned.

Translation: I'd rather get hit by a semi.

It was nearing four o'clock when we left the cafeteria. When I finally saw his guardian's red Jeep pull to the front of the awning, I turned into Karen 2.0 and thanked the Lord for His impeccable timing. I made my way across the parking lot, which was empty for the most part, considering it was Friday and the only people still at school were nerds, teachers, and those with no life. The minivan was parked in what everyone called the last-minute section at the farthest end of the lot. Splattered chocolate milkshake was smeared along the driver's side where some moron had been too lazy to move three steps closer to the garbage can. I vowed to take my chances with handicap towing next time.

It had been another dragging day. Go figure. As

uneventful as it was, I'd had more than sufficient time to dwell on all the things I hated. My depression. My friend-lessness. My pending date with doom and worst people manifestations (see: family reunion). And Snake. Snake the cheater. Snake the survivor. Snake the Twizzlers addict. Snake the poser filmmaker extraordinaire. Snake the douchelord.

Carla's Snake.

I dwelled extra long on the last one.

It wasn't easy having two classes with her, especially that day, when she kept looking at me like I had stabbed her in the back with a pencil and asked for the lead back. Something had happened after I left last night. Something had happened with Snake. Well, things had happened with me, too. In my mind. A change. And I didn't want that change to leave me in a state of Carla, with puffy eyes and desperation and loneliness. But Snake had a way of making crazy people crazier. And although I was almost embar-rassed for thinking it, I kind of felt like Carla and I were weathering Hurricane Snake together.

I fumbled for the van keys at the bottom of my mes-senger bag. As I struggled to get ahold of them, I heard a familiar voice a few feet away.

I went through the checklist of the kinds of people who stayed at school until four o'clock on a Friday. Nerds. Teachers. Those with no life.

Carla definitely fell into the third category.

"Hey, Snake." She paced by the trees, twirling a strand of red hair around her finger as she spoke into her bedazzled phone. "I've left at least five messages. It's four o'clock —you're twenty minutes late. I thought we agreed you would still come today. Maybe I heard wrong. Call me back if you're coming. Oh, and bring—" She paused and drew the phone from her ear. "Dammit." She pounded the screen and grabbed her forehead with her hand.

Ugh. I was going to have to do a good deed. I resented people like Snake who made other <u>people like Snake</u> (see: me) pick up the pieces of <u>Snake-like victims</u> (see: Carla) and do <u>good deeds</u> (see: torture). I gave up on my keys because, frankly, they were too tangled for me to care, and I had to talk to Carla fast or I would burst with glitter and fairy dust and go-team positivity.

She didn't see me until I was nearly a foot from her, but she bore the weirdest expression when she did. Her mouth opened and she let out a breath, blinking her eyes at twice the rate. Was she relieved to see me?

"Hey," she whispered, wiping her mascara like I didn't already know she was a blubbering mess. "I didn't see you there."

"Really? I could hear you wailing from the library."

"What?" she gasped.

"Kidding. Relax. You're pregnant, you can get away with the constant hormonal tears."

She glanced down the street. "He didn't come."

"Who didn't come?"

"Snake. He was supposed to take me to birthing class, and he won't answer his phone."

"Oh, maybe he'll show—"

"I know something's going on with you two," she blurted. I tried to keep a poker face, but I was terrible at lying. And poker. "You can stop pretending like you barely know him."

Her voice quivered a bit too loudly to be ignored. Then the lip biting started. And after that, the grand finale. The bursting of the emotional floodgates. At least she had the decency to cry into her hands and not subject me to one of those horrible, nostrils-flared, mouth-agape cry faces. Because I would have laughed, and the whole "do good" thing would have been shot.

"Why are you crying?" I asked.

I waited for her to pick either A) because I'm pregnant, that's why!, B) because my boyfriend's a cheating asshole, or C) I just realized how bloated I am. (I knew she wouldn't pick option C—I tossed that one in there for shits and giggles.)

"Snake hates me," she cried against her snotty hand.

"Did he say that?"

"No, but he does." She reached into her pocket for a Kleenex. She would fare well in therapy. "Can we talk in your car?"

"Well . . ."

"Please."

Etched into stone since the universe's creation is this basic law of humanity that you have to give pregnant women what they ask for, or else you'll be haunted by the gods of fertility and die a virgin. Not quite ready to take my vow of celibacy and invite the ghosts of pregnant women past upon myself, I gestured to the van. When she clumsily climbed into the passenger seat, she was still crying. I was still hating my life.

"Can you not? You're getting your emotions all over my mom's seat covers."

"I'm hormonal, okay?"

"You're also covered in snot." I handed her a fresh tissue from the console. "Get yourself together."

"He hates me."

"He doesn't hate you."

"We broke up last night. And I dumped him, in case he tries to spin the story."

"Why?"

"I had my doubts about us before, but seeing my aunt

die made me realize that life's too short to waste it with people who don't care about you." She blew her nose. She even snorted like royalty. "And my dad highly encouraged it."

I didn't want to slip and make it look like I cared. I didn't do the caring thing. They broke up—big deal. They broke up, and it meant nothing to me. It didn't change anything. They could break up or get married or have seven kids or be madly in stupid love, and none of it would matter.

Except that it did matter. I hated that it mattered.

She held her stomach. "And he doesn't love Little Man. Not the way I do, anyway."

"Little Man?"

"I haven't picked out his name yet." She looked at me like the new Carla. Puffy-eyed. Lonely. Resentful. When she wasn't crying, new Carla was becoming, dare I say it, mildly tolerable. "He doesn't love him, does he?"

I didn't say anything, because I honestly didn't know. Somehow, it never came up.

"I can accept that he doesn't love me. I think I always knew that he didn't. Even when he said he did, he didn't."

"He said he did?"

"Yeah, sometimes."

I wondered if he ever meant it. He probably tossed it out there as a crutch, as a safety net to keep her happy. A happy Carla was a less miserable Snake, after all. His self-ishness repulsed me.

"I can accept that," she repeated, wiping her nose. "I just wanted him to love Little Man. And, I don't know. I don't know if he does." She tried to breathe, but ended up wheezing like a pack-a-day smoker. "Did you know about Snake and me? When you guys started doing . . . whatever."

"We didn't do whatever," I clarified. "I don't know what Snake told you."

"He told me that he couldn't keep trying to make himself feel something for me." She folded her hands over her belly. "It's kind of pathetic when you're having a guy's baby and he still doesn't feel something for you."

"That's Snake's fault, not yours."

"It's both of us. Anyway, whatever you're doing is working. He said you make him feel long-term, or some Snakeism like that."

"Snakeism." I laughed. I was mad I didn't come up with that myself.

She turned to me. "So you didn't know?"

"I did, but nothing happened. I didn't intend to rouse his long-term feelings, whatever that means."

"I was hoping you could tell me."

"I can tell you one thing. Snake is a jerk."

"Isn't he, though?"

"And conceited. And what's with the Twizzlers?"

"Ohmigod, it drives me insane. My dad calls him Sugar Rush."

"I hope he has good dental insurance."

We were smiling. I, Reggie Mason, was sitting in my mom's minivan on a Friday afternoon gossiping about a boy with what appeared to be my up-and-coming BFF over a pack of tissues that smelled like peaches. My identity was slipping fast.

"Can I be honest with you?" she asked.

"As long as you stop crying about everything."

"I can't make any promises."

"Fine. What?"

She looked down at her engorged feet that were like two pears squeezed into ballet flats. Despite her splotchy eyes and soiled tissues, she was oddly at peace with losing Snake. I think she knew she'd lost him to something she would never have been able to compete with anyway.

"I don't have friends anymore."

"You have plenty of friends."

"Not now. Not anymore. I mean, they tried to be there for me. Olivia came to an appointment or two. And Ellie was going to throw me a baby shower, but got busy with gymnastics and lost track of time. I think I just became, literally, dead weight to them. I guess I tried to make it work with Snake for so long because . . ." She looked at me again. The loneliness from last night was there, and it was poignant. But it was a peaceful loneliness. "I don't have anyone else."

"I've never had friends," I said, tossing another pack of tissues at her. "You, on the other hand, have had them by the dozens. And yet we both ended up here, sitting in the school parking lot on a Friday night bitching about our pointless lives to the only person who will listen."

"That's kind of depressing."

"It's honest. Friends are just two people who mutually use each other to get what they want. You're not missing much."

Neither of us said anything for a few minutes. We sat in my favorite perk of living, silence. It seemed appropriate since nothing made sense. I was feeling sorry for Carla Banks. And she was being nice to me. And we both hated Snake, only one of us in the good way. And he'd told her he loved her. And I wondered what that meant. And we were both alone, still only one of us in the good way.

She glanced down at her blank phone screen. Snake had never responded. "In an unlikely turn of events, I need to ask you a favor."

"You need to use me?"

"Is that your Reggie way of proposing friendship?"

"Not on the life of your ginger squash."

She looked confused for a second before shaking it off. "Since my ex-boyfriend slash your current, whatever, is a no-show, I would really appreciate it if you would take me to my birthing class."

"Excuse me?"

"Please, Reggie," she begged. "I know we've never been close. And you probably hate me, and I'm kind of angry at you right now. But I'm terrified of having this little person come out of me, and I really need this class." She looked like she might hyperventilate. Good thing I had the numbers of over a dozen psychiatrists on speed dial. "Will you be Little Man's dad today?"

"I would rather get punched in the face."

"Don't make me beg."

"That wasn't begging?"

"That was asking nicely."

God, she was relentless. No wonder Snake always catered to her every whim and called her babe and handled her like glass. I was genuinely afraid of Didn't-Get-Her-Way Carla. Now I was the whipped one using the Official Carla Voice to keep *that* version from erupting.

I stuck the key in the ignition. "Where's the class?"

She smiled because she'd won. She always did.

Two stoplights and a box of tissues later, I found myself sitting next to Carla on a baby blue yoga mat among a throng of emotional pregnant women and their similarly emotional husbands. The woman next to us was referring to her husband as Sugarkins and her fetus as Baby Sugar, and suddenly Carla's Little Man didn't seem so cheesy. There was a foldout table in the back with a sign that said HEALTHY SNACKS, as if the words *healthy* and *snacks* should be allowed to share the same sentence space. We were in a dance studio–type room, surrounded by mirrors on every side. It seemed warped to me, considering there weren't going to be mirrors in delivery, and no woman has any desire to see what she's going to look like when she shoots ten pounds of human out of her lady cannon.

Carla changed into black yoga pants and a pink T-shirt that was so absurdly tight I was sure I could see the baby waving to me from inside the womb. She was eating a banana and breaking into a cold sweat before we even began warm-ups.

"I'm the only one here without a partner," she said as she chewed.

"Must you use the term *partner*? We already look like Snake's moms."

"Oh my God, I didn't even think about that. Are people going to think we're dating?"

"Just don't call me Sugarkins, and maybe no one will notice."

"I can't have people thinking I'm dating *you*. Ugh. If I were going to date a girl, I'd at least pick one with better taste." She shot a disgusted look at my oversize sweatshirt.

"Time for damage control." She pushed up on her knees and handed me her half-eaten banana.

"What are you—"

"Excuse me!" she yelled. "This is my friend Reggie. We are NOT dating. I repeat, NOT dating."

Everyone stared at us in the most hostile, hard-core-judging way that made Snake's pimple stares seem pleasant.

"We're not friends either," I added. "Just to clear that up."

She fell back on her butt, and the mindless chatter resumed.

"If you weren't pregnant, I would kill you," I whispered, handing her the banana.

Sugarkins woman leaned across her mat and touched Carla on the thigh as her husband massaged her neck. I wondered if he ever considered wringing it.

"Is this your first class, sweetheart?" she asked.

"I was taking classes at Boomers, but I switched," Carla replied in that sickly sweet voice that made mothers weak in the knees.

"How far along are you?"

"Eight months."

"Boy or girl?"

"Boy."

"Boy." The woman smiled. "Boys are such a blessing. I

have two boys myself. My first girl on the way." She rubbed her ginormous stomach.

"Congratulations."

"You too." She looked at me briefly. I'm sure she wondered what I was doing there. I wondered that myself. "It's nice that you have friends by your side. Pregnancy is the most beautiful experience, but it can also be such a difficult process."

"Tell me about it," I huffed.

"How old are you, darling?"

Carla hesitated. "Seventeen."

"Oh." The woman tried not to reveal her true identity as Miss Judgypants Mom, but the look in her eyes didn't match her kindness. "Well, I wish you the very best." She glanced at me. "And you're lucky to have such devoted friends. You're going to need them."

She retreated to her mat and proceeded to further annoy Sugarkins with her baby talk and cheek pinching. I felt his pain.

The instructor snapped her fingers at the front of the room to summon the group's attention. She was no older than twenty-two. She was wearing square glasses and had a head full of multicolored hair that curled down her Free People shirt. I doubted her credentials the moment I saw her college ID badge clipped to her workout pants.

She welcomed everyone, talked about herself, talked

about the phenomenon of birth, talked about herself. Then she announced we were working on mock births that day. I didn't like any of the words in that sentence.

"Dads, position yourselves between the mother's legs to prepare for breathing techniques."

The mothers spread open like swinging doors as the dads kneeled before the vast expanse of no-man's lands before them. Carla smiled at me apprehensively.

"Reggie?"

"I'm not going down there."

"You have to!"

"Not a chance."

"I bet Snake would do it if he were here."

"Snake's already been between your legs. I, on the other hand, have no desire to venture."

The instructor began reviewing the first technique.

"You're going to make me look stupid!"

"I'm going to make you look stupid? Not the planet orbiting beneath your boobs?"

"Reggie!"

The mothers started the inhale-exhale routine.

"Fine," I grumbled. I crawled to Carla's feet and held her legs apart and imagined that I was absolutely anywhere else.

She was beginning the inhales when the instructor insisted, "Faster now."

All the *hee-hoo*s were like a broken fan.

"Slowly begin to push," the instructor ordered. "Dads, it is your job to support the mother as she undergoes this difficult step in the birthing process. Be encouraging. Talk her down. Help her with her breathing. Remember what we've learned in past weeks."

Carla fake pushed like a pro. She could have been an actress on one of those *What to Expect When You're Expecting* DVDs.

"Encouragements, please," she demanded through clenched teeth.

"Uh . . . I hope your baby isn't a ten-pounder?"

"That's not encouraging."

"Sorry. I didn't have time to grab an encouragement-for-the-day calendar on my way over."

She was actually breaking a sweat over pretend pushing. Man, she was good.

"Talk about prom," she said. "That's encouraging."

"Prom?"

"Yeah. It's next weekend. I know I won't be able to go this year. Pretend like I did." The instructor sped up the birthing music. Had there been music playing this whole time? "Tell me how much fun I had."

Prom. The Met Gala of small-town celebrities. A competition to see who could spend the most money on a more-often-than-not ugly gown that they would never wear again. It was large-scale excitement that fell to even larger-scale disappointment when the night of everyone's dreams turned out to be a glorified game of Pretty Pretty Princess. Frankly, I would never have wasted my time. But Carla wouldn't hear of missing it unless something <u>tragic</u> (see: getting knocked up) happened. Carla Banks would have been prom if prom were a person.

"Yeah, you went to prom," I said.

"Did I look pretty?"

Bite your tongue. Bite your tongue.

"Uh, sure. You wore a pink dress."

"Purple," she corrected.

"Okay." I rolled my eyes. "A purple dress. And Olivia was there, and Ellie, and all of your snobby user friends."

"Did I have a date?"

"A date? Yeah, you did."

"Snake?" She opened her eyes and stopped faux pushing.

We stared at each other, my blue eyes reflected in her brown ones. "Do you want it to be Snake?"

The music ceased, and the instructor clapped her hands, congratulating everyone on the progress they made, as if clenching their abs to a techno beat prepared them for real-life contractions and hard labor. The class went on for another thirty minutes, but nothing was as eventful as the synchronized birth routine. When it was over, the moms barked at the dads to fold the mats and wipe their sweat and grab fruit and go pull the car around. The husbands obeyed without complaint. I think they feared death by belly smothering if they rebelled.

I waited at a picnic table outside for Carla's dad to pick her up. She still had beads of sweat on her hairline from the strenuous imaginary birth, her eyes locked onto a piece of chewed gum on the sidewalk.

I must have been going soft and spineless, because all I could think was that Snake should have been there.

"You're good at fake labor," I said.

She kept her eyes on the ground. "Let's hope I'm as good at the real thing."

"Don't forget that there will be a human coming out of you at the real thing."

"Trust me, I haven't forgotten." She scrunched her forehead like she was concentrating. "It's entirely new to me, you know? Having a baby. What if I'm a bad mom?"

"You will be."

"I'm serious."

"Me too. You're used to being perfect, and you won't be. You're going to screw up and forget stuff and want to jump out of your window half the time because life will suck, but that's not you being a bad mom. That's you being less than perfect." I laughed to myself. "That's you being me."

"That's more terrifying than labor."

We didn't speak as we waited. I didn't know if I should take the silence to explain what happened with me and Snake, to assure her that I hadn't tried to cause problems. But I doubted that she cared. She didn't seem to be all picking-petals-off-of-flowers googly-eyed about him the way I thought she would be.

It was Carla who dissolved the quiet when she said, "I'm sorry, by the way."

"You?"

"Yeah. We've known each other since we were five, and this is the first time we've ever hung out. I mean, besides work and school."

"That's because I've never liked you."

She smiled the way Snake did when I insulted him. "I guess I've never liked you much either."

Her father's BMW pulled up to the walkway. She looked at me in a Carla way that wasn't like all of the other Carlas. Her eyes were uncharacteristically sincere. Like Snake, it was her best look. "Thanks for coming with me today. You're the last person in the entire world I would have wanted to spend a Friday night with, but it actually wasn't too bad."

"The disgust is mutual."

She grabbed her duffel bag and tossed it over her

shoulder. As she walked toward her dad's car, she paused turning back to look at me. "By the way," she called, "the answer is no. I wouldn't want my date to be Snake."

Thirty minutes later, I ended up on Snake's front porch, ringing his doorbell a thousand times until someone had enough nerve to answer. When the door swung open, it was Jeanine, flour spattered across her floral apron.

"Reggie," she said. "I wasn't expecting you."

"Where's Snake?"

Her smile faded the moment I mentioned him. I waited for the next words out of her mouth to be he was sick, dying, or dead, because that is all that would have justified ignoring Carla and making me her go-to by default.

"He's having a rough day."

"I bet."

"There was an issue last night."

I knew she was talking about Carla dumping his sorry ass.

"Is he in his room?"

She nodded. I scooted past her without asking, because I was quite honestly all cared out. When I made it to his door, I could see that the lights were off. There was no shine beneath the crack. I pushed the door back.

Darkness. Computer screen shut down. Blinds closed.

TV off. A hump of covers. I recognized the scene as if it were my own. Classic Stage 3. Snake was in Disconnect.

I found him exactly where I expected, lying in his bed with the blanket pulled to his nose. His phone was on the nightstand. Untouched. He had a set of earbuds in his ears, a reverberating noise leaking into the quiet. Drums. Screamo. The Renegade Dystopia.

He didn't see me, and it wouldn't have mattered if he had. Disconnect made you as good as dead, which was why I decided not to do what I wanted to do. Yell. Scream. Put up a fight. Tell him off the way he secretly wanted me to.

His only cop-outs were sickness, dying, and death.

Disconnect was all three.

I wasn't sure if it was Carla he was mourning or the consequences of yet another mistake. That mistake being me, of course. He probably regretted me, but he probably still wanted me because he knew he shouldn't. And it hurt him and it made no sense and it was useless, and he needed it. He needed to need because it made him feel. Unfortunately, feeling wasn't always such a good thing.

As I peeled the covers back, he glanced up at me with glassy, distant eyes. Disconnect eyes. I lay down on his bed, twisting on my side to face him. He was looking straight at me. But he wasn't looking at me so much as through me.

I pulled the covers to my neck and reached my hand to

his earbuds. I took one out and put it in my own ear. He didn't move.

"You're a day early," I whispered. "Wallowing in self-hatred is supposed to happen on Saturday."

He didn't say anything. He didn't acknowledge me at all. We lay together for an hour as the Renegade Dystopia screamed into our ears. It really was a crappy band.

CHAPTER eleven

I SPENT MY ENTIRE SATURDAY MORNING shopping for baby clothes (see: corporal punishment) with Carla Banks. Apparently, my stand-in-dad stint at birthing class gave her the wrong impression. I got the call after I left Snake's the night before. A chatty little voicemail that said:

Reggie? Snake texted me your number. Hope you don't mind. I was wondering if you'd go baby clothes shopping with me tomorrow? I know that's kind of awkward, but I don't have anyone else to go with. Call me back!

Like birthing class, I would have rather been punched in the face. But the list of reasons I was indebted to Carla was endless and unrelenting.

1. I might have sort of kind of had a thing for her ex-boyfriend/baby daddy.

2. She didn't try to catfight me in the school parking lot during our confrontation about reason 1.
3. Her dad was my boss.
4. It was bad karma to shun a pregnant girl whose aunt had just kicked the bucket.

So there I found myself, moving from rack to rack, hordes of giraffes and butterflies bombarding me at every turn. Flashburn didn't even have a real mall. It was only a few outdated stores shoved inside a building the size of a warehouse. I only went to the mall for one reason and that was when I was craving a soft pretzel. Or when Karen was forcing me to help her pick out bath towels (see: capital punishment).

"This is so cute!" Carla exclaimed, lifting a sweater vest with a matching bow tie. It was yellow and argyle and so ugly I could have barfed on it. "What do you think?"

"You don't want to know what I think."

She hung her head and hooked it back on the hanger.

"What about this?" I asked, waving a mini white T-shirt bearing the phrase WORLD'S MOST ELIGIBLE BACHELOR.

She laughed in disgust. "Ugh, Snake would love that."

"If it were a few sizes bigger, he'd wear it."

"Ohmigod," she said, sifting through the animal-themed section. "Right after I told my dad I was pregnant,

Snake showed up to my house in a Darth Vader shirt that said WHO'S YOUR DADDY?"

I slapped my hand over my mouth to keep from bursting. "He. Did. Not."

"I swear to God. My dad almost drop-kicked him right there in my living room."

I rounded the corner and snorted into my hand, the weirdest, most uncomfortable sensation I'd felt in weeks. Lately, laughing felt a lot like opening my mouth to speak and hearing my words flow out in a foreign language. Carla, of all people, was laughing alongside me, talking back. It was like we both understood but didn't know when we'd learned to.

"Olivia hates him," she said over her shoulder. "I mean, she thinks he's hot. Obviously. But she also thinks he's a prick."

"That's because he is a prick."

"Yeah . . ." She dragged it out like she wasn't sure. Like she was agreeing just for the sake of agreeing. "He wasn't always like that, though. You know?"

I wanted to have enough knowledge of Snake to agree. To have the memories Carla had, to be able to say, "Remember that one time he did that awesome thing?" But I didn't know him before, I barely knew him now, and it was pointless to pretend it would have mattered either way.

"Tell me," I said.

She glanced at me and scrunched her forehead. "Tell you what?"

"What he was like before."

A poutiness seeped into her expression, and I feared I was encouraging Crybaby Carla to make an appearance. "Oh, um . . . I don't know. He was just . . . different. Like, he'd always say he was excited about Little Man, and kiss me when we'd just be sitting there watching TV, and tell me I was beautiful . . ." She looked away shyly. "Never mind. It's stupid."

I bit down on my tongue. "It sounds like he really liked you."

"I thought he did." She shrugged, her eyes vaguely scanning the heaps of baby crap piled around her. "Maybe I just wanted to believe he did. I don't know."

"He did. And he probably still does."

I barely knew why I said it, or why there was an almost rude-sounding confidence in my tone when I did. Carla's blank stare met my angry one, and it annoyed me that I couldn't unscowl my face.

"Did he say something to you?" she asked defensively.

I managed to loosen my jaw long enough to say, "No. It's just kind of obvious."

She placed her hand on the table behind her and leaned

against it, her belly and chest inflating with her breath. "I just don't get him. He loves me, then he doesn't love me. We're making out, then we're breaking up. His mood swings give me serious whiplash."

They're not mood swings, you idiot! I wanted to yell. It was so clear to me as someone who was constantly shifting, drowning, that there were reasons behind his douchebagness. But for a person who'd never felt it, depression couldn't be watered down to a game show–style Q&A.

Question: What makes a person go from "this indescribable happiness is what it means to be alive" to "this is so painful it might just fucking kill me"?

Answer: Depression.

"It doesn't matter," she said, pushing herself back onto her feet. "Point is, he changed. And maybe I did too, I don't know. Whatever, I'm sick of talking about it."

A salesclerk interrupted us, ogling Carla's stomach and leading her to a rack of designer baby clothes in the front of the store.

I stood motionless and a little sick, clinging to Carla's memories, hating that she got to have them. Worse, hating that she had to keep them. I knew what harboring memories felt like. It felt like owning the most expensive item you could get your hands on and having it taken away and replaced with an inferior version of itself. You recognized the imitation, the smell, the texture, the design, but it was off. It was a replica of the expensive thing, but not the thing. Just a shitty version of what you wanted.

Checking to make sure Carla was still distracted, I hurried to the back of the store and hid behind a tower of children's books. My thigh was sore from holding the weight of my phone, and I couldn't stand it anymore. I slid the screen and dialed the number.

One ring.

Two rings.

Three rings.

The fourth ring was my death sentence. Always. But I needed it. Some sickness inside of me was fed whenever I heard the phrase.

This number is no—

"Reggie?"

Carla stood beside the books, a pack of blue onesies draped over her arm. A panicked look kicked into gear and her lips parted as she spotted me shoving my phone in my pocket.

"You weren't calling Snake, were you?"

"No, Carla—"

"Did you tell him what I said? God, thanks a lot. Now he thinks I'm over here going on about how I still have feelings for him."

"I wasn't on the phone with Snake," I said.

I stared at her feet and not her eyes, because it was too hard to look at them knowing that Snake had seen them smile and liked what he saw. Knowing that my phone wasn't finished damning me, and if I stayed here long enough, completely subjected myself to it, Carla had the power to damn me a second time. There was nowhere to look but down, so I did.

"I didn't mean that," she mumbled. "I don't still have feelings for him."

"It's okay."

"No, it's not. I don't want you to think I'm like, replaying all of this stuff in my head all the time. I'm not hung up on him. I just . . ."

"Wish it were easier to let him go," I finished.

She relaxed, her shoulders slouching, seemingly relieved that I got it, whatever it was and however the hell it made things better.

"It feels wrong to be with him, and it feels wrong not to be," she said, brushing her hand through her fiery hair. "And now I'm not. And I should be happy or whatever, but I really just feel like shit."

There was only one illusion with Carla, and I don't think it was that she was genuinely afraid Snake had never loved her. I think it was that she was afraid that he had, and it scared her that someone could be there and whole and yours and then be somewhere else entirely.

"Take it from the girl who considers 'shit' her favorite emotion. You can feel like shit whenever you want, and you shouldn't let people make you feel bad about it," I said.

She bowed her head and rubbed her hand along the bottom of her bump.

I gestured to the clothes on her arm. "Those are hideous, by the way."

She giggled and stuck out her lips. "I think they're adorable."

"You would."

She stared at me too long, Snake-long, and that time, I looked into her eyes. They were hopeful and terrified and downright lost, and it didn't strike me as strange that all those feelings, as different as they were, could be observed in equal measure.

"We should hang out more often," she said.

All I could do was laugh it off. It was so much easier that way.

"No we shouldn't."

CHAPTER twelve

THE DREADED <u>DAY OF RECKONING</u> (see: family bonding) had arrived. A chilly breeze attacked my hair, which was annoying because I had actually taken the time to style it. I didn't have much of a choice, considering it was Sunday, and according to Karen, you had to look presentable in church because all those Bible verses about the state of your soul being superior to your outward appearance were obviously just filler chapters. My brother, Frankie, and his wife —I called her Blondie—were sitting beside me on the picnic blanket as baby Killian drooled a mucus river between my legs. I didn't like children. I only semitolerated Killian because he did kind of have a cute gap between his teeth, and I was a sucker for chubby, gap-toothed babies. Other than that, he was just drool and stench.

We were having a family picnic by the pond. The rich

kid pond. The enchanted swamp of fish piss pond. Snake's pond. I could see his house from where I sat next to a tree that smelled like sap and bark and other gross outdoor smells. When I'd asked Karen if Snake could come, she basically quoted half the book of Romans along with a number of inapplicable metaphors.

"I'm sorry, Mama K," Blondie said after Killian spat up all over my mother's new blanket. She smiled behind her bright pink lipstick. "He hasn't been feeling well, car sickness and everything."

"Don't apologize. Frankie was the same way."

Frankie never spoke much. When he did, he was just one inspirational quote away from being the pastor version of my mother. That's why the only person keeping me sane was my dad, who also never spoke much, but managed to touch on sports and politics and things that I wasn't entirely sick of hearing about yet when he did. I watched him eat his PB&J in total silence, and imagined he resented being there as much as I did.

"How was Dad's appointment?" Frankie asked. He addressed the question to my mom, because it wasn't like my dad was sitting right there and could speak for himself or anything. "Our entire congregation has been praying for him."

"We're trusting the Lord right now," Karen answered as she touched her heart. "The doctor says his palpitations are probably stress related. He's been taking it easy, but he needs lots of prayer."

"How about we pray right now?" Blondie suggested.

This was not happening. At even the slightest mention of prayer, my mother turned into the Flash, grabbing my hand quicker than Frankie could start the opening "We praise you, Lord."

"Lord, the great healer, the protector, the alpha and omega, the beginning and the end, nothing is too big for You. We lift up Dad today and ask for Your healing hand of protection on his heart. Keep him safe. Relieve his burdens. Your word says, 'Come to me all who are weary, and you will find rest.' Give Dad rest today. Bathe him in Your love and keep him safe. Thank You for all You have blessed us with and continue to bless us with each and every day. We love You, our Father. It's in Your Son's name, Amen."

I'd been raised not to make fun of prayer. Karen said it was sacrilegious, and God might send down a giant pillar of fire from heaven to teach you a lesson if you did. But I couldn't shake the plain truth that that prayer was an utter load of crap. No offense to my dad, who was probably as confused as I was that we were praying for him like he was on life support when all he was trying to do was eat his sandwich in peace. So he had heart palpitations, big deal. I had chickenpox once — didn't mean I was dying of a flesh-eating bacteria.

When I opened my eyes, the first thing I saw was the same scene. Frankie. Blondie's painted face. Drooling Killian. My terminally ill (see: perfectly healthy) dad. Karen being Karen.

Then I saw a familiar face. His neck tattoo. His unwashed hair. His ripped jeans. His black T-shirt that said I DO MY OWN STUNTS. He was walking toward us with a fishing pole in hand, his bulky camera strapped on his back. It kind of made me wonder what I'd been subconsciously praying for.

"Snake?"

"Hey, Masons," he said, giving my mother premature wrinkles from how intensely she was frowning. "What brings you all to the pond?"

He knew we were going to be there. I'd told him Friday night when I left his house. Like always, he was being a rebellious douchebag. I definitely hated that in the good way.

Frankie stood to his feet with his customary diplomatic air and shook Snake's free hand. "Frankie Mason, Reggie's brother. Part-time prayer leader, full-time youth pastor. And you are?"

"Snake Eliot. Part-time filmmaker, full-time stud. Still fuzzy on the who I am thing."

"Do you go to church with my family?"

"No, Frankie." I stood up, shooting Snake a mean look. "Snake is my friend from work."

"The soft serve business is booming these days." Snake smirked. "I like to think of Reggie and me as partners in cream."

I couldn't believe he'd said that out loud. Frankie and Blondie cracked up, corny humor being their niche and all. Karen wasn't amused in the least, to no one's surprise.

"Would you like to stay for the picnic?" Frankie asked. "We have plenty."

"I'm sure the young man has plans," Karen interrupted. She didn't look at Snake or me or anyone, really. She coddled baby Killian and talked to the top of his bald head. "He has a fishing rod. He was probably on his way to catch some trout."

"This old thing?" Snake shook the rod. "Nah, I just tote it around so it looks like I'm doing something. I come down here to film a lot, can't have people thinking I'm a creep. I live up on the hill over there." He pointed to his house.

"Well, then, take a seat," Blondie offered. "We have plenty of sandwiches for everyone."

He was fearless, almost vicious in his neglect for rules and conventionality and polite behavior. The name Snake had never fit him so perfectly.

He moved to sit by me. Karen hesitantly dipped into the

cooler, pulled out a chicken salad sandwich, and handed it to him with extra caution. She couldn't have her holy hands graze his hellion fingers.

He took a bite. "This is great, Mrs. Mason," he said with full jaws. "I'll have to get this recipe for my moms."

Karen froze, looking to see if Frankie noticed the plurality of that statement. He did. Snake smiled, because he knew exactly what he was doing.

"It's a family recipe," she said. "I'd rather not share it."

"I get it. Family recipes are sacred stuff. That's like, one of the Ten Commandments, I think. 'Thou shalt not share recipes with unbelievers.' I don't know, something like that."

"That's not a commandment." Frankie frowned. "I can list them for you if you'd like."

"No, I know them. Adultery. Lying. Stealing. Something about cows."

"Brazen images," Dad said. He hadn't spoken all day. It was weird to hear him talk.

"*Ding. Ding. Ding.* We have a winner." Snake grinned. "It's always the quiet ones."

Dad smiled. I got the feeling he liked Snake, or at least appreciated him. I was glad I wasn't the only one.

Baby Killian hadn't taken his big blue eyes off Snake from the moment he sat down. It was like Snake was like the biggest, newest toy in the playpen. He reached out his tiny hand and cooed to get Snake's attention. Blondie patted his hand down, but he only raised it again.

"I think someone wants you," she said to Snake. Frankie shot her a look like she should have kept her mouth shut.

Snake took the last bite of the sandwich and wiped his hands on a napkin. "What's his name?"

"Killian," she said.

"That name's kick ass." He put his hand over his mouth. "Sorry. I mean kick butt." He tilted toward me and whispered, "I hope Carla picks out something cool like that."

Killian smiled his gap-toothed smile and reached both of his chubby arms in Snake's direction.

"Can I hold him?" Snake asked.

A little triangle formed between Frankie's eyes, which was always a sign of him being super uncomfortable or super aggravated. He was most likely both. Snake did have a proclivity for bringing that out in people. Blondie happily replied, "Of course!" before Frankie could shut her down.

Snake reached across the blanket and tucked his hands under both sides of Killian's back, cautiously drawing him into his arms. He held Killian in his lap and shifted his face into ugly formations to keep the baby entertained. I thought Killian was going to get a hernia from laughing so hard.

I didn't want to look at him with Killian and imagine how he would be with his own kid, because the idea of

Snake being someone's dad was kind of gross and disturbing and, selfishly, obnoxious to me. But he was a natural. He was gentle and playful and funny. I'm not saying he was dad-of-the-year material, but maybe he wouldn't be so bad if he gave it a sincere try. And that bothered me. Damn, that bothered me.

"You're great with kids," Blondie pointed out. "Have you worked with children before?"

"No. I'm an only child, so I've never been around them much. I'm working on my skills, though."

"You should. You'll be having your own someday, I'm sure."

He glanced at me from the corner of his eye. "Yeah," he mumbled. "Someday."

Someday being a month from then. In a month from then, Snake's picnics would look entirely different. Snake Jr. would be giggling on his daddy's lap. Carla would be doting on his every impulse. They would take embarrassing white-shirt beach photos like the one hanging in Snake's house. His life would be a photograph of inescapable realities that wouldn't change no matter how much I did or didn't want to be a part of the disaster that was Snake Eliot.

Snake handed Killian back to Blondie. He drooled a puddle of chunky spit all over her silky church dress, and subconsciously I wished that some of it would have landed on Karen. I glanced at her, and she was staring Snake down in an I-can't-stand-you-yet-I'm-praying-for-you way that only Karen could pull off. The smirk Snake had worn since showing up made it clear that Karen's hostility hadn't slipped past him. Of course, it was at his expense. Naturally, he loved it.

"Did everyone enjoy the service this morning?" Frankie asked, trying to ease the tension. He really needed to pick up a book on effective icebreakers, because religion was definitely not one of them.

"Snake," Karen said, her tone as hostile as her narrowed eyes, "I don't believe I've seen you at church. Does your . . ." *Spit it out, Karen.* "Family attend?"

Then came the Twizzler. It was bound to surface eventually.

"We're free spirits ourselves," he replied. "Sun. Wind. Moon. Nature calling. Listen to the sound of your heartbeat. Paint with the colors of the wind."

"You never attend services?"

"Sometimes we meditate next to a statue of Buddha while smoking hookah and listening to a Celtic orchestra, but that's only after my moms have been drinking."

He glanced at me from the corner of his eye, wearing the most absurdly mischievous expression. This was a Snakeism, being so blatantly rebellious in the most polite of forms that no one could challenge him without being proven an unworthy competitor. After that, Karen didn't speak to him again. She couldn't keep pace. Who was she to compete with a Snakeism?

"Reggie," Snake said, chatting louder than usual to make sure everyone would hear, "you want to go out on the water?"

"Sure, let me pull my yacht around," I taunted him.

"You could do that. Or, we could ride one of those." He pointed toward the pond where a white and blue water wheeler was bobbing against the dock. It was tied to the peg by a rope and had WATER-TO-GO painted in pink across the plastic.

"That's a pedal boat. Too much exercise for me."

"You could use it."

"Says the guy who can't go five minutes without eating."

"Come on, I'll pick up the slack." He smiled in this odd, flirtatious way that was repulsive and insanely cute at the same time. It was bizarre how he could do that. He should've added it to his list of talents (see: singing), since he didn't have many to claim. "I'm used to doing the hard stuff, anyway."

Was that sexual? Did he really just make a sex joke in front of my parents and my older brother? I mean, Karen was so pitifully naïve, anything of the sexual variety was lost on her. But Frankie, the self-proclaimed shepherd of lost teens, was no stranger to innuendo. He and my dad perked up in weirdly perfect sync. My family was sure to combust from Snakeisms by the time this day was through.

I looked to Karen, whose forehead was fixed into a wrinkly frown that would take years of antiaging cream to remedy.

"We're going to go out on the pond," I told her.

We were at the dock before anyone in my family could try to stop us. Snake untied the rope and bent to his knees, grabbing ahold of the side. He glanced up at me and squinted as the sun blinded his eyes. "Get in."

"You can take it like that?"

"Yeah, the pond committee bought a few for recreation."

"The pond committee?"

"Yes, the pond committee. My moms are on the board." He patted the boat. "Get in."

I jumped in gracefully (see: tripped) and landed in the far seat as freezing water splashed against my face. "Jeez." I shivered. "The prestigious pond committee isn't wealthy enough to heat the water? I'd have thought they would have invented a pond radiator by now."

"Budget cuts." He jumped in behind me and landed gracefully. I liked him better when he was klutzy and awkward.

It turned out to be easier than I thought. Circular

motions. One foot up, the other down. It was like riding a bike, except that steering was nearly impossible, and there wasn't a way to brake while I pedaled us toward our <u>rocky death</u> (see: the bank).

"Turn, Reggie," Snake ordered.

I tried. I failed.

"Turn," he repeated. "We're gonna hit the bank."

"Maybe I want to hit the bank."

"Or maybe you don't know how to turn."

"I know how to turn. I'm choosing not to."

I had no idea how to turn.

"No, you're so unbelievably stubborn that you would crash yourself into a rocky bank just to prove that you don't need anyone's help." He glanced at me and grinned, his eyes squinted. It was different than usual, or it might have just made me feel different. I wasn't sure.

He grabbed my leg right beneath the knee, moving me in the direction we needed to go. With his help, we missed the bank by an inch. After, he slid his hand upward, his fingertips skimming my thigh before letting his arm fall at his side.

"Smooth," I mocked.

"Actually, quite prickly. Have you considered shaving?"

I punched his arm harder than I meant to as we drifted toward the west side of the pond, away from Snake's house and my <u>family</u> (see: ragtag team of psychos).

"It's nice out here, right?" Snake asked. He said it like he wasn't sure.

"It's trees, water, grass, and sky. I could get it on the Discovery Channel."

"Yeah. But experiences are better than the replications, aren't they?"

"Our experiences are just replications of other people's experiences."

"Nothing new under the sun."

"That's from the Bible."

"I know." He smiled. "My family doesn't really smoke hookah next to a statue of Buddha while listening to a Celtic orchestra."

"Good," I said, smiling back at him. "Celtic orchestras suck."

He steered us toward a white-blossomed tree that was vomiting flowers onto the water and took his foot off the pedals to let us drift. Then he looked at me kind of intensely and said, "This is where I take the time to make an absolute fool of myself to apologize for making an absolute fool of myself."

"Sounds foolish."

"Oh, it is. And I probably won't come away from it a better person than before, but I need to tell you I'm sorry for not showing up to Carla's birthing class the other night and making you liable by association. I would say symptom of depression, but I'm starting to think depression is a symptom of me."

"It's not a symptom of anything," I corrected him. "And you can't control Disconnect, Snake. I'm not judging you for it."

"Disconnect?"

"The third stage. I look at it in three stages. Disconnect is where you were the other night. It's that nonfunctioning state where you feel nothing. Numbness. You just want to listen to music that makes you miserable and take Prozac and sleep for eternity. So I get it. You're not really up to taking your pregnant girlfriend to a parade showcasing the miracle of life when you feel like dying."

He was watching me intently. His boring eyes seemed less boring every time I saw him. I couldn't tell if it was because he was getting better or I was.

"I like the way you see it," he said, pumping his feet to spin us in gradual circles. "When I first got on Prozac, my moms started blaming themselves, like I needed something they couldn't give me. I think they felt powerless, or something. But it's because they were viewing it all wrong. We don't always feel pain for a reason. Sometimes we hurt because it's better than nothing. We hurt to feel alive."

"I think that's where you and I are different. When I got on Zoloft, I might as well have been diagnosed with cancer as far as my mother was concerned. I was a lost soul. I didn't have Jesus. I needed to pray. Karen blamed it on everything and everyone but me. It's like she couldn't accept that maybe I hated to feel because it's overrated. I didn't need feelings, I needed the world to slow down." I reached over the side of the pedal boat and picked up a blossom. "The world's too fast to stop, though."

"It feels pretty slow out here."

"Yeah."

I didn't expect that I'd feel the same. But he was right. Somehow, he was right. We weren't spinning.

"Feeling's not overrated. I don't think you do enough of it."

"And I think you do too much," I argued, tossing the blossom to the water. "We only have a scrap of useful passion. It's a shame to spread it thin."

He didn't answer. We bobbed toward the bank again, but he successfully steered us back onto the pond and toward his house. This time, he pedaled slowly. He went slower than he had on the way to the quiet side. I could tell that he didn't want to waste his moments. But I almost wondered if our moments were better off wasted. Empty. Wouldn't it have been better that way? To let our feelings drain so that nothing could be lost when the moments were over?

"How was it?" he asked. He didn't seem himself. Nervous, even. "The class? I've been to a few, and they were the closest semblance to physical torture I could imagine."

"I ended up between Carla's legs while she pretended to push a child out of her body to a techno beat. The torture was very much physical."

I didn't mention what Carla told me at the mall, about the feelings she might have still had for Snake. Telling her secrets felt like sticking a thumb on her bruises. As a person with a lot of wounds, I knew how badly that could hurt.

"She texted me yesterday," he said. "She wasn't upset with the way things ended. I kind of got the feeling she was relieved to be rid of me."

"I hope you know you're not really broken up. And you'll never be rid of each other, either."

"Do you want me to be with her?" He stopped pedaling again and was calculating my reaction under disheveled hair. "You act like you think we should be together."

I didn't know if *want* was a term I would use. And I knew that *want* was all he used. And it was the most honest and unusual question, but it didn't have an obvious answer.

"You know what I think? I think we're too young and imperfect and unpredictable to decide who should be with whom and who is the proverbial 'one' and what draws us together apart from the simple bias of human obligation to the concept of love. So I don't care if you're with Carla, or convincing yourself you're without her, or pining after wants you can't obtain because the bias of love falls short on you. You can want what you want, but there are some things that never change. And Carla's presence in your life is one of them. So, the answer is no. I wouldn't say I *want* anything in particular."

He didn't grin. The one time I was brutal to a fault, and he wasn't cheerful about it. But he wasn't thrown. Rather, expectant.

"Who am I to forsake obligation?"

"No one." I rubbed my eyes. I couldn't believe I was about to say it. "You actually have one more obligation."

"What's that?"

"You need to take Carla to prom."

He almost laughed. "Um, what?"

"Personally, I find it ridiculous. But Carla is wired to need it, and you should know all about that." He was watching me with more feeling than I liked. Like everything else he did, it was too much. "Friday night. Take her."

His blue eyes were too dull against the water, and the sun was brighter than he would ever be, and he lied to himself every day, and he was too presumptuous, and I was pointing out all of his flaws because I was beginning not to notice them anymore. It was like the first time I met him. He was beautiful and average. Only this time, minus the average part.

"I really, insanely, undeniably hate you in the best way," he whispered.

"Reggie!" Karen called from the grass. She had the picnic blanket rolled under her arm while my family headed uphill toward the street. "Come on. We're leaving."

The pedal boat reached the dock. I turned to Snake, and he lifted his hand. "After you," he said, motioning for me to leave. Every ounce of me protested.

I jumped out of the boat and clumsily climbed onto the dock without his help. I didn't need it. He was crawling out behind me when I took off and sprinted toward my mom. I didn't look back.

He was probably soul staring me. He was probably waiting for a response that would ease his hunger. He was probably wanting too much.

But there was no probably when it came to what we both knew.

I really, insanely, undeniably hated him in the best way too.

CHAPTER thirteen

HE NEEDED A SUIT. IT WAS no revelation to discover that Snake Eliot had never owned a suit in his entire seventeen years of living. Not a church suit, not a funeral suit, not a for-the-heck-of-it suit. Nothing. So that's where I found myself Monday night after work, shopping for suits at a mom-and-pop retail store for a guy who was too pretentiously unpretentious to buy a suit worthy of his price range, so he could attend junior prom at a school he didn't go to with his pregnant ex-girlfriend who didn't really want him there.

"She said fine." He laughed, modeling in front of the dressing room mirrors. He was wearing a navy blue tux that swallowed his arms, still insisting he try on sizes that were totally beyond him.

I sat in what I could only deem the girlfriend chair. It was the only explanation I could come up with for the white plush pillows and *Cosmopolitan* magazines on the glass table.

"How did you start it?" I asked as I flipped through an article about what men look for in the ideal woman. Because nothing said female empowerment like a commentary from the <u>peanut gallery</u> (see: patriarchy).

"I started it off like, 'Hey, babe.' She said, 'Don't call me that, jerk.' Then I said, 'I know you're mad, and you're not in the mood to hear from me, but I really want to take you to prom.' She kind of got quiet and was like, 'I'm not going. I'm too big for all of the dresses, I'll look ugly, yada yada.' And I was like, 'You're beautiful. Come on.' And that got her, you know. Vanity and all. Then she said, 'Fine.' That was it. Fine. I thought I would at least get a thanks. Jeez."

"You knock her up, tell her you have feelings for someone else, don't show up to her birthing classes, and then ask her to prom." I tossed the magazine on the table. "You're lucky you got a *fine*."

He spun around and held out his arms in a sweeping gesture.

"What do you think?" he asked. I couldn't concentrate with the crooked bow tie beneath his chin.

"You look ridiculous."

"I think I look like James Bond."

"Maybe his deranged stepson twice removed."

"You're a harsh critic." He grinned, unbuttoning the

tuxedo jacket to reveal his white T-shirt underneath. "I'll have to remember to never come to you if I need an ego boost."

"Your ego needs no boosting, my friend."

He stepped down from the pedestal and grabbed a hanger from the rack. "Friend, huh?" He smiled. "Is that what you're telling yourself these days?"

He hung the jacket inside out, probably because his hair had gotten so long he couldn't see what he was doing. Or he was just an idiot. There was ample evidence for both.

"Would you call it differently?"

He took a seat in the chair beside me. He still wore the baggy tuxedo pants with his tattered white T-shirt, holding the fluffy throw pillow in his lap. Despite his shaggy hair, I could see his eyes sparkling as they teased me. He was some piece of work (see: smug bastard).

"See the thing is, I've gone above and beyond to make my feelings remarkably clear. However, you seem to hate me in fluctuating patterns, which lead me to rocky conclusions, which, in the grand scheme of things, don't matter at all. Because whether you hate me in the bad way or you hate me in the good way, you're still thinking of me. So I believe that we're either A) very passionate friends or B) masochistic lovers." He smirked with desperate flirtation. "I prefer B myself."

"I prefer C) try on another tux or I'm leaving."

"That wasn't an option."

"I'm not playing this game." I jumped from the seat and walked to the rack of hideous and oversize suits. I grabbed the one he let me pick out that was in his size. "Try this one. Maybe you'll get lucky and won't look like the before shot on a Weight Watcher's infomercial."

"Ha. Ha." He strolled to where I stood and stepped as close to me as he possibly could without completely needle-popping my personal bubble. "Masochistic lovers it is." He took the hanger and disappeared into the dressing room.

When he returned, I barely recognized him. He was in formfitting black, with a long, skinny tie and sleeves that accentuated his arms. I could tell he'd messed with his hair, because it kind of had this swoopy thing going on that wasn't there before. His stupid tattoo was covered, too. For once, he looked like the preppy rich boy he was trying so hard not to be.

"You can't tell me I don't look good in this one."

"It's only because I picked it out. I have impeccable taste."

"I have to give you credit," he said, checking himself out in the wall mirror. "Carla won't be able to keep her hands off of me."

"Only if she's strangling you."

He laughed. "She's not as violent as you are."

"I bet you just adore that about her."

"It's a perk." He glanced back at me with a playful smile. "Are you jealous?"

"Jealous?"

"Yeah, because I'm going to prom with Carla. Because that was your brilliant idea, not mine."

I rolled my eyes. "I couldn't care less what you do or don't do with Carla."

"Reeeeally?" He stretched the word as far as it would reach. "So if Carla and I go to prom, and we dance to some sappy song, and she starts getting emotional as we reminisce about the night we met, and we start making out and professing our undying devotion, that would be perfectly okay with you?"

"First of all, sloppy drunk sex is hardly something to reminisce about. Second of all, good luck slow dancing with her jumbo belly between you. Third of all, the whole public-make-out thing is gross." I stood up and tossed my messenger bag over my shoulder, fed up with his grins and suits and sad flirtation attempts. "Pay for your damn suit."

As I turned to leave, I heard him yell, "Wait!" He walked to me with a sort of pained look in his eyes. I didn't care why. "I just want you to know that if the situation were reversed, it would drive me crazy seeing you with someone else."

"Then you're a sucky person," I snapped. "Because I'm not doing that to you. I'm putting myself second to do right by people I don't even like just so I can . . ."

"Just so you can what?"

"Nothing."

He touched my cheek with the back of his hand. It was a simple gesture, one I'd seen him try on Carla a thousand times. I should've shoved him away. I should've told him to screw off like I wanted to that first time I met him at the pharmacy. But I never could because he was Snake. Infuriatingly persistent, charmingly sincere Snake.

"I don't think you're putting yourself second because of anyone *but* yourself," he said. "You're afraid that you could feel something for me, and that terrifies you."

"Feeling is overrated, remember? I don't feel things for people, Snake. And I don't need you to feel anything for me. And I definitely don't need you telling Carla that I make you feel long-term, because it's never going to work."

"Never going to work because of the baby?"

"Never going to work because you and I are toxic. I learned that from a bottle of Zoloft, weeks of therapy, and a doctor who prescribes me pills every month. And if you think we're stable enough to make something work, especially with you having a baby, you're even stupider than depression."

He looked at the ground and didn't look up again. I'd succeeded in hurting the feelings he esteemed so highly. And it wasn't even that I meant to; it was that I didn't want him to make this harder. Despite everything, he always hoped and believed and trusted, and I just . . . didn't. I couldn't.

"I better change," he said, undoing the buttons on his jacket.

He disappeared into the fitting room without another word.

I called Snake later that night, prepared to mend whatever it was that I'd broken at the store. Unsurprisingly, he ignored all three calls. Texts, too. I'd struck him somewhere that did a lot of damage, and while it was more than a little vindicating, it mainly hurt like crazy.

I knew it was stupid to fall into a depressive state over a few dodged calls, but I wasn't exactly the master of my depression. So I stopped trying to dominate my uncontrollable insides and let myself go. I cried. I blew my nose into a school permission slip on my nightstand because I mistook it for a tissue. I swallowed my Zoloft.

And then I thought about how alone I was. And how painful the mere act of breathing could be. And what it meant to be whole, because I always felt more like a million origami shreds glued around an inflated balloon. And if

I would ever be stupid enough to be happy. And if people would stop being people and be permanent instead.

I reached for my phone again, dialing the number I knew by instinct. The number that wouldn't change. The number that would be immortalized inside my head, regardless of what could never physically or otherwise exist on the other end of the line.

This number is no longer—

"I miss you."

—in service.

CHAPTER fourteen

MY MUCH-NEEDED THERAPY SESSION WAS RESCHEDULED for Tuesday. When I arrived, Dr. Rachelle bent forward in her chair, paying me what I labeled her creepily undivided attention. I had a tissue in my hand even though I wasn't crying, because she insisted I be ready. I didn't think I could produce any more tears after the debacle from the night before.

"It looks like you've had a rough day," she said, invoking her killer instincts (see: common sense).

"It's me. Your expectations should be pretty low by now."

"My only expectation is that you be genuine. That's what counts."

"I don't feel like being genuine."

"Why is that?"

"Because I have no one!" I yelled, surprising myself.

She slid on her horn-rimmed glasses, something she always did when she predicted that our session was about to get real.

I wrung my hands, buzzing through past phone calls, through robotic voices that wouldn't, couldn't, humanize. "You know how many times I've called her since she's been gone?" I asked.

"Who?"

"One hundred sixty-two," I said. She studied me long, not keeping up. "I've called her one hundred and sixty-two times. And you know how many times she's answered?"

A recognition sparked in her eyes. "Ah."

"Never. She's never answered me, not once. Because she can't. She can't come back, even if she wanted to. She's gone for good, right? That's what you said the first time I came to you. That I had to accept that she was gone for good so I could learn to grieve."

Dr. Rachelle waited for me to keep going, to cry and fit and rage. But I didn't see the need. And I wasn't sure I had the strength. "But you didn't fully grieve, did you? Calling a canceled line one hundred sixty-two times doesn't sound like someone who's moved on."

I tugged at my sleeves and looked everywhere but her face. I knew what she was doing without having to watch.

She was cocking her head, squinting her eyes just a little. Sometimes, it was all too predictable. "How am I supposed to move on when the only person I trusted after that screwed me over? Oh, and left. Left and screwed me over."

"Alex," she said. "Say his name. Say both their names."

"I don't want to."

"You don't want to because it's uncomfortable and hits at all of your triggers, but that's the only way to confront grief. Grief doesn't digest. You have to feel it until it passes through."

Dr. Rachelle was always good for a metaphor. Unfortunately, she was right about this one. As much as I wanted to disregard her advice, she was right about most things. Plus, she was the only person I could be open with who wasn't allowed to fight back or tell me that I was wrong. I didn't want to hear someone talk; I wanted someone to hear me talk. And to listen—and pretend to care, useless or not.

"Alex." I held my breath for ten seconds, then let it out. Another method Dr. Rachelle had taught me. "Bree."

"Alex. Bree," she repeated, inching her chair closer. "What does that trigger in you?"

"Disappointment. Heartbreak. Sadness."

Talking about my emotions was easy as long as I pretended they were filler words. If I replaced them with something else, they had no meaning at all.

"I think you're forgetting one that's very central to who you are," she added.

I knew what she was going for. It was another word I pretended was empty. A word that ironically was empty when I considered it.

Loneliness.

There was nothing more frightening to talk about. Not because I never felt it, but because I felt it too much. It was sacred to me. Loneliness was like my own imaginary friend; the more I acknowledged her existence, the more real she became. Losing people, having nothing, it was all a matter of the mind until I made it tangible. Until I acknowledged that it was there.

"The loneliness is my own fault," I told her, scanning her brown eyes for a reaction. I got only a blank, waiting stare. "I would have never been this miserable if I hadn't let myself care so much. When I lost them, it gutted me. And I can't let that happen again. I'll take the void and the Zoloft and the three stages over having to go back there."

"You think caring about them with the profoundness you did is what hurt you?" she asked. "Not the acts themselves?"

"Someone told me once that caring was just a way to survive. He said that you're damned if you do and you're damned if you don't. So you might as well do. But, I don't agree. I think you're just damned if you do. Nothing good can come from caring too much. It's painful when it's justified, and it's painful when it's not." I looked at my hands. I had to commend myself, because I'd never talked this much in a single session. And I didn't want to be genuine, but I wanted to be okay. Just okay. It wasn't too much to ask. "I don't want to get hurt like that again."

"I understand. And you're afraid that you'll get hurt by forming new relationships, by getting close to people."

She was steel-gazed, urging me to blow a gasket and erupt with my deep, dark secrets. Like that I wanted to be with Snake. And that seeing him with Carla drove me insane. And I didn't know what to feel because I was actually starting to like her. And I wanted them to do the right thing and be together, but I wanted them to be apart.

If only hiding the truth made it hurt less.

"Bree's never coming back," I whispered.

Never coming back.

It wasn't filler. It didn't fit.

"I could call her a hundred thousand times, and it wouldn't bring her back."

"You're right. It wouldn't. So what do we do with that?"

"I don't know. Every time I think about it, it kind of feels like I'm standing on a street corner watching everyone pile into a car and drive off without me."

"Loss."

"Yeah, loss. I can't chase it down or outrun it. It just goes and goes and takes everything with it."

She slid closer. "It's awfully lonely, isn't it?"

I didn't answer. I'd said too much already, and if I dug any deeper, I feared I would fall into a pit (see: Stage 3) I couldn't climb out of.

Scribbling something down, she said, "I'm assigning you a different project this time on the off chance that you'll do it."

"What?"

"Same task as last time, except now I want you to journal what *loneliness* means to you."

"Doesn't it mean the same thing for everyone?"

"Loneliness isn't a blanket feeling. There's all different kinds." She looked at me, hopeful. "Tell me what you think you should do when you're alone on a street corner."

I slouched on the living room floor in front of my dad's recliner, scrawling doodles (see: nth-degree boredom) in my journal. My essays for the week had all been written, thanks to Polka's tutoring in the cafeteria after school. It was nice having Polka around to help, given he was a brain on legs that was willing to spend most of his time with me in spite of my complete indifference toward his life outside of Hawkesbury. Sometimes I felt like a jerk for never investing in his life. But he knew me well enough to know I didn't invest in anyone, myself included, and he would be wise not to take it personally.

"You write nice today, Reggie," he'd said, leaning closer to me, but not so close I needed to give him the elbow.

I didn't look up. "Well, superhero stories practically write themselves."

"The idea give lot of potential, but only good writer write a good story."

He wasn't speaking in his usual monotone. I brought my gaze up from the page to find his small black eyes watching me back, emotionlessly, his lips quirked upward on one side. Was Polka smiling? I didn't think his mouth could go up instead of down.

I felt my own lip slide up in response, using the remaining bit of my concentration to deflate it. "That might be the first compliment you've ever given me, Polka."

He'd smiled full throttle, his teeth bared. It was a cute look for a perpetually frowning face. "I should give compliment more often. You earn it."

"Dude, are you flirting with me?" I'd teased, punching his shoulder.

His mouth fell flat, his eyes turned down to the table. He adjusted the purple bow tie beneath his chin, back to the Polka I tolerated/mildly liked. "What is it with Americans crushing on teachers? It a weird society."

His cheeks reddened a shade when he said it, proving that he had, in fact, been flirting. Which was totally weird, and not something he, or I, was likely to ever talk about later. It did feel kind of nice, though. Having someone at school who liked me as distantly as I liked him, someone who wouldn't try to push me into matching friendship bracelets, or into a prom-king-and-queen relationship. We could write cool essays and eat lunch and not have to exist to each other beyond the perimeter of a building.

"What are you working on there?" Dad asked over my shoulder, snapping me out of my daze. My hand immediately flew to the page, protecting the word *LONELINESS* scribbled out in blue pen.

I closed the journal and set it beside me, resting the back of my head against the armrest of his chair. "Nothing. Just stuff for Dr. Rachelle."

He sucked in a breath as if he was prepping to ask me more, then closed his mouth with a swallow. We both sat quietly for a minute, listening to my mother humming praise songs from the kitchen. It began to storm outside, a crash of thunder shaking the walls. The clouds were black in spots and white in others, like the sky was a checkerboard, or a series of dominoes.

Dad knew I hated thunderstorms, so he closed the

blinds. "I read a story in the newspaper today," he said, getting comfortable in his chair. I craned my neck to nab a glimpse of him. "Said some doctor in Chicago is working on a drug that will make people permanently euphoric, like a heightened version of an antidepressant. Claims it'll help with America's crime problem. People will be so happy, it'll be like living in a utopia."

"How does he suggest people take it?"

"Injection, mostly. He's still testing the chemicals, but hopes it'll be ready for consumption in the next few years." He grinned under his shaggy mustache. It was getting long on the sides, growing into the <u>Fu Manchu</u> (see: facial mullet) he was working toward. His eyes shot to the kitchen, making sure Karen was distracted. I checked, too, just to be sure. I didn't know why she wasn't allowed to hear what he had to say, but I was excited to find out.

He bent down a few feet from my face and whispered, "Do we call bullshit?"

My mouth fell open. "Dad."

"Your mother can't hear, don't worry." He popped his eyes up to the roof and pointed a finger to God. "I'll apologize to you later."

Our eyes aligned, both slyly holding in the secrets we couldn't say to Mom, or to each other. Secrets like my dad was pretty freaking awesome when he gave himself half a shot. Secrets like it was hard to be miserable to the best of my ability when Dad was cursing like a guy who might have been cool if he hadn't married Karen. Neither of us needed to validate the other. We shared a silent respect on both ends.

"I think anything that promises eternal happiness is utter bullshit," I answered.

He nodded. "I think so too."

My phone buzzed on the ground, slicing through our wavelength. I read the screen, a prickle of hope, of relief, sprinkling across my skin. Snake's name was at the top.

I hadn't talked to him since our episode at the tux place on Monday. He'd probably been moping around in Stage 2 for days, waiting for me to bend or for his willpower to break completely. He wanted me to turn a blind eye, to be willing to encourage his fantasies. The ones where we were getting by on a rope rather than a fine strand that was sure to snap with time. As if his persistence could outlast my commitment to misery.

I didn't know what to expect when I read his text. I only knew, in typical Snake fashion, it would make me hate him in all the ways that would draw me closer in the end.

I need help with my film.
Thought I'd borrow you for
a few shots. You interested?
(P.S. I'm sorry for everything.)

I didn't hesitate to text him back and tell him that he, like Dr. Optimism, was full of shit.

CHAPTER fifteen

OF ALL THE GODFORSAKEN PLACES I could experience what was sure to be the most mind-numbing afternoon of my existence, it just had to be in the Hawkesbury High parking lot. It was Thursday afternoon, the sun heavy against my pale skin, my exposed arms turning a reddish pink. The parking lot was vacant, since all the students who had lives to live had gone out to do so. Captain of the Lifeless Squad (see: Snake) was adamant about two things in regard to shooting this particular reel of footage for his indie documentary crap fest (see: movie). And I, like the idiot I was slowly becoming, indulged him to a fault.

One, it had to be captured at the epicenter of our lives, where we spent most of our adolescent time, in spite of how little we cared for it, and how little it cared for us.

Two, it had to encapsulate every single aspect of who Snake was as a person, including each individual facet of his life, like the pipes, knobs, and wires that comprise a well-oiled machine.

Translation: He wanted Carla and his ginger squash to be a part of it.

"Tell me where to stand so I can get this over with," I grunted, folding my arms over my T-shirt in protest.

"You're good right there." He squinted behind the camera, half his face scrunched up to reveal only one side of his teeth. "Babe, can you scoot back a step?"

"You've lost the privilege to call me babe," Carla pouted. She took a dramatic step backward, limply clutching a circular reflector in her hands. "And you said you'd do my shot first so I could go home."

"I was planning on it, until I considered which one of you would cause me more bodily harm if I kept you here too long. Sorry, but Reggie beat you in a landslide victory."

The red light clicked on, indicating we were rolling. I glared into the camera with more gusto than a celebrity in a DUI mug shot.

Snake peeked at the camera, drawing away to look at me in real time. "The camera still hates you."

"And I still hate it. This game of who can say the most obvious thing is really quite tiring, isn't it?"

He laughed. "Okay, so, tell me your name. Age. And worldview."

My worldview? There was a certain caliber of stupid I expected this film to be, and he was already exceeding my expectations.

I smiled ruefully into the glass lens, watching my own contempt for Snake and all his ridiculous hobbies reflected back at me. "My name's Reggie. I'm seventeen. My world-view is that we're all spiraling toward a vast and gaping obscurity we can't escape, and if we're lucky, we're doing so alone. Also, I despise you. And by you, I mean the general human population."

Carla's eyes expanded three sizes, gauging Snake's reaction. And, naturally, he was smirking. It was exactly the response he expected from me. But Carla, who lived on Rainbow Unicorn Island, had no way of knowing we were on a page she just wasn't on.

"Ohmigod, for real?" she squealed, dropping the reflector to the asphalt. She stepped beside me and fixed her fiery curls. "Give me a turn. I can do so much better than that. No offense, Reggie."

"If I were any less offended, I'd be dead." I moved out of her shot and picked up the reflector, purposely standing too close to blow out the hue. She was already ghastly pale. If I made her any whiter, she'd just be pink lips and a giant belly.

She smiled her best Little Miss Flashburn smile. "I'm Carla. I'm seventeen. My worldview is that—"

"Wait," Snake interrupted. He readjusted the camera to balance it on his shoulder and leaned his head around the mass of metal to look into Carla's eyes. "I'm doing something different with you."

She glanced at me, as if I knew where Snake was going with this. He hadn't told me anything about the plot of his movie apart from the footage I'd already seen. It was basically all *The Onslaught* and Carla and a smidge of me, which I guess was a fairly accurate depiction of that uselessness he loved so much. I couldn't be too hard on him. If I were making my own movie, the cast would include myself, Dr. Rachelle, and a shit ton of disappointment.

"Tell me about the most significant thing that's ever happened to you," Snake said, moving one foot length closer.

Carla touched her stomach on instinct. "Snake," she griped, her voice cracking. She was going to cry again. Her constant sobbing was oh so <u>pleasant</u> (see: infuriating). "That's not fair."

His face remained hidden behind the camera. "Why not?"

"Because you know I have to say Little Man, or I look like a bad person."

"Not necessarily. You could say winning Little Miss Flashburn, or getting that autographed Taylor Swift album when you were in New York, or—"

"I can't say any of that."

"Because?"

"Because the most significant thing that's ever happened to me might not have even happened yet." She rubbed her palm across the top of her stomach, a black tear escaping her eye. "Little Man and I. We have a whole lifetime of possible great things."

"Don't forget me," Snake said.

She blushed. "We wouldn't forget you."

Snake pulled the camera away from his face, watching Carla with his sappy, doting, boyfriend eyes. And he wasn't even her boyfriend anymore. It shouldn't have bothered me as much as it did, seeing him feel something genuine and real for a girl that he owed a lot to. They were tied to something too big for both of them, and it was logical and factual and right that they would connect differently to each other than they would to anyone else. But just because it made sense didn't mean it didn't completely suck.

Carla pressed down on her stomach, her frown twisting to a smile. She jerked her head up to Snake, giggling. "Come here—you have to feel his foot."

Snake shot me a glance, gesturing to his camera. It was

like he had forgotten I was there until that very moment. "Reggie, you mind? Keep the camera rolling just in case."

I took the heavy camera from him, impressed that Snake could hold something that weighty so easily on his shoulder. I watched through the viewfinder as Snake walked to Carla and offered a hand. She pressed it to her left side so his fingers rumpled her silky pink dress.

He grimaced. "Ew. Why is it sticking out like that?"

"Don't say ew," Carla protested. "It's the way he's sitting."

"It feels like a Gungan. Like you got a little Jar Jar Binks in there."

"Who's Jar Jar Binks? And don't call your kid a racial slur."

"Gungan isn't a racial slur. It's from *Star Wars*."

"God, I might as well have had this baby with a Gungan."

Snake peeked up at me, his hair hanging like a sheepdog's over his eyebrows. His mouth struggled as if it wanted to smile, but there wasn't enough energy stored in his face to make the muscles move. "Reggie, you got to feel this."

"Your alien fetus holds no interest for me."

"Aw, come on," Carla begged, reaching pinnacle Nagging Carla. She peered at me with expert-level doe eyes, her bottom lip poking out. "He's just a *wittle baby*."

"Which precisely explains why I don't care."

Snake grinned and turned his attention to Carla. "Well, I think it's pretty awesome."

Her whole face lit up in reaction.

They stood there locking eyes for a few good seconds like a page ripped from a cheesy teenage romance. It may have just been in my head, but it felt like I was third-wheeling it hard. Like, as hard as a girl on New Year's Eve who watches her friends make out as she drinks tequila and plots what size apartment to rent to fit all twelve of her cats. If this was how they were planning to be at prom on Friday, I was growing increasingly worried that Snake wasn't joking about them rekindling whatever it was they'd had over the past few months. Which I had originally thought was just an obligatory relationship between two idiots too stupid to use a condom, but wasn't so sure about anymore.

Whatever. It didn't matter. I wasn't going to prom. I wouldn't have to be subject to <u>precious</u> (see: disgusting) moments like this one. Assholes. Screw him. Screw both of them, actually.

Snake removed his hand from Carla's belly and walked back to where I stood. I unloaded the camera from my shoulder, ignoring him as he pinched my waist and tried to rattle me up in one of our back-and-forths. He gave it another go, but I shook out of his grip.

"One last shot?" he asked quietly and exclusively to me. "Please?"

Not one fraction of my being had any desire to be there anymore. I hadn't wanted to help him in the first place, and especially didn't want to after watching his sickeningly sweet family video. As if having Snake's reality shoved in my face made it any more concrete than it already was. I would always be watching his life from the outside, close enough to delude myself into believing I was a part of it, but still far enough away to know the truth.

Besides, I had my own reality. One Snake wasn't present for, one Carla only vaguely knew about, one my mom never cared to unearth. But at least in my reality, I didn't give anyone a reason to think that they could get closer than arm's length. I never tried to convince anyone that they were more special to me than they really were, or that I had any plans for a future together when I could barely see the present.

I stood next to Carla, a strong wind whipping through the trees across the lot. My black hair and her red locks glowed in the screen.

"Make this quick," Carla pleaded. "My dad's going to be here in a few minutes."

Snake grabbed a Twizzler from his jeans and chewed it. "Final question," he said, biting down harder. The blinking light sped up. "Why does all of this matter?"

Carla's face milled through expressions, settling on a frown. "What do you mean?"

"I mean," Snake continued, swallowing the last bite of Twizzler, "this. You, me, Reggie, Little Man, our lives. Why does all of this matter in the greater scope of the universe?"

Carla was stumped, her eyebrows dipping in concentration. I stared at Snake's one blue eye above the lens, at the reflection of Carla's swollen cheeks and belly, at my own dark circles and soon-to-be-sunburned skin. At the trees and the narrow road and the houses across from us. At the wooden sign that read HAWKESBURY HIGH: FOUNDED IN 1973. There was only one conclusion to reach, one answer to a question so incomprehensible that it made my blood go warm in anger. Because I wished to God that it wasn't as incredibly real as it had to be.

"Maybe it doesn't," I replied, shrugging at my own mirror image. "Maybe nothing we do matters at all."

On Friday night, I sat in my room and stared at my phone, waiting for a text from Snake like one of those desperate, pathetic girls who had nothing better to do on a Friday night than obsess over some jerk-face guy. And like those pathetic girls, I received no reward. No text. No call. Nothing.

It was seven o'clock. Prom was starting. He'd probably picked her up at her house. They probably took pictures, and he drove her in his girly, soccer-mom Prius. He was probably calling her babe, and she was telling him to shut up. They were probably experiencing one of those <u>possible great things</u> (see: romance) Carla had talked about in Snake's film. He probably wasn't thinking about me at all.

"Reggie." Karen was in the doorway, folding a shirt from the laundry basket. "If you're not doing anything, you should work on your final paper."

"It's prom night," I muttered. "No one types papers on prom night."

"Well, you decided not to go to prom."

Like she would have let me go even if I'd wanted to. Karen hated proms. She called them the devil's playground and said they tempted teens into committing sexual immorality. Because we nutty teens aren't aware that there are another 364 days in a year in which our no-no parts fit together just fine. Clearly, we can only have sex if we dance to shitty pop music first.

"If you're in for the night, you should get it typed."

"I'll do it tomorrow."

"You can't keep putting everything off."

"I can if I want to."

She sighed as she pulled the door cracked. "At least write something," she called from the hallway. "If you don't want to do schoolwork, then it's a perfect time to use that journal."

Man, she was annoying. And kind of right, unfortunately. Did I have anything better to do? Snake wasn't going to call me. He was probably asking Carla to dance the very moment I heard the pitter of the washing machine blade grinding against the metal. She was warming up to the idea of him again. He was praising her beauty; she was eating it up. They were falling into the stupid and nonexistent ideal of love to the rhythm of a John Legend song.

I grabbed my black notebook and pen and wrote down words without even thinking. I had done enough of it.

What Loneliness Means to Me: Lying in your bed on a Friday night listening to your mom do laundry while the guy you hate in the good way is at prom with his pregnant ~~girlfriend ex-girlfriend~~ *WHATEVER.*

After I reread my words a thousand times, my secret little friend was alive and banging around inside. In my stomach, in my blood, in my veins. Loneliness. She was alive because she was breathing, and she was breathing because I was pumping air into her lungs. I was making her real. The louder she became, the deeper my resentment. But I didn't resent that she played these games with me, I resented that she always won.

Unable to shake her any other way, I frantically scratched out the words and wrote new ones underneath. I didn't know what they meant. I only knew that Dr. Rachelle had said them, and they meant something. It was better than nothing.

What should I do when I'm alone on a street corner?

The washing machine clunked out.

Piece of crap.

CHAPTER sixteen

SLEEP HIT ME LIKE A TRUCK. Zoloft always knocked me out cold, but it was way more intense when getting knocked out cold was something I was gunning for. I won't say that I hit Stage 1 and cried until ten o'clock, because that's deplorable . . . but I cried until ten o'clock. My eyes stung, and the walls were suffocating, and I could hear my heartbeat, and I hated the thump of heartbeats, and Stage 2 was way more miserable than Stage 1 because my chest felt sharp and penetrating and every sound made me want to die. Thank God the washing machine had broken, or I may have had a full-on mental breakdown. Mental breakdowns were a bitch.

I was in my ugly, drug-induced slumber when I awoke to the sound of a clinking noise. I jumped upright in bed. My head spun and part of my brain still sank below the thick bed of unconsciousness I had fallen into. The room was pitch-black, the flicking sound growing. Louder. Faster. I sat in total quiet and concentrated on the noise.

Clink. Clink. A hushed curse word. *Clink.*

Something was being tossed against my window. I grabbed my phone and checked the time. Midnight.

Springing from my bed, I stumbled to the window, tripping over my laptop, which all but broke my pinky toe. I hopped to the window and pulled up the blinds.

Clink.

I nearly fell backwards as something red spiraled into the glass and bounced off.

Clink.

This was really happening. I wasn't dreaming. The clinking against the glass was red licorice. I looked down at the driveway and there he stood, still wearing the fitted suit that made him look significantly manlier than he would ever hope to be. He had to go and ruin the sexy undercover spy vibe by sporting a gray beanie that shoved his thick hair completely over his eyes. He was holding a bag of Twizzlers in his hand, and one was aimed at the window.

He fired.

Clink.

I unlocked the window and forced it open just as one of his licorice bullets went airborne and smacked me in the eye.

"Sorry!" he called up.

"Snake!" I yelled. "What the hell are you doing?"

"I'm being romantic," he <u>whispered</u> (see: screeched). "I'm tossing theoretical pebbles at your window like those medieval romance movies with the guys in drag."

"No, you're wasting food and acting like an idiot."

He dropped the empty bag on the asphalt and stretched out his arms. "Soft, what light through yonder window—"

"Shut up," I interrupted. "Are you drunk?"

"No. Are you?"

"I was sleeping, you moron."

"You're meaner than the girls in the movies."

A light blinked down the hall. I could hear footsteps and I shut my window. I held my breath until the bathroom door closed, then let it out slowly. I pulled the window open again to the cry of Snake singing some atrocious melody.

"If you don't shut up, I'm going to throw something at your head!" I called down. He stopped and pouted. "What are you doing here?"

"Look." He leaned his neck back and pointed to the cloudy sky. It was black in spots, emitting a purplish hue.

"It's about to storm. What's your point?"

"Not just storm. A cold front is moving in from the east. They're calling for a lightning storm. It's starting in about fifteen minutes."

"What are you, a meteorologist?"

"Filmmaker." He smiled. "And I have a movie to finish. A lightning storm is just what I need for my last few shots."

"Good luck with that." I grabbed the window and yanked it down. "Don't hit my mother's ceramic angel on your way out."

"Wait!"

"Shhh." I pulled the window back up. "What now? My mom is right down the hall."

"Come with me. There's a hill behind my house where you can see everything. I want to watch the storm come in with you."

"Stop trying to be romantic. You're bad at it."

"Fine. Of all the conceitedly self-sufficient loners in town, I thought I would be able to slightly endure your company. And do something with your hair. You look worse than you usually do, and that's saying something."

"That's more like it," I commended him. "But I can't."

"Why not?"

"For one, it's midnight and I just took Zoloft. It's a wonder I'm even coherent right now. Second, my mom is awake. She'll hear me leave."

He stroked his chin, searching all around him for divine intervention. And then he looked up and gave me that telling, mischievous grin, and I knew. I don't know how I knew, but somehow I knew exactly what he wanted me to do before he even proposed it.

"Jump," he said.

"Are you insane?"

"Yes."

"I'm not jumping. It has to be fifteen feet down."

"It's not that high. Come on, I'll break your fall."

"You're weak. You can't catch me."

"I didn't say I'd catch you. I said I'd break your fall. I carried Carla up to her room after prom, and she has to be at least as heavy as a baby elephant."

"Why'd you have to carry her?" I asked, trying not to sound jealous.

"She was tired, and her feet were swollen, and—" He shook his head. "Never mind. Irrelevant." He moved to the side of the house, only a few feet from the brick. "Slide your legs over and then push off with your arms. You'll land on top of me, and we'll plummet to the ground together. Deal?"

"I'm not jumping out of a building for you."

"Then why do you have a leg on the ledge?"

I glanced down and realized that I had mirrored his instructions. One leg rested on the metal frame, both hands white-knuckled against the brick.

"I don't trust you," I said.

"Rude. I trust you."

"Duh, because I'm trustworthy. Unlike you, Mr. I-Want-to-Ask-You-Out-Even-Though-I-Have-a-Girlfriend."

He spread his feet and bent his knees in ready position. "You're still hung up on that? I consider that a minor infraction, compared to everything else I've done."

"Are all guys as oblivious as you?"

"For the sake of humanity, I hope not." He opened his arms. "I'm ready for you now."

"You can't handle me."

He scrunched his nose. "Are we still talking about jumping, or has this conversation gone PG-13?"

I didn't really know what I meant by that. It just sounded like something someone would say in a movie, and I thought Snake would like it. Truthfully, though, there was one thing I had to know if I was about to plunge to my death with this oddly tolerable jerk.

"I'll jump, but answer me this."

"What?" he sighed.

"Do you . . ." I was about to cross the great unspoken line. I was about to use the *L* word. I braced myself, though I knew Snake was blissfully ill-equipped to combat it. "Do you think that you love Carla?"

He stood up straight and looked at the wall. I'm guessing he concentrated, though I couldn't see his eyes very well beneath his hair. My brain was dancing a victory routine because, for once, I had shocked him.

"Why do you ask if I *think* that I love her?"

"Because love is a futile disposition fueled by hormones and stupidity, which I think we both know you're exceptionally well-versed in. So how hormonal and stupid are you when it comes to Carla?"

He smiled, not his usual close-mouthed, lazy grin. A real smile. A bright smile.

"Let me put it this way," he said. "I'm not standing in front of Carla's window at midnight holding a bag of Twizzlers and wearing a tuxedo amid a killer lightning storm to ask her to risk breaking my back and/or killing me just to spend the latter part of an evening with her." He bent into ready position again. "That sounds pretty hormonal and stupid, if you ask me."

The dude had a point. I was the one he bothered round the clock. I was the one he practically stalked whenever he thought he could get away with it. I was the one on the receiving end of his embarrassing romantic gestures that he would certainly regret one day. But I still knew that Carla had something I didn't. That he would always see her differently.

The bathroom door opened.

Footsteps.

"My mom's coming!" I yelled down.

He bounced on the balls of his feet. "Now or never."

To this day, I swear, if I had to stand trial for jumping out of a window to my death just to escape to another possible death, I would plead temporary insanity. And yet, I found myself with a leg on the ledge, both hands on the brick.

My trembling feet despised me, almost as much as the rational part of my brain. But there was another part of my brain that told me to go for it. I didn't know what part that was, but it was louder than anything else.

Momentary confession: I was an idiot drunk on the allure of a <u>futile disposition</u> (see: love). And all of its uselessness and futility and pain awaited me on the ground with skinny arms wide open. I knew I could have hurt myself, or him, or both. We could have shattered to a million pieces on the asphalt. We could have been irreparably damaged. And that was the scary part. Not the idea of falling, but the fear of getting hurt.

So I jumped. I jumped because the fear of getting hurt wasn't unbearable. The only unbearable fear was living my entire life with only one leg out the window.

Next thing I knew, I had two hands on the cool grain of the driveway with Snake pinned beneath me. I could smell him. Strawberry. Cologne. A hint of Carla's expensive perfume. I could hear him. He was making a moaning sound, but it was more of a showy moan than a necessary one.

I opened my eyes gradually. Hazy darkness and lavender dotted his pasty skin. I glanced down at his face. He was staring at me like his life depended on the memory of what my eyes looked like under a purple sky. I could tell by his broken breaths that he was in some pain, but it was sufferable. He could handle hurt.

Falling hadn't killed us. Not yet, anyway.

"Are you okay?" I whispered.

"Pretty comfortable, actually."

"Your hand's on my ass."

"Oh, sorry." He slid his hand to my hip. "Better?"

I pushed up on my palms, standing with a leg on either side of him. I swung my right leg around and reached a hand down to help him up. "No," I said. "That's better."

He accepted my help and pushed up onto his feet. "Ouch," he breathed, rubbing his hand across his lower back. He turned to me, stepping one foot length too close. I didn't mind. "You're lighter than I thought. I could have caught you if I had known."

"No, you couldn't have."

"I'm stronger than you think."

"It's not about underestimating your strength. It's about overestimating my weakness."

I think we both knew we weren't talking about my Olympic dive from the window at that point.

We hopped in the Prius and were at his house in ten minutes. The house was dark except for the twinkle-lit sidewalk, buzzing like fireflies in the shadows. He led me past his screened deck, where there was a master grill like the ones in those fancy commercials. As we went through the backyard, I was staring at the sky, dazing off as the gray gave way to black.

"Reggie?"

Snake was staring at me again, but it was more of an earth-to-crazy stare this time. I looked around and noticed that we were on a hill a good few yards behind the house, not a huge one, but high enough to provide a great view of the neighborhood and the pond. He untied the camera from his back.

"Are you going to lay the blanket down?" he asked.

I forgot I had been carrying a hand-stitched quilt his grandmother had made for one of his moms when she was a baby. The pattern was Jacob's ladder in patriotic colors, and I knew that because Karen had instilled in me every possible design of quilt that any human could ever not need to know. I spread the blanket across the dewy grass and sat down. Snake sat beside me, his arm pressed to mine.

The lightning had already begun on the car ride over. There were little flashes here and there, but nothing significant for his documentary. He clicked the camera on just as brighter sparks electrified the horizon.

"Why do you need lightning shots, anyway?" I asked as a bolt struck above his house. The sky was honey in an instant, and bruised purple in the aftermath.

"Because it's ironic," he said from behind the lens. He had one eye squinted into the viewfinder as the sky erupted. "A lightning storm in Flashburn. Who could pass up the opportunity to capture not only our uselessness, but the predictability of our existence?"

"We are exactly what we say we are. No surprises."

"None except one." He pulled away from the camera and looked at me, a flash of pink blinding half of my vision of him. "You're the only person who's ever surprised me."

"I'm not that complex."

"On the contrary, you're so exclusively complex that you only have one predominant behavior." He kept the camera rolling, but set it on the ground in front of his feet. He leaned closer to me, his eyes electrified by lightning and something of an entirely different kind of nature. "Hate. It encompasses you, but barely scratches the surface of who you are. And I'm still not sure how that can be."

I didn't want to be repetitive even to my own conscious, but this guy. This presumptuous guy. He was roundabout, complimenting me like he always did, sprinkling his assertions with arrogant assumptions. It used to make my skin itch. Now, it was comfortable. It was the kind of lightning that only bothered the sky.

"So I'm a little complex."

"No kidding. I can't tell if you hate because you're inherently hateful, or if hate is your love language."

"What about you, huh? You're surprising."

"No, I'm not," he mumbled.

"No? I see a kid refilling his Prozac and find out that this guy has a cool talent, awesome moms, a girlfriend, whether or not he wants one, a baby on the way, and he's clinical." I shrugged. "Doesn't make much sense."

"I'm sorry my depression isn't listed on the periodic table of logical depression. Do I have to draw up a map of why I feel the way I do, or can we accept my defects as one of the unexplainable mysteries of life and let them be?"

"No, I get it. People always want reasons. My therapist always asks me, 'What was your initial trigger?' and I used to not answer, because I didn't know. But then I just got tired of the nagging and this idea that misery must be attached to reasons why, so when she asked me for the thousandth time, I said, 'Birth.'" He laughed. "Yeah, my therapist hates me. And not in the love language way."

"My therapist always tells me, 'To have a friend, you first must be a friend.'" He yanked a blade of grass from the ground and tied it around his thumb. "That's it. That's the eighty-dollars-a-session advice that I couldn't possibly get anywhere else, like from my moms or a minivan bumper sticker." He looked at me as lightning struck behind the trees of his neighbor's house. "I guess loneliness is my hatred. One screwed-up movie we're in, huh?"

I looked away right as more lightning exploded, rosy hues kissing the gray. The flashes were like light bulbs across the atmosphere, like the gods were paparazzi taking pictures of the lost and broken little humans wandering aimlessly beneath their thumbs. I looked at Snake, who had snatched up his camera to make sure he got the perfect shot. I hated myself for thinking it, hated myself for not hating how stupidly happy I felt beside him.

And I couldn't help but think of how pointless it was to live in the imaginings of lightning, to believe that they were fireworks and the universe made them so that we could be futile little humans in love with our own futility.

"Her name was Bree," I whispered against the show.

Snake turned to me, setting the camera down as the lightning simmered. "Who?"

"My trigger, if I had to pick one." I watched a cloud be torn apart by the sparks. "The friend thing never worked much for me either, believe it or not. I guess my good looks and general charm were too threatening."

His eyes rounded at *charm*, and he chuckled.

"I met Bree in the bathroom on the first day of seventh grade after I spilled Cherry Coke all over the crotch of my pants. She offered me her gym shorts to wear for the rest of the day so it didn't look like I'd peed terminal red piss all over myself. We sort of had to be friends after that. The only problem with friends is, you care about them. A lot. And then they get hit by a drunk driver a few weeks into freshman year and die before they were ever given a chance to feel the things the rest of us get the opportunity to feel all our lives."

He gasped under his breath. "Holy shit. Wow. Um . . . yeah. That's . . . I'm sorry."

"It's okay. I get the feeling I would have ended up miserable regardless, but it sucks for her and her family, you know?" I ripped up a chunk of grass and tossed it to the side. Snake sat completely motionless, not bothering to do that thing people do where they pretend they understand. It's ridiculous how much trouble people have admitting that they don't understand everything. "Anyway, when something like that happens, there's no good way to move on. So I did my best. Tried to bury myself in schoolwork and books and stuff, but it all felt, well, useless."

His mouth morphed into a sad smile.

"So I started hanging out with this guy in my geometry class that I'd known since he was just a nerdy kid in kindergarten. But I couldn't help but notice he wasn't such a hopeless dork anymore. He was awkward and cute and told me lame stories about the space robot invasion from his favorite comic book. And I didn't care about the robots or the book, but I cared about the nerdy boy who did. Especially when he told me he loved me and said that he wouldn't ever leave like Bree did, and that even though he was moving to Vermont at the end of the summer, I would still be a part of his life. But then when he moved to Vermont, I never heard from him again. Saw online that he had a girl there he'd been talking to all school year, the daughter of this guy his dad knew, and that was it. He never talked to me again. And there I was believing that I had someone who would never leave, and he was never really there to begin with. That's when I realized that caring isn't a way to survive. It doesn't prevent pain, it encourages it."

I looked at Snake. His lids were heavy, but not like he was tired. Like he was hurt. Sad, even. "That was my trigger. Absence. Realizing its inevitability. I cared too much about Alex from geometry, and he left. It's human nature, I suppose. Temporariness. Tightropes into oblivion."

"The Onslaught."

I tried to smile at him, but knew I looked unhinged. "One point for complexity, right?"

He was exuding multiple Snakeisms at once. His pervasive staring. His Twizzler chew. His grin that wouldn't even complete a full upward turn because it was defiant toward the mouth that made it. "I never imagined there was a point in time when Reggie Mason was anything other than a total misanthrope," he teased, trying to lighten the dark cloud I'd tossed over the evening. "That's not one point for complexity. You just won the whole complexity game."

"What about you?" I asked. "What's your kryptonite of choice?"

"I wouldn't call it a choice." He shut his camera down for good. I prayed the audio hadn't been on for my humiliating oration. "And I don't know. I wish I did. In some ways, I wish I had a Bree, or Alex from geometry, to make sense of it. Maybe it's friendlessness or only-child syndrome or something. But I didn't have a trigger. It was sort of a slow burn, I guess."

"How did you know you were depressed?"

"How does anyone know they're depressed? You feel equally alive and dead and have no idea how that's even possible. And everything around you doesn't seem so full anymore. And you can't tell if the world is empty or you are. That's how I knew. I realized it wasn't the world that was empty."

He forgot the part about the walls closing in and threatening to suffocate you when you're already barely breathing, but it wasn't my depression we were talking about. And he was right about the empty theory. Except he was wrong about one thing.

He wasn't empty. Not to me, anyway.

"Look at us," I said, motioning to the blanket damp

from the evening dew, his three-piece suit, and my pajama pants. "We're a wreck. No wonder people don't want to hang out with us."

"No one except Carla. She thinks you two are best friends."

"What?"

"Yep. You've been propelled right into the friend zone."

"I would like to remain in the silently-loathe-one-another-from-afar zone."

"She isn't that bad. I promise. A tad conceited, but not wholly insufferable."

"So you're telling me that prom wasn't insufferable?"

"No, prom was hell. The DJ only played reggae, and the punch tasted like poisoned apple juice."

"Now you know why I don't go to Hawkesbury functions."

He scrunched his face like he didn't blame me. "Horrible party planning aside, Carla and I actually had a pretty good time. Granted, her friends weren't hanging out with her, which I think had more to do with me than her, but still. We hung out. We mainly sat around and talked about you and baby stuff."

"Me?"

"Your budding friendship. And you and me."

"What about you and me?"

"She said that she didn't totally hate you. And that she didn't totally hate me. And if I liked you, I should go for it and stop wasting her time." He shot me a playful look. "She put it differently, but I'm telling you the clean version."

"You've never said you liked me to my face," I pointed out. "You're too much of a coward."

"I said I hated you in the best way, which I thought was the same."

"Do you mean it?"

"Yeah."

"Then tell me you like me." It shouldn't have surprised him that I was demanding his affection so I could mock it. He knew too many layers.

"You're going to call me a name and tell me to get over myself."

"Probably. But if you're going to continue your sad attempts at winning me over, at least man up and say what you want from me so I can properly reject it."

"If that's what you want." He grinned with a dash of hopefulness as he leaned toward me and said, "Reggie, I really like you."

I rolled my eyes. "Get over yourself, douchebag."

He looked down and shook his head, the tips of his hair swishing against his bottom lashes. I watched him smile to himself, pleased with my dismissal of his affection. And for the first time, I understood why he liked being hated. It was so much easier to mock our feelings than indulge them.

"I should go home," I said after he yawned. "If Karen's still awake, she's probably sent out a search team."

He tied the camera around his back. "I'll drive you."

It took fifteen minutes to make it home when it should've only taken ten. Snake was driving twelve miles an hour under the speed limit, stopping extra long at every stop sign. He claimed that he needed to get the engine checked on the Prius before the baby arrived because it was a heaping pile of junk, and Carla wouldn't want her kid cruising in a safety hazard on wheels. It would've been a great excuse if the check engine light had been on to back up his story. That idiot was driving Miss Daisy to buy himself time with me, time he was afraid he wouldn't get back. I would've called him out on it at the very first stop sign if I hadn't been willing to pay it in full.

When we reached my house, it was lit on both levels. I was a dead girl walking.

"I think you're screwed," Snake whispered, shutting the headlights off.

"Sentence predictions?"

"A month. Solitary."

"Generous. I'm going to take your month and up you another. Also, possible execution."

"I would bet you on it, but it feels wrong to gamble with a dead person."

"I appreciate that considerate decision."

The light in my bedroom disappeared just as the hallway light made its debut in the *Signals of Reggie's Imminent Death* show.

"I'm going to go before the whole house turns yellow," I whispered, turning to Snake.

The porch light flashed on, and I knew I had to act fast. I grabbed him by the arm and pulled him close, kissing his cheek lightly. His skin was smoother than most boys', and it smelled of a cologne that reminded me of those cheap samples that come in magazines. He was too cool for magazine cologne.

When I backed away, he was staring at me with a keen smirk, like he was winning a game I hadn't known we were playing. In a squeaky voice that was supposed to be a mimic of mine, he whispered, "Snake, I really like you too." Then he smiled and said, "It isn't that hard."

I opened the door and slammed it shut, the window shivering in the socket. The entire house was shining, my window still swung open from my dive to the pavement. He held his smirk as he sped down the street, nearly flattening my neighbor's trash can with his reckless driving. Skid marks dotted the asphalt like footprints to the pond.

I watched him leave and felt that familiar deep-seated

fire, a sensation with which I was well acquainted. The emotion to end all emotions.

Hate.

Apparently, it was my predominant behavior. I was hating again. But, for once, I wasn't hating him. I was hating the absence of him.

I smirked back as he vanished.

CHAPTER seventeen

"REGINA LORRAINE MASON," KAREN HISSED THE second my boots touched the carpet. She was clad in her pink floor-length night robe with her whale-spout hair cocked messily to the side of her head, her glasses balancing crookedly on her nose. She pointed to the love seat across the room. "Sit down. Now."

As I made my trek to the couch, I noticed my dad reclining in his La-Z-Boy, struggling to keep his sagging lids peeled. He wore pinstriped silk pajamas and tiredly watched me with a sad sort of irritation. The creases that cornered his eyes said more about my presumed rebellion than any sinner's prayer my mother was preparing to make me recite.

She stood beside the couch, staring at me with

<u>quarter-size crazy eyes</u> (see: slasher-movie status). "You have ten seconds to explain where you've been. Go."

"That's not enough time to come up with a good cover story. Come back in five minutes, it'll have machine guns and everything."

"Don't start that tonight, Regina," she snapped. "I'm not in the mood."

"Saving a cat from a burning tree?"

"Regina!"

"Fine." I sighed. "I was with Snake."

Her scowl all but froze her face. She wasn't shocked, though. She knew. Moms always know. "Where did you go with him?"

"We were out having sex and doing drugs . . . and something with machine guns—"

"Reggie," my dad interrupted. He yanked the lever on his chair to push himself up. He frowned at me the way he did when I'd lied to my mom about stealing the communion bread at church or when I'd called her Jezebel because I thought it was the absolute worst Bible insult I could dish out. "Tell your mom the truth, and you won't get in too much trouble. I promise."

Truth. Honesty. Authenticity. If only Dr. Rachelle were there to applaud my efforts. "Snake showed up after prom and asked me to help him film some shots for a movie he's making," I explained. "We went to his backyard and filmed the lightning storm, and he brought me home. That's it."

"You're lying."

"Yeah, Mom. I made up that incredibly lame story because holding a giant hunk of metal in the middle of a lightning storm makes me sound like such an intelligent individual, and I thought you'd be impressed."

"He didn't try anything with you?"

"I guess you missed the having sex part."

"Be serious, Reggie." She rubbed her eyes and smeared leftover makeup across her cheeks. "I don't trust that boy. I've heard rumors about him in my ladies group."

"What your mom heard has been very unsettling for her," my dad added. It didn't slip past me that he emphasized the *her* in that explanation. I never heard a *me*. "She has a lot of concerns."

"What about you, Dad?" I asked. "Do you have concerns?"

He blinked at the ground, his brow wrinkling. "I suppose I do, yes," he mumbled after he gave it some thought. But I wasn't sure he meant it. He wasn't good with humans, especially ones like Snake and me. Unlike dead animals, we weren't so easy to repair. "If it's true, of course."

"And these rumors are . . . ?"

He looked to Karen for support. She sighed, sitting

next to me hesitantly. She paused for a moment and kept her eyes on the ketchup stain on the carpet as she said, "I heard he's the boy who got little Carla Banks pregnant."

Little Carla. Ever since we were kids, my mother had always referred to her as Little Carla. Why wasn't I friends with Little Carla? Why didn't I ever invite Little Carla to my house? Why didn't I ever want to go to Little Carla's parties? I imagined it was hard to see Little Carla as Pregnant Carla or Mommy Carla or Less-Than-Perfect Carla when my mom had always not so secretly wished her daughter were more like precious Little Carla Banks.

I looked directly into her nervous eyes as she waited for a response. There was no point in lying to defend Snake. He was who he was. And if he'd been beside me in that moment, he wouldn't have made a single excuse for himself. He would have owned his wrongs. He would have enjoyed the ensuing scorn. I had to respect his absence, the mistakes he made to keep himself sane.

"Yeah. He is," I admitted.

Shots fired. Karen down.

Her skin flushed red. She crawled through the steps of the premental breakdown breathing routine. My dad stood up and walked to the couch to lay a hand on her back, but she only shook him off.

"Listen to me, Reggie," she choked. "I don't want you to see that boy again. He's a bad kid. I don't know how else to put it. You're better than that. I won't have my daughter getting involved with someone like him. Do you understand me?"

"You don't know him."

"I know enough."

"You know one mistake."

"It's a very big mistake, Reggie."

"You don't know him!" I shouted, the pent-up bitterness from every judgmental look and raised brow seeping through my teeth as I confronted her warped conclusion about the boy I knew. The boy she wouldn't bother to understand.

She didn't know Snake the way I did. She didn't know the way he grinned with only part of his lips, or the way he spoke about whatever random thought popped into his mind in a passing minute, or the passionate way he filmed the dullness of our lives, or the way he cared about everything, no matter how ineffective he knew it to be. She didn't know the Snake I knew.

"It's my job as a mother to protect you from people like him," she said, wiping her nose with the back of her hand.

"Guess what, Mom? I *am* a person like him. He's as bad at being human as I am. But I guess that just gives you another reason to resent him, doesn't it? It certainly gives you plenty of reasons to resent me."

"I'm not going to deny that you struggle, Reggie. But

you're better than him. He's not a good person. It's as simple as that."

I stood up, my fists clenched at my sides and my bones rattling. I was having a near-Hulk experience. "Because you've never screwed up, right? You're so damn holier than thou, it amazes me."

"Don't talk to your mom like that," my dad interjected. His tone was too soft and unimposing to be taken seriously.

She jumped off the couch, standing nose to nose with me. "You sulk around and make your smart-aleck jabs and pay no mind to anyone else, and I'm sick of it. Start behaving with some respect."

"Give me something to respect!" I yelled back desperately. "All you ever do is judge me, judge Dad, judge Snake, judge his moms, judge, judge, judge, and I'm the one who's sick of it. How about you stop acting like you were directly appointed by God to be everyone's keeper, because you're no better than anyone else."

As I tried to move past her, she stepped in front of me and grabbed my wrist. "You are not to leave this house for two months. Only school and work. I hate to do this, Regina, but I've had as much as I can take. I don't know what made you this way. I don't know why you can't just . . . just be normal."

She was staring straight into my eyes, like she knew the parts of me that were in the blue and nothing underneath. I saw a distorted image of myself in the lens of her glasses.

The truth of it was, there was too much underneath for her to know. For me to fully know myself.

My dad sat down on the couch. He stared at the wall like he couldn't comprehend what was going on. If I wasn't so fully hating, I might have tried to explain that none of this was his fault. But I was so far past being reasonable.

I jerked out of my mother's grasp and stormed up the steps. When I made it to my room I slammed my door, nearly knocking it off the hinges.

I raked my hands through my hair until my scalp hurt. My stomach was tied in a legion of knots, each aching and pulsating and throbbing to the point of near explosion. I kicked my bed and my laptop toppled onto the floor. Watching it hit the carpet was like a gunshot, detonating a built-up rage that had lived inside of me for the past year.

My heart wasn't an organ with valves and blood and arteries. It was another creature entirely. One that couldn't be ignored, no matter how quietly I told it to beat.

I grabbed a pillow and screamed into it.

The first scream was for my mother. One loud, screeching, teary cry for my mother. I hated her. I wasn't supposed to say that, and maybe one day I would regret letting myself think it, but I couldn't stop. I hated that she didn't try to understand me. I hated how she turned her nose up when she walked by my room at night and saw me crying. I hated that I wasn't the kid she bragged about to her friends in church group. All she saw in me was a walking mistake, a sin to be forgiven, a disease to be cured. I hated that she looked at Snake and saw the same.

Then I screamed into the pillow a second time.

I screamed for myself. I screamed because she was right. I was a disease. I was sick and vastly spreading and untreatable. But I wasn't my depression. Depression was a symptom of another illness. Being human. Being me.

I screamed again.

The third time, I didn't know who I was screaming for. Maybe Snake. Maybe my dad. Maybe another pity round for myself. The shriek clawed from the cords of my throat without intention. But once it was out in the open, sucked into the pillow, it became increasingly clear.

My screams were of lost souls and Cherry Coke and acrobats and geometric shapes and pill bottles and uselessness and flashing red lights and lightning and loneliness and babies crying and brevity.

I hated having to live each day knowing that, good or bad, I would never get it back. And I hated to resent time simply because it couldn't be taught to stay. And it took me until that moment, falling to my knees at two o'clock in the morning, to realize that all the things I hated, I hated only because they wouldn't let me hold on. Because they didn't know how to outlast themselves.

I hated that the world wasn't empty, but I was.

Whispers from the living room interrupted my Stage 2 breakdown.

"She will never be okay," I heard Karen say. My dad was trying to shush her, but she only got louder. "She's been dealing with this depression issue for an entire year. I prayed about it and meditated on it and talked to Pastor James, and, against my better judgment, tried the antidepressants and the therapy, but nothing works. And now she's running around with this boy, God help her. He's only going to tear her down. It won't be long before she's the one having his baby. What are people going to think? I can only hide so much."

"She's being a teenager," my dad said quietly. He didn't sound like himself. "They all go through rebellious phases. You went through one yourself."

"I would have never shouted at my mother like that."

"I agree. She shouldn't speak to you that way. But she's lashing out. This will pass, Karen. It's a phase."

"You always make excuses for her," she snapped.

There was a brief silence in which all I heard was heavy breathing. And then the sound of the couch shifting as someone stood. It was my dad's voice, a shallow whisper.

"I don't think you make enough excuses for her."

I had to leave. That was what all the screaming and pillows and echoing conversations amounted to. I couldn't stay there that night. I needed to think. Needed to breathe.

Needed to be anywhere but there. I grabbed a pair of jeans and a white T-shirt, shoving the clothes into my messenger bag. I sat crumpled on the floor for minutes, focusing on nothing but *depression issue. Depression issue. Depression issue.*

The words whooshed in my ears like a wave crashing against my eardrums. Depression was a symptom of me. Depression was an issue. I was an issue. A problem. A mistake.

I had no logical place to run to that late. I had no logical person to turn to. None but one, and he was hardly logical.

When I went downstairs, I headed straight for the front door. My mother sprang from the couch, her brows furrowing the moment she noticed my bag.

"Where are you going?" she asked.

"I'm leaving."

"No you're not."

My dad met me where I stood, watching me with a hint of something my mother's anger lacked. "You don't have to do this," he whispered. "Let's talk."

"There's nothing to say. You married a lunatic. There. We talked."

"She loves you." He laid a hand on my shoulder mechanically, observing me through his glasses. His gray eyes were fading. Had they always been so lifeless? "I love you."

"I know. I know you do. But you can't speak for Mom. You may want your words to replace hers, but they don't."

My mother moved toward me. "Regina," she said, anger ebbing in her tone. She wasn't even looking in my eyes anymore, but at my hands clasped tightly to the bag. "I love you. I want you to stay."

I love you. Three words. She wanted three words to rectify a year. She wanted three words to heal two completely different people. It was a nice idea, that words could do that. That they had the power to fix and repair and transform even the most shattered of people. But unfortunately for us, words were nothing more than a string of nice ideas.

"Why am I depressed?" I asked, grasping at the niceness of ideas until they vanished.

She looked surprised. "What?"

"Why am I depressed?"

She glanced at my dad, who was watching me, maybe knowing the answer. Maybe wishing there wasn't one.

"Well, it . . . it was what happened to Bree," she stuttered, still eyeing him for help. "But now? I don't really know."

"That's the problem, Mom," I said, tossing the bag over my shoulder. I opened the door and it creaked in the stillness. "You don't know me."

My dad held my mother back and ordered her to let me go as I took off running through the front yard and down the street. It was the ideal dramatic exit. The girl leaves her overbearing parents behind and runs to the boy without ever looking back. It was cinematic perfection. It was real-life destruction.

My feet were clunky like wooden blocks and my chest wouldn't lift to let me breathe and my temples were throbbing with an excruciating headache unlike any other I'd experienced. The streetlights were guiding me forward, but the sway of the clouds was drawing me back. I stopped running the instant my brain caught pace with my rage. I was trying to run to Snake's house on foot. Snake, who lived at the pond a ten-minute drive away. And me, who couldn't run for more than a half mile without getting a side stitch. I stopped in front of this hideous yellow house down the street that my mom always said reminded her of a lemon. I dug my cell phone out of my pocket and texted Snake.

> I'm in front of an obscenely
> yellow house near the end of
> my street. Please come pick
> me up as soon as possible.
> I may have barely survived
> that execution we were talking
> about.

I plopped down on the curb and waited. It had only been nine minutes when blinding headlights flashed in my direction, the word *Namaste* glowing in the darkness. The

Prius came speeding around to the curb, nearly leveling my feet against the road. Snake parked. I jumped up, swung the door open, and dove in.

"Thank God for you," I panted as I shut the door.

I turned to him. He was watching me calmly, wearing only gray sweatpants and no shirt, his hair flopping from his scalp like a mop. I kept telling myself not to stare at his stupid, hard chest. At the curvature of his abs that weren't really abs, but close enough. At his waist that formed the perfect shape of a . . . crap. Okay, so I was <u>staring</u> (see: drooling).

"Where's your shirt, loser?"

"Under my bed." He hit the gas and took off down the road. "I was almost asleep, but the damsel needed my saving."

"Call me a damsel again. I dare you."

He laughed. "All right. Fill me in."

"Nothing abnormal," I said as he turned onto the main road. "Karen found out about your upcoming transformation to world's most underqualified dad the same night that I break my curfew so we can sneak out together, disregarding the fact that I'm forbidden from seeing you. As I'm sure you can imagine, she took that very well."

"I'm not that underqualified," he argued.

"Wow. That's all you got from that."

"Sorry. From where I'm sitting, it doesn't sound like

anything new. Shouldn't a knockdown-dragout have been expected?"

"Yes, but—" I tried to think of a reason why this time was different. A nasty word or a banishment to the nearest convent or a fist brawl to the song "Kung Fu Fighting." Something. But it wasn't different. The only difference was that I ran this time. The only thing that was different was me. "It doesn't matter. I need time away, okay? Can I stay with you tonight, and we can figure the rest out tomorrow?"

"Sure. But my family is leaving tomorrow."

"Leaving?" My stomach rose to my throat.

"Not forever." He grinned, smugly delighted that the idea of him leaving bothered me so much. "Just for the day. Remember when I picked you up that first time we went out, and I told your mom that my family goes to Cedar Point every summer?"

"Yeah."

"Well, we haven't missed a summer since I was six. My moms arranged for us to go tomorrow. We have to do it early this year since the summer is going to be super hectic with the baby and everything."

"Oh." I tried to picture Snake at an amusement park with his moms and a head-size cotton candy on a stick, but couldn't conjure the image.

"You can come with us," he said as we reached the stoplight, his bare skin draped in red. "We can buy you a ticket."

"I don't want to put a damper on your postcard family outing."

"It *will* be torture having to listen to you make fun of old men's fanny packs all day, but I'll survive."

"I don't do heights. No Ferris wheels or drop towers or anything like that."

"You jumped out of a window," he noted.

"Because I knew I would fall on you."

"Well, then, pretend like the ground below is a bunch of concrete mes to break your fall . . . and kill you, but that's besides the comforting point I'm making."

We pulled into his driveway. The house was completely black except for a single light shining from his bedroom window upstairs.

"My moms are asleep. Be very quiet," he whispered as we walked up his porch steps.

"Are they going to be mad that I crashed?"

"No, they're cool about stuff like that."

"Carla Banks. Exhibit A."

He scowled and opened the door, placing his index finger over his mouth like he was a kindergarten teacher at naptime. He led me upstairs, past the nerdy beach picture that seemed to get nerdier the more I looked at it, as if the spike cut and buck teeth could get any worse. He stopped at his door and turned to me, suddenly fidgety and awkward and . . . was he nervous?

"I'm sure you have a guest room in this fine estate," I whispered.

"You don't have to whisper up here. My moms' room is downstairs. And yeah, it's that one right over there." He pointed across the hall to a room diagonally across from his. The door was cracked slightly. "There's a bathroom in there, too."

"Where's the basketball court and indoor pool?"

"Basketball court is undergoing renovations, and the pool is being cleaned. You forgot about the exercise room."

"I didn't forget. I only asked about the rooms you'd find me in."

He smiled and lowered his head, his blue eyes fixed on the ground. His shoulder was pressed in the doorway and the light from his bedroom reflected against his smooth skin. I bit down on my lip so hard it went numb. I'd never been much of a lip biter, mainly because I found the habit to be flirtatious and very Carla-ish, but Snake inadvertently gave me a new tick just by being so boyish and so shirtless and so freaking close.

He glanced up. And that time, it was me who was nervous.

"I should probably go to bed," I whispered, pointing behind me. I was pretty sure I pointed in the wrong direction. My brain was so Snake-high, I didn't know which way was up.

"Okay." He nodded. Then he took an extended breath, his hard chest lifting, and said, "You could stay in my room if you want."

I want. I want. For the love of—

"Stop flirting with me."

"I don't think I can."

I didn't want to go to the guest room. I didn't want to go to bed within ten feet of him and not with him. I didn't want him to stop flirting with me. I didn't want to be the one to admit it.

He took me by the waist and pulled me against his chest, wrapping his arms around me tightly as if he thought the girl within his grasp would float away in an instant. And I might have with anyone else. But not with him. He felt safe and warm, and still had that magazine cologne scent on his chest. He was breathing heavily into my knotted hair, my ear against his heartbeat. And even though I didn't like heartbeats, I liked his. His heart wasn't just blood and pulsation. His heartbeat had a rhythm. A sporadic, insecure, perfect rhythm. It was like mine, a beast all its own.

"I just want you to know that there are still streaks of purple in the sky from the lightning," he whispered into my hair.

I lifted my head from his chest and looked into his eyes. Comfortingly dull. Hidden. Wanting. "So?"

"So not everything leaves," he said, his hands sliding

away. And then his chest wasn't so close to my cheek. And his cologne smell was vaporizing. And I didn't know what the tingling against my skin meant. He glanced down the hallway and back at me. "Good night."

I was able to drag myself to the guest room. The décor was exactly what I would have expected: a king-size bed with an ornamental wooden headboard, mint green curtains to match the striped bedspread, unburned incense on the bedside table. The guest room was so incredibly Jeanine, just like Snake's room was so incredibly Snake.

My tiredness didn't register until I fell on the bed and felt the foam against my spine, melting my body against the mattress. I clicked off the lamp and lay on my back beneath the covers, gazing up at the empty ceiling.

Light filtered through the blinds. No color, just figments. No color, except one. A shade.

A streak of violet.

I closed my eyes for the last time that night, and I swear I could still hear his heartbeat.

CHAPTER eighteen

ROAD TRIPS WERE AMONG THE FEW pleasures in life I hadn't learned to hate. Whether it was being free, riding seventy miles an hour with the windows down and the bass pounding to the same rock song on repeat until that band got buried in my never-listen-again pile, or the sense of escape, from leaving a town that only held me down and from people who couldn't have cared less where I ran to or even why I ran. I didn't know what it was about running that drew me so much. All I knew was that I didn't want to stop.

That's where I was that Saturday morning, somewhere between carefree rock bands and sweet escape. Snake sat beside me in the back seat of the Prius, controlling the radio from his iPod that was hooked into the cigarette lighter. I'd made him swear before we left the house that he wouldn't play anything remotely resembling the Renegade Dystopia. He was doing a decent job so far.

Jeanine was driving, her silky jet-black hair braided in a fishtail down her back. Snake's other mom, Meg, rode shotgun. She had a frizzy blond afro and virgin skin, virgin because she didn't wear a speck of makeup, yet somehow managed to still be pretty in that organic, borderline-hippie, au naturel kind of way. She'd packed us a cooler brimming with "healthy snacks" (see: vegetables) and that Jeanine had stuffed with chocolate and Cheetos the moment Meg turned her back. Snake had hidden money in his pocket for edible food once we got to the park.

The morning had gone more smoothly than anticipated. I received all of six voicemails from Karen—as opposed to the estimated twenty. Naturally, I didn't listen to any of them.

Snake's moms called him down for breakfast at eight, completely unaware of the fugitive crumpling the sheets in their guest room. Snake came to get me, and we confronted his moms together in the kitchen. He said my parents had gone out of town and were okay with me staying over. Once his moms' maternal instinct questionnaire (see: "Are you *sure* your parents are okay with this?") had been answered, the Cedar Point trip was a go.

Snake was right about his moms being cool with guy/girl sleepovers. The only disapproval I got from Jeanine was when I failed to finish a third pancake and she scolded me for not making myself at home. Jeanine had liked me from the first time we met, though my douchelord speech about her only son should have sent me right over the edge of parental approval. Meg seemed to like me, too, but it was harder to read her, considering she rarely spoke and was studying a nature magazine for the majority of breakfast.

I caught my eyes wandering multiple times that morning, glancing from Jeanine to Snake to Meg and wondering how life would have been different if I'd been raised like Snake. If my parents had been willing to try to understand me. If I could have gotten away with harboring runaways in my guest room. But the more I wondered, the more I realized, Snake still swallowed his Prozac every night. Snake still blew his nose into lubricated tissues while his therapist pulled out every weapon in the arsenal to make him spill his depression-filled guts. Snake was still a symptom of himself. I guess none of us was perfect.

"Snake, turn it up!" Jeanine called from the front seat. "I love this song!"

"Mom, it's Ultra Drain. How do you even know about them? They aren't on your old-people CDs."

She glared at him in the rearview mirror, the yellow lines of the road streaking her eyes. "Dana plays their songs in cardio, thank you," she replied with a huff. "Now, stop talking, I'll miss the chorus."

Snake shot me an embarrassed glance and clicked the volume up.

She began to <u>sing</u> (see: yelp).

And I'd thought Snake's vocal efforts were agony.

"I see where you get your horrid singing voice from," I called to Snake over the music.

"Hey!" Jeanine protested. Meg glanced at me over her shoulder and winked. I felt immediate pity for Meg, the most patient woman I'd ever known, who had to live with the two worst singers the good Lord ever created.

Snake spun the volume to the max decibel and held his head back proudly, leaning toward Jeanine. He opened his mouth and joined his mom on the chorus, squawking like the seagull from *The Little Mermaid*. I thought the windows were going to shatter.

And that was the two hour car ride to Cedar Point. Jeanine trying to sing. Snake trying to harmonize. Meg, who I had concluded was a genius, tuning out the wailing with earplugs. And me, mocking their attempts and secretly enjoying the music. Despite their horrible voices and pitiful duet endeavors, their singing was everything they were.

Bearable.

It was the best road trip I'd ever taken.

We made it to the park by eleven. Given the Snoopy dog statue dancing on the sign, I took it this park was a little below us. That assumption was proven true when a nearby middle school showed up hosting a Saturday at the Park event, and we were fortunate enough to stumble upon the rousing extravaganza of <u>preteens</u> (see: people worse than the worst kinds of people).

Once we were able to worm our way through the excessively perfumed and braces-faced crowd, we were inside and ready to ride whatever roller coaster didn't have a line of screeching almost teenagers. The GateKeeper it was, a twisty blue coaster with an aggression level of 5. I had no idea what an aggression level was, but aggression was my favorite hobby, and 5 was higher than all the 4s I was seeing. I wasn't stoked about how tall the coaster looked, but the line was only ten minutes long. Hopefully, the ride was short too.

Jeanine and Meg waited on a bench outside of the pavilion. Meg claimed the velocity of roller coasters made her stomach sick, and Jeanine had brought a book to read until we got to the family section of the park so she could ride the swings. They even took Dramamine to sit on a bench. Typical nonadventurous, blaming-their-boringness-on-motion-sickness parents.

While Snake and I waited under the pavilion, I spotted a guy in front of us with his young son. There was no way that kid was getting on the ride, considering the top of his spiked hair struggled to reach his dad's thigh, but at least he was willing. His dad wore a GUNS N' ROSES T-shirt with faded jeans, filming his son's excitement through a silver portable camera.

"That's you and your kid in the future," I said to Snake, nodding in their direction.

He looked at the man and scrunched his nose. "I wouldn't be caught dead with a Polaroid. Worst digital brand they make."

"Not the camera, stupid. The filming your kid's every uneventful move."

"Oh, that." He watched the man and the boy, his focus shifty. "Maybe. I don't know."

"You don't know? You film me every time I breathe."

"I feel like it will be different with him."

"Why?"

Bringing up the inexorable truth that Snake would, in fact, be a dad in less than a month tore at something deep beneath the surface. Something so far-reaching, the mere mention of "your kid" dove headfirst into his complexities. A complexity he didn't want me to know about. A complexity he might not have recognized himself.

"I think he's going to resent me in a lot of ways," he said. "For the way things happened."

"Because you and Carla are so young?"

"That." He dropped his head, knowing his hair would hide his eyes from me. "And because we won't be together."

"You don't know you won't be together. And even if you aren't, what matters most is that you both take care of him. And don't get in a nasty custody battle like those teenage parents on MTV, because that's just embarrassing."

"That's incentive to not film our lives post-baby right there." He grinned.

"All I'm saying is, don't do that thing where you make idiotic mistakes and try to fix them by making more idiotic mistakes. Be in his life and don't be a deadbeat, and you'll be golden."

He nodded, but I could still see him doubting. Silently mistrusting himself. Plotting how he would try to keep his son from hating him. Wondering if he was doing anything right at all.

"How did Carla tell you she was pregnant?" I asked, interrupting his self-evaluation. I was pretty sure he was failing it, anyway. "I'm sure it's an entertaining story."

He shook away his thoughts, beginning to smile again as we moved up in line. "She called me after school and asked me to meet her at the pond. We'd been hanging out since the party. I wanted to ask her to be my girlfriend, but kept getting nervous."

"Why? She obviously wasn't going to say no."

"Well, because I . . ."

He trailed off, and I could finish the sentence for him.

Because I really liked her.

"Anyway, when I got there, her eyes were all red like she'd been crying. I thought she was going to say she didn't want to talk to me anymore. I started mentally preparing my breakup playlist for later. Pretty much everything by the Renegade Dystopia." I rolled my eyes. "Then she told me she was pregnant. I took the news about as heroically as you'd expect . . . I threw up under a tree."

"No you didn't."

"Swear. I vomited three times that night. I told my moms I had food poisoning."

"You're so pathetic." I laughed. "What did you say to Carla?"

"I asked her if she was sure over and over until she threatened to push me in the pond if I asked again. When she said she was keeping it, I promised I would be there for her as much as she would let me."

We moved farther up in line. The boy and his dad were getting strapped in, and the kid could barely see over the harness.

"And your moms?" I asked.

"They cried for at least a few days straight. Which I get, you know? I hadn't even turned seventeen yet. I was still a kid to them. They asked if I wanted to marry her or anything, and I said no. I wasn't sure if that made it better or worse."

"That's brutal."

"It was a big mess for a few months there. Hats off to Prozac for dragging me through it."

"You could be a testimonial for their commercials," I joked. "Snake Eliot the Prozac poster kid."

"I never needed it as much as I did then, I can tell you that. At least I wasn't entirely alone."

He wasn't entirely alone because he had Carla. I could picture it like I'd seen it on the big screen, Snake and Carla running from their problems when things with their parents became too much, when the only two people they had were each other. I wondered if Carla ever called Snake from the side of the road at one in the morning. I wondered if he sped to her rescue. I wondered if she slept in his guest room. I wondered if it was on those nights, when no one understood them but them, that Snake told Carla that he loved her. I wondered if in the darkness of their loneliness, he really meant it.

"What about now?" I asked. He raised his brows at me. "How do your moms feel about Carla now?"

I thought about how strange Jeanine acted whenever Carla was mentioned. How no one ever talked about her except for me. It seemed like they wanted to pretend she didn't exist.

"They like her for who she is. They just don't like her for me."

"Why not?"

His eyes found mine instantly. "Because they like what makes me feel good."

I held back a smile. "That's a slim list."

It was our turn to board. A redheaded kid with a pale face shrouded in acne ushered us onto the ride, helping us lock the buckles on our harnesses. His quivering fingers were hardly comforting to someone who was deathly afraid of doing anything not involving having both feet planted firmly on the ground. I looked at Snake, who was sitting beside me already strapped in. Apparently, he'd been staring at me the entire time I was getting locked.

"Stop staring!" I yelled over the machine noises. "You know I hate it!"

"You said no heights!" he yelled back, a sly smirk parading on his face.

"I meant heights where we're hanging for a long period of time!"

"Technically, we will be! You're contradicting yourself!"

"No, I'm not! We drop fast!"

"You say one thing and mean another!"

"So do you!"

"No, I don't!"

"You said you loved her!"

The words flew off my tongue so fast it was like we

were already riding. His whole expression shifted from lightheartedness to confusion. I'd succeeded in shocking him again, but it didn't feel like a victory that time. It felt like a loss.

The recording began to play, welcoming us to the GateKeeper and instructing us to keep hands, arms, and legs inside the ride at all times (and a bunch of other safety nonsense no one cared about). Some kid behind me was crying. The couple in front of me was taking a picture on a cell phone they were going to lose in ten seconds. And Snake was still staring, not at all in the good way.

We took off.

The remainder of the ride was a haze of track, sky, and terrified screaming. I even swallowed my gum on one of the coaster loops. That was pretty memorable. Memorable because I was choking for the last few seconds of the ride and prayed my mother's infamous Jesus-take-the-wheel plea before I realized that I would, in fact, live.

Snake didn't ask about my outburst after that. By the time we hopped off the GateKeeper, he was so ready to surge his adrenaline on the next ride, he all but forgot about it. Jeanine and Meg patiently waited on every parent-ridden bench in every neck of the park until dinnertime, when we forced down Meg's homemade gluten-free tuna sandwiches at the picnic tables. Afterward, Snake bought us hot dogs when Meg was in the bathroom, and we scarfed them down so fast we could have given the Nathan's Hot Dog Eating Contest winners a run for their money.

At eight, we made our way to the family side of the park where the <u>middle-aged parkgoers</u> (see: Jeanine & Meg) took their inner daredevils for a spin around the carousels. Snake, unenthused by the concept of sitting on a plastic unicorn while a harmonica track crooned a slow and torturous tune, led me a little ways down the hill toward the far end of the family section. The sun had almost fully set by then.

Twinkling multicolored lights strung by ropes glimmered against the sky. A classical song was drifting through the noise. Snake retained bits and pieces of the melody and hummed it quietly.

As we trekked down the hill, I knew exactly where he was leading me. Straight ahead, prismatic and rotating against the sky, was the dreaded Ferris wheel. A line was backed up to the bathrooms, a bunch of crazies waiting to dangle from faulty cords above asphalt demises. Okay, maybe I was overhyping the likeliness of imminent death. Regardless, it was still the scariest thing I would have ever done if I agreed to it. Second to jumping out of a window, of course.

"Aren't you slick?" I taunted once we reached the line.

"Butter me up like you're taking me somewhere special, and we end up at the wheel of peril."

"Taking your aversion to a beloved theme park attraction into account, I still concluded that it would be romantic." The yellow, blue, and pink lights from the wheel cast colorful dots across his face, enhancing his usually dull eyes.

"Because I would be scared, and you'd have to hold me? Get some new material, dude. That method is tired."

"You mock it now, but once we're up there, you'll be in my lap. Guaranteed. And I may have used a cheap and worn-out method, but I'd still be winning."

"Meaning?"

"Meaning, you'll need me and have to painfully admit it."

"Ha." I laughed. He never failed to wow me with his expertise in being a presumptuous dick. "Once we get up there, we'll see who needs whom."

He smiled as a dash of pink flicked on the wheel, glowing against his teeth. The line moved faster than expected, five-year-olds putting me to shame with their smiley anticipation. And in spite of the fact that I grew closer to peeing my pants with each step we took toward boarding, I held a smug grin on my lips so Snake knew just how much I didn't need him.

Gluten-free tuna sandwich almost found its way back out of my mouth when my phone buzzed in my pocket, stunning me out of my terrified observation of the wheel freezing at the tiptop. I was going to die up there for sure.

I checked the phone screen. A text from Carla.

> Hey, Reggie. I was just
> making sure you were okay
> because your parents came
> by my house this afternoon
> looking for you. They said you
> didn't come home today. Are
> you with Snake? Let me know
> if you need anything. Not like I
> care, obviously ;)

Great, my parents were scouring the town for me. Who knew how many people my crazy mother had harassed? My dad was probably being towed around on his leash all day, while my mom stapled flyers to telephone poles and plastered my face on milk cartons. The wheel of peril wasn't looking so bad after all.

"Is that Carla?" Snake asked, reading over my shoulder.

"Nosy much? And yes."

"Did she say anything about me?"

"I'm genuinely curious how your head fits on your body."

"I'm not being arrogant. I'm just wondering, jeez."

"She was informing me that my parents went to her house looking for me this afternoon. Which proves that Karen doesn't know me at all, because one, I would never have a sleepover with Carla Banks. And two, I would never have a sleepover with Carla Banks while the dam around her uterus could burst at any moment."

"The doctor said it'll probably be a few weeks. And your mom, while a tad on the screwy side, is doing what any good mom would do."

"I don't think we're talking about the same mom."

"All I'm saying is, don't make idiotic mistakes and try to fix them by making more idiotic mistakes."

"Don't use my words against me. Idiocy is your thing."

"Idiocy is widespread. And you should be grateful that she cares, at least. Even if you resent the way she does it."

He was giving me this bizarre, raised-brow, life-coach expression that was very dadlike and particularly unsettling. Snake had never looked like he could be someone's dad until that moment. And even then, he was a deranged, pretty-boy-meets-grunge-dude version.

We made it to the front of the line, and Snake bumped my shoulder as the girl motioned us into the cart. I slapped him so hard the girl shot me a troubled look before she closed our door. Snake wearing a white T-shirt that read ALWAYS THE VICTIM wasn't helping my case.

Snake cuddled next to me in the middle of the seat (a completely unwarranted move, I might add). He held his hand on his thigh with the palm facing upward, waiting for me to grab it. He would be waiting a while.

"When the ride starts moving, just think comforting thoughts," he said, as a family of four loaded into the cart in front of us. "Like how you'll be on here for the next fifteen minutes without a chance of getting off, and if we get stuck at the top, the fire squad has to take us down via crane. Also, a cord snapping is always a feasible outcome."

"As long as you think about how your not-so-clever little plan to get me in your lap will end with you suspended in the air next to a very mean and very angry girl who will have no witnesses for the things she could do to you."

"Is that supposed to be a threat?" He smiled. "Sounds pretty great to me."

Of course it did.

A creaking noise resounded, and we began to move. Backwards. Slowly. I shut my eyes, holding my lids together so tightly it gave me a headache. I could feel Snake's warmth beside me. I could feel him staring. One thing was different, though. He didn't smell the same.

Keeping my eyes shut, I said through clenched teeth, "Snake?"

"You need an arm around the shoulder? A handhold, perhaps?" He was smiling that overconfident, got-this-in-the-bag smile. I could hear it.

"Shut up. I find it necessary to point out that you haven't eaten a single Twizzler all day."

He didn't say anything. With a swell of bravery and desperation for headache relief, I opened my eyes.

Don't look down. Don't look down.

For future reference: Telling yourself to not look down only encourages you to look down quicker. Yeah, I looked down. And screamed. Out loud. At a shrieking decibel I didn't know I was capable of. We were stopped somewhere in the middle. We hadn't even reached the top, and I was ready to sing my hallelujahs and bow out.

"Shhh." Snake laughed, trying to calm me. "It's okay."

I made an inhuman noise.

He grabbed my hand and laced his fingers through mine. "You win, okay? I'm the one who needs it."

I looked into his eyes. They were smiling back at me. "But you're not. You're fine."

"It's not heights I'm afraid of," he whispered, his breath cloudy against my skin. "Trust me, you won."

The ride started up again, pulling us toward the blue-blackness of the sky. I dug my nails into Snake's hand. He groaned in the back of his throat, but tried not to show it. We stopped again, two spaces from the top. I was shivering, from cold or fear or Snake. I hadn't figured myself out yet.

I had to admit, disappearing into the sky was a whole lot easier holding Snake's hand. He felt like a vision. He felt safe.

"I haven't gotten the urge," Snake said, gently rubbing his thumb against my hand.

"The urge to what?"

"Chew. You said I hadn't eaten a Twizzler all day. I haven't gotten the urge."

"Where does it come from? The urge."

"I don't know. Depression, I think."

The ride kicked into gear again, and I knew the next destination was the top. Once we made it, I was used to the feeling of suspension. It didn't bother me so much. I could notice things my fear wouldn't let me.

The air was chilly. We were next to the lake. It was a full moon. Orion and his belt marched across the skyline. Stars. Lots of stars.

I turned to Snake, and he was watching me. I knew that face too well. Desperate wanting. Excessive needing. Desire. He leaned in, his lips parted.

"You can't kiss me on top of a Ferris wheel," I whispered into his open mouth.

"No?" he breathed.

"It's cheesy. They do it in every chick flick."

"That's why we have to do it. It's expected. So expected that the predictability of it is undone when you do it aware of the expectation. It's reverse irony. It's so expected, it's unexpected."

"That makes no sense."

He let go of my hand and wrapped it in my hair, clenching tight. His eyes were hungry. Enlivening. Unusually interesting. I leaned into his touch, into his waiting body. I leaned because I wanted to. I needed to.

"We don't make sense," he said. A smile escaped him, and his lips touched mine so softly I wondered if I'd imagined it. "Now, shut up and let me kiss you before I'm out of my moment."

He drew my lips against his in one smooth tug. His breath was hot against the cool wind, seeping into my anxious, eager mouth. He traced his fingers along the back of my neck, and my whole body chilled.

I remembered the first time we kissed, how simple he'd kept it, how it was just an awkward first kiss to get to the slightly less awkward second. But this was the second, and there was nothing awkward about it. There was nothing routine about the way he stroked the skin along my neck or how he gently grazed my lower lip with his teeth or how he tasted like boy instead of candy. He had been holding back on me the first time. Damn him.

We began to descend from the top, or at least I thought

we did. We could have been sitting on a park bench or lying in the grass or floating aimlessly through outer space, and it wouldn't have felt any different than riding a deathtrap in the sky. I could only feel his curly hair tickling my cheeks, his silky lips mastering the curvature of mine, his hands . . . well, everywhere.

When his lips released me, we sat with only a cold, powdery breath between us. His hand was still gripping my hair, and I felt motion sick, or dizzy, or something that had nothing to do with the ride. His eyes were amazing. How had I never noticed how amazing they were? The blue alone was more alive than I ever was, the only difference being his eyes didn't have a heart trying to claw its way out of its chest.

Of course, my heart was its own monster. A selfish one that kept only itself alive. The rest of me, on the other hand, hadn't fared so well. I died on top of the Ferris wheel exactly as I'd thought I would. Just not from the kind of falling I had predicted.

Snake and I ran up to his room the moment we got back to his house. I sat on the edge of his bed as he dug through his dresser for a pair of pants. I wasn't ready to go home yet. After last night, I'd be grounded for life. I figured there was no better way to spend my last moments of freedom than <u>hiding out</u> (see: making out) with Snake.

He yanked out a pair of mesh shorts from the bottom of his drawer. "These okay? They're the smallest pair I have."

"Ugly, but they'll do."

He moved to the edge of the bed. "Funny. I could say the same about you."

"Jerk!" I yelled. He was close enough for me to reach him. I grabbed him by the waist and tackled him to the bed. Unfortunately, my sneak attack backfired. He landed directly on top of me, my chest crushed beneath his weight. "Can't breathe," I mouthed.

He pushed up on his elbows. His hair was dangling in my eyes, a leg perched on either side of my waist. Passionate eyes, the eyes from the Ferris wheel, regarded me through wispy curls. But it wasn't his eyes I was focused on. It was his lips. His soft, skillful, capable-of-anything lips. I wondered just how much he was still holding back.

"I don't mean it," he whispered breathily. A finger glided along my cheek, making an agonizing journey to my neck. His eyes were focused on something too. And it sure as hell wasn't mine. "You're crazy beautiful."

"As beautiful as Carla?" I quipped.

Great. I had brought her up again. I must have been trying to break the record for most stupid comment to make when you're about to make out with a guy. Bring up his ex-girlfriend—that'll do the trick.

His fingertip paused at the bottom of my neck. "Stop talking about Carla. That's not fair."

"That's not an answer."

"You want an answer? No. You're not as beautiful as Carla. Come on, the girl's worked seventeen years for that title. She earned it. To compare you would be to put you in the same category as her, and I can't."

"Then what am I?"

"You're terrifying," he whispered, stroking my face. "And destructive. And overwhelming. And, let's face it, a little violent."

"So all horrible things?"

"Strong things," he said, breathing slowly. "All the things I'm not ashamed to want."

I gripped his hair with both hands, clutching two fistfuls of soft locks between my trembling fingers. "I hate you."

Relief swept across his face, his eyes glowing like stars and rainbow-colored lights. He'd finally gotten what he needed. And in some bizarre way, so had I. I couldn't help but think that maybe he was right all along. Maybe hatred really was my love language.

"I was hoping you'd say that." He pressed his lips to mine, kissing me so hard it felt like I was suffocating under his touch. We collapsed against each other, his mouth frenzied. Wild. I could feel his tongue slide between my open lips. I reached for his shirt and yanked it over his head, tossing it to the floor. My hands were on his back, my nails digging into his skin. The only thing I could hear was his heavy breathing, scorching as it sank inside my ear. His lips traveled along my jaw, all the way down to my collarbone.

"Maks," I panted.

He stopped completely, snapping his head up. "You mean Snake," he gasped between breaths. "This is awkward."

"No, I mean from *The Onslaught*."

"You're picturing Maks from *The Onslaught*?"

"No. Ew. Bear with me." I rubbed his neck and pulled him closer. "I was just thinking about *The Snake Project*. And, I mean, I have no interest in watching the source material, so just tell me. Do Maks and Margaret end up together?"

He smiled guiltily. "No. They both die."

"Wow, that's bleak. You said it was a romance."

"I said it was doomed from the start."

I gave him a half smile, despite the anxiousness buzzing in my stomach. "Isn't everything doomed from the start?"

He watched my mouth as he ran his fingers along my cheek. Then he looked me in the eyes, really looked at me, and said, "I like to think people doom themselves."

I wanted to ask him what he meant. If he thought the reason we were here in this position was because of some inherent fault of our own, and not a matter of forces beyond our control. I wanted to know if he believed in fate.

But instead of ruining yet another moment, I kissed him. I pulled him tight enough to memorize the sound of his heartbeat, no matter how irregular it was in the space between his chest and mine. The harder I kissed him, the more I wanted him to strip me open, dig out all of my pain, and have the choice to hate me or want me or leave me or forget me. I wanted him to regret me the way I would regret him later. If only in the midst of those ragged breaths and reckless kisses, I wanted our idea of enough to be the same. But it wasn't, and that was an inescapable truth. Except for once, I didn't want the truth. I wanted someone to lie to me the way only Snake could.

He slid his hands beneath my shirt, and it was gone. Skin to skin. I didn't know how far I was willing to go, and it didn't make a difference. I was only an empty shell trying to pretend there was a person inside. A full, living and breathing person capable of staying that way.

"Reggie," Snake breathed against my neck. I couldn't find a way to respond. He repeated my name, glancing up at me. "Your phone's ringing."

"I don't care," I whispered, pulling him to my lips.

"You know it's your mom."

"Then I really don't care."

We ignored it. It stopped ringing, then started again

only seconds later. Snake groaned, tearing himself off of me and sitting up. "You need to get that. It's distracting."

The piercing ringtone jolted me back to my surroundings, ripping the veil from my brain and making everything clearer. Suddenly, I realized that I was in my bra. And Snake was shirtless. And his door wasn't fully closed, and his moms were downstairs. And we had almost just pulled a Carla.

I grabbed the phone and found my mom's name lit across the screen.

"I'm not answering it."

"You have to."

"No."

"Reggie."

"Fine." I grunted and slid the green button. "Long time no see, Karen."

She let out a dramatic sigh. "Oh, thank God. Are you okay? Where are you?"

"I'm fine. And out." A man's voice rumbled lowly in the background. It was confident. Professional. "Mom? Who's that?"

Silence. Usually a privilege. But not that kind of silence. It was panic silence. Terror. I had a gut feeling this wasn't about me running away.

"Mom?"

"We looked for you all day," she cried, sniffling into the

phone. "I left you voicemails, and we went around town. Your dad. Your dad isn't supposed to get worked up . . ."

"What happened to Dad?"

Snake moved beside me and rubbed my back. I could see my fear reflected in his eyes.

"You need to come to the hospital as soon as you can."

My mind wasn't catching up. "Why?"

Silence. Too much silence.

"He's had a heart attack."

CHAPTER nineteen

DEER. A DEER WITH GIANT ANTLERS. They were called bucks, I had been told. Male deer with giant antlers were called bucks. And they weren't smart. They ran out in front of moving cars and walked directly in front of hunters without knowing it and always somehow ended up at my dad's shop, stuffed with hardened powder and staring blankly at the remains of their own hides stretched out across my father's fixing table. Dead. That was their one common trait. Not that they were deer or bucks or stupid, but that they always ended up dead.

"They aren't dead," my dad would say, stitching the finishing touches on a six-pointer someone had brought in from a hunting excursion. I sat on a stool across the room, drinking a juice box and keeping my distance. When I was a kid, I had this irrational fear that one would eventually come back to life on my dad's table and take revenge on all the humans who had had a part in his slaughter. None ever did.

"Yes, they are," I argued. "A hunter killed him. And now he's dead."

"What's dead about him?"

"His heart doesn't beat anymore."

My dad set down his knife and looked at the buck. He ran his fingers along the antlers and touched the space on his chest where hearts were supposed to beat. An empty space. "So, a heartbeat is what makes us alive?"

"Yes."

"That's interesting," he said, his hand lingering on the empty cavity. He studied the buck above the rim of his glasses, as if he knew it before it was nothing. As if he truly cared about what happened to it. "He still has a spirit, though. Doesn't he? Doesn't he make you feel something when you look at him?"

I observed his giant antlers, his body twice the size of my own. He looked like someone's dad. A leader.

"He makes me feel . . ." I struggled for the right word. "He makes me feel sad."

"Why?"

"Because I think he was someone's dad. And his baby probably misses him. And he might have had a lot of friends. And they probably miss him too."

My dad smiled. He didn't smile often, but when he did, it was always a stamp of approval. It was his expression of pride. Pride in himself. Pride in me. "Then he's alive," he said, picking up his knife and resuming his diagonal cuts of skin on the buck's back. "He has a spirit. As long as his spirit touches something living, he'll always be alive." He looked at me, and I swear to this day, it was the most strength I'd ever seen in his faded eyes. And then he said, "Nothing ever dies. Not really."

Snake was speeding to the hospital, flying fifteen over like he was bolting from the cops. I was wearing his baggy, uncomfortable basketball shorts and couldn't stop pulling on the string and thinking about my dad and bucks and dying.

My mom had told me he wasn't looking good. His heart attack had been severe enough that the doctor insisted she call my brother in New York. He said my dad had coronary heart disease, where the arteries to his heart were tightened and clogged and couldn't pump the blood the way they were supposed to. Basically, his heart didn't like him very much. It didn't want to keep him alive. And maybe he was right about hearts doing a sucky job at keeping people alive. But I didn't want my dad to be the buck. I didn't want him to only be alive because I felt a certain way about him. I wanted his heart to like him. But I guess Snake and I weren't the only ones with untamable hearts.

It was eleven when Snake dropped me off in front of

the hospital. He called to me as I was hopping out, something about parking the car or going home or good luck. I wasn't listening.

When I got inside, I rode the elevator to the third floor. That was where the people with sucky hearts went. They ended up lying in hospital beds on the third floor, with IVs tacked under their skin and crappy hospital food served to them on trays once their bodies decided they could eat again. My dad was on the far end of the hall, with the people whose hearts were just a little too greedy for their own good.

I spotted my mom standing outside his room once I got there. She was in <u>ill-fitting pants</u> (see: mom jeans) and a Winnie-the-Pooh pajama shirt, a tissue clasped tightly in her hand. I fidgeted with the string on Snake's shorts and looked down. I couldn't face her because I might have been wrong to run away, and all of this might have been my fault, and she might have hated me. I didn't know how to handle it if she did.

She looked up briefly to scan the hall and saw me standing by a nurse's cart, in clothes not my own, with hobo hair and a guilty twitch on my lips. It was too late to avoid her now. I trudged forward, still pulling on the string.

"How is he?" I whispered once I got close enough to be heard.

She paused for longer than she needed to. It was like

she was trying to spite me in between her words and the stillness. "He's stable," she answered. Her voice was as aloof as her eyes.

"Can I go in and see him?"

"No. He's sleeping right now."

"Oh." I twisted the string around my finger.

"Those aren't your clothes," she pointed out. Immediate judgment. I should have been prepared for it.

"They're Snake's," I muttered.

"I see. So that's where you've been."

"Can we not talk about this right now?"

"We tried to find out where he lived, but not many people knew him." Her voice was trembling, leftover frustration trying to find a passageway out. "Little Carla told us his address. We rang the doorbell ten times, but no one ever showed up. I assumed you weren't there."

"Technically, I wasn't," I said, staring at a brown mark on the tile. "I went with his family to Cedar Point for the day. We just got back an hour ago."

A tear slid out from under her glasses. It was an inevitable repercussion. Hurting others. A side effect of me.

"Your dad was so desperate to find you," she whispered as another tear fell. "He regretted letting you walk out that door. He said he forgot how stubborn you are."

"It was only one day. You guys didn't have to be so dramatic."

"One day?" Her eyes were wet and angry and terrified in one look. "What day was it, Regina? Hmm? Do you know what day it was?" She glanced at the clock on the wall that read 11:10. "What day it is?"

"Saturday . . ." I said slowly.

"Guess again."

"I'm not doing this, Mom."

"It's your dad's birthday." She wiped her eyes with the tissue in her hand. "He spent his entire birthday looking for you."

"I'm sorry. I didn't know."

"Of course you didn't know. Because you spent the whole day thinking about you, just like you always do. It's always about you, Regina."

"I said I'm sorry!" I yelled. She put a finger over her mouth to quiet me, which only made me angrier. "What do you want me to do about it now?"

"I want you to open your eyes. I want you to see that your depression is selfish."

"What?" I mouthed.

"You heard me," she continued. "It's selfish to be so miserable that you let your own unhappiness consume everything around you. You hate your life so much that you've let yourself believe it doesn't matter, that the things you do don't affect people." She motioned to the door. "But I want you to look at how loved you are and still try to convince yourself that your life is worthless and the things you do don't matter. Because all-consuming hatred is selfishness. And the people who love you, really love you, don't deserve to be victims of your depression."

She took an accomplished breath, like she had been rehearsing that speech since the day I was diagnosed. Her words rushed into my brain all at once. I couldn't subdue them. I couldn't arrange the sensations they stirred into any cohesive whole. All of the emotional mush produced one dominating response. Anger. How could she hate me so much that she didn't even try to understand?

"I'm selfish?" I whispered. I wanted to yell. Scream. Explode. Do something that would get her attention. I wanted her to see me. To listen. And then, after everything was bared, I wanted her to look me in the eye and tell me who I was to her. But I couldn't find it in myself to fight anymore. "Do you even know why I'm depressed? Do you know what day I go to therapy each week? Do you know one single thing I've talked to my therapist about? Go ahead. Guess, since we're obviously playing games."

"Reggie."

"You don't know. Just like I forgot Dad's birthday, and I ran away, and I pick battles with you, and I make more mistakes in a day than most people do in a lifetime. And maybe that's selfishness to you. Maybe my depression makes me selfish. But what is it that makes you selfish? All you do is pray for me, and preach to me, and tell me how wrong I am for letting myself hurt. You've never tried to understand me. Why don't you want to understand me?"

I wiped a tear that I didn't even know had fallen until I tasted salt on my lips. She looked at me briefly, so briefly she didn't see me at all. She didn't want to.

"It's not that I don't want to understand you," she said, still focused on the wall. She might as well have been talking to it. "I'm just afraid that if I did, I would want to fix you. And, apart from an act of God, I don't know how to fix you."

"I don't want you to fix me," I whispered. "I don't want you to see me as broken."

"Well, I do. I can't help it. I can't help it when I hear you crying in your room when you think I've gone to bed, or see you staring at walls for hours on end, or catch you running around with a boy who is going to do nothing but break an already broken heart." Her eyes fogged over, as if she wanted to cry but didn't know what she was crying for. "That boy will destroy you. By then you'll be so broken, I'm afraid you'll be unmendable."

"He makes me feel," I justified, to the benefit of no one but myself. "He makes me feel like I'm more than just a sack of blood and bones with a stomach full of antidepressants. That sounds ridiculous, I know. But I don't fear anything with him. I don't know why I'm telling you this. You won't understand."

"I'll tell you what I understand," she said. "I understand he may treat you well, and pay you attention, and give you all of these feelings. And he may mean every bit of it. For now. But what happens when that little girl has her baby, and he is suddenly responsible for taking care of another person's life? What happens then?" She watched me with pity I didn't want. I didn't want to need it. "You'll never get the best of him, sweetheart. He's going to leave you like the one before. And I don't say that to knock you down. I say that because you've already lost people you've loved. I don't want to stand by and watch it happen again."

She doesn't know Snake, I tried to remind myself. But it wasn't comforting. I didn't know if it was her sincerity that propelled my doubt, or the unchangeable reality that hearts are fragile machines, made to be broken. I might have already known that Snake would break my heart if I let him. If I gave him a heart to break. He would never be permanent. Like ninth grade year. Like best friends. Like nerdy boys from math class. Like circus people.

Snake Eliot was incurably human. And like all humans, he was wind and fire. A gust of life. A wake of destruction. And I would soon be a broken heart. An unmendable machine.

"I want to see Dad," I said. I couldn't think about the inevitable. I couldn't let myself dwell on what I knew I was going to have to do to preserve the tiny pieces of me that remained intact. That kind of hurt could wait.

"I told you, he's asleep."

"I'll be quiet. Just let me see him, okay?"

She rubbed her exhausted eyes. I knew she didn't have the willpower to tell me no. And the careful way she slid away from the door, the way she looked at me with something reminiscent of my dad's compassion, told me that she didn't want to.

When I walked into his room, the lights were dimmed. He was hooked to stacks of metal by small tubes and needles. His eyes were closed tightly, and his square glasses weren't on his face. He looked even more helpless and fragile than he usually did. I stared at him, probably in the pimple way that I didn't like. But I couldn't help staring, and wanting to help, and feeling guilty because I was selfish. I was so astoundingly selfish.

There was a cushioned chair stationed by his bed. I sat in it, close enough to see the pastiness of his skin, the purple hue of veins drawn beneath it, the lifelessness of sucky hearts. I wouldn't touch him.

"Happy birthday, Dad," I whispered, so quietly I wasn't sure I made a sound.

I tried to arrange some grandiose speech to appease

my conscience, something about remorse and lost time and wishful thinking. But, like all the pages ripped from my journal, words weren't good enough. They didn't express enough. Give enough. Mean enough. My mind wasn't bound by words, but doses of memories. And sunlight. And odd smiles that didn't seem to fit. And a wolf above the fireplace. And regret.

"You told me once that nothing ever dies," I whispered; his eyes were still firmly shut. "But you lied. Things die every day. Poor children in Africa and people in car wrecks and cancer kids and old people and animals. And yeah, they have spirits. And yeah, the impression never leaves. But people do die, Dad. We die because we're decay. We're the wolf above the mantel. We are and then we aren't, and that's the truth of it. That's our nature. We can't stay any longer than time can have us." I wanted to reach for his hand, but I was afraid he would wake up and hear me. Some things were better left unsaid.

One of his devices beeped loudly, lines rising in V-shapes and falling again. I stared at the heart lines, waiting for a doctor to hurry in and rush him away. But seconds later, the sound subsided, the lines mellowing. He never opened his eyes. He never moved.

I contemplated touching his hand, and that time found the courage. I wrapped my fingers around his. They were colder than the metal of the bed. I traced my fingertip along an icy blue vein, but he didn't seem to feel my touch. A sleep that deep must have been nice to someone with a heart like his, a necessary relief from overbeating.

"I wish the world had a pull cord, and whenever it spun too fast, you could yank it and stop everything dead in its tracks." I studied the vein. It was thick, protruding from the skin. Blood pulsated under my thumb. "Wouldn't that be nice? To convince yourself that the universe and time and life are willing to pause for you? Maybe I would be happy then. I think I wouldn't have wasted so much time not appreciating the temporariness of you." I thought I saw his eyelids flutter, but it was probably more wishful thinking.

"Time is in a race with itself. And we're the gunshot that sends it running. By the time it comes back around, we've already made all of our mistakes. And people like me have already hurt ourselves and taken our pills to the bottom of the bottle and hated everyone and everything along the way. And people like you are left with the pain we cause. But we don't mean to cause you pain; we just want to cure our own."

His hands didn't grow warmer with touch. My fingers were sweating against him, yet he felt as cool as he had when I first laid my hand on his. I stood from the chair, bending toward his face. I would have thought he was gone already had it not been for his breath, slow puffs against my cheek.

"You want to know a secret?" I whispered into his ear. "Something's killing me, too. It's called depression. And it's not a symptom of anything but me."

I touched my hand to his chest. His heart was beating, but not enough. It was beating only because it chose to. It would stop only when it chose to. He, too, was incurably human.

"I guess people die in all kinds of ways."

CHAPTER twenty

ONLY THREE HOURS LATER, I WAS awakened to a rush of nurses. My mom was bewildered, tossing out questions returned with silence. Machines were ringing at excruciating decibels. Personnel were shouting all of these medical words I didn't understand. Mom and I were exiled from the room without the chance to say goodbye.

Fortunately, goodbyes weren't in immediate order. Unfortunately, they weren't off the table. The doctor informed us that his condition had caused him to slip into a comatose state (see: coma), which could be as mild as a few hours of unconsciousness to the severity of days. Apart from monitoring his heart and vitals, there was nothing more to do. My dad's life was a waiting game.

Karen did the only thing she knew. She prayed. And I didn't mock it. I didn't particularly mind it, either. She meant every word she said. She asked me to pray, but I didn't even know where to start. But Karen actually said something that helped me. She said praying isn't about the words you say, it's about the meaning you put behind them. So I prayed for nonsense. And I let myself hope. I hoped that, if no one else did, God understood me.

We sat in the waiting room near the elevators. Karen was on the phone with Frankie, explaining the situation as he promised to make it to town by noon. It was Sunday morning, maybe six. I hadn't checked my phone since I got to the hospital. I took it out of my pocket to see the time and noticed three missed calls from Snake. There was a text spread across the screen.

> I wanted to make sure you
> were okay. I'll be outside if
> you need me. Call me back
> when you can.

He'd sent it at two in the morning, right around the time my dad slipped into the comatose state that we all knew was a coma but refused to classify. There was no way Snake was still outside. He must have waited for a while and left when he got no news. He must have gone home when I didn't respond. Then again, I wouldn't have put a hospital parking lot all nighter past him.

I glanced at Karen, who was in deep conversation on the phone. I nudged her and mouthed, "I'll be right back." She threw up a dismissive hand.

When I reached the parking lot, there it was in its gold, soccer mom, yoga wisdom glory. The Prius (see: wimpmobile) was parked next to the hospital sign on the edge of the road. Snake was sleeping in the front seat, his head resting on the steering wheel in the most uncomfortable sleeping arrangement in the history of makeshift car beds. He looked peaceful, though. Calm in his unconsciousness. I didn't want to wake him. I didn't want to serve the long-time-coming blow that was needed and unavoidable and possibly the most painful absence I would ever demand. In my selfishness, I wanted to keep him for a little longer. I wanted to bask in his presence and forget how momentary the pleasure. But God, if I ever prayed for nonsense, it was to not have to walk this tightrope alone.

He jolted awake when I knocked on the window, disoriented before he wiped his eyes and remembered how he got there. He opened the door and stepped out of the car, his chaotic hair electrocution-level crazy. His dull and amazing eyes were watching me with concern.

"How is he?" he asked, reaching to hug me.

I backed away, staring at the pebbles of broken pavement on the ground. "Not great," I answered, my voice nearly gone. I was just like Dad, there and not at the same time. "He slipped into a coma early this morning. They don't know how long it will last."

"Oh," he breathed. He knew something was off. There was dread in his tone. "I'm really sorry."

"Thanks. You should have gone home."

"I wasn't going to leave you."

"Why?"

"You were freaking out on the way over. I was worried about you."

"I can take care of myself, Snake."

It wasn't necessary to remind him. But I couldn't stop myself once I knew how badly this would hurt.

I looked into his eyes for the first time.

He was what I expected him to be. Tense. Upset. Overwhelmed in a controlled kind of way. "I know?" He took a step toward me. "What is this about?"

"We need to talk."

I regretted how horribly Breakup 101 it was to say that. Next thing I knew, I'd be saying "it's not you, it's me" and waiting for him to beg so I could toss out the old "we can still be friends."

"Reggie," he whispered. His face was discolored like he was going to be sick. "Please, don't do this. I know what you're going to say, and I'm begging you to let me be ignorant for just a little while longer. Okay? Let me pretend like you want me the way I want you."

"I want you, Snake," I said. It was like admitting that I was the one who stole the crown jewels. It was like confessing to a homicide. It was liberating and horrifying in one beat. "That's the problem. You've always wanted too much, and I never wanted enough until now. And it feels like dying, to be honest. It feels like Prozac seizures and frenzy and Disconnect, because I know how tragically temporary this is. How tragically temporary you are."

"It's only as temporary as we let it be," he said, panic sweeping across his face. "I know I haven't shown you the rest of my film yet, but if you give me a chance, you'll see that I understand exactly how you feel. That's the outlook. Temporariness. And it doesn't have to change anything. Just give me a chance to prove that to you."

"I can't," I insisted, my voice catching. It would have been unforgivable to cry. I bit my lip so hard it throbbed, and I could still feel the tears threatening to overwhelm me. "My dad is in there dying. Not the you-and-me version of dying. The real kind. The kind Zoloft can't alleviate. The kind therapists can't write prescriptions for. Heart-stops-beating, dirt-on-the-casket dying." He was shaking. I could see Stage 1 in his twitching fingers, in his disbelieving eyes. "I've been neglecting him all this time. I've been so focused on you, and that's great. Really, Snake. You've been the only thing keeping me alive. But you have a bad case of human. You were made for two things, to make people want you and to leave them still wanting. And I can't do it. I can't stand around waiting for you to leave me."

"So you're going to leave me? Is that it?"

"It's going to happen eventually. Might as well save ourselves the melodrama."

He raked his fingers through his hair, trying to process. He was going to cry the unforgivable tears. Maybe they weren't so unforgivable.

"You're such a fucking coward," he said, watching me angrily. It was <u>sad anger</u> (see: depression anger). "You're so terrified of being left that the second something good happens to you, you destroy it. This"—he motioned to the two of us—"this is real. I'm not Bree. I'm not Alex from geometry. I'm standing here promising you that I'm not going anywhere, and you won't let yourself believe it. You won't be satisfied until you're alone. What, do you think loss is easier when you choose it?"

"We could have never made it work," I whispered, the sun beginning to rise over the houses across the street. A beam glowed behind Snake's head, the tips of his hair lit orange. "We're too much alike. All we would have done was prolong each other's unhappiness."

"I never believed in happiness, but I was wrong." One of those newly forgivable tears escaped from his eyes. He bowed his head so I wouldn't see. "It's not only for stupid people. I was happy whenever you were around. And whenever you told me you hated me. And whenever we kissed. I was non-Prozac, fully aware, smart person happy." He looked at me with an intensity that was disarming. I thought I was breaking up with him, but I wondered whose heart I was breaking. "I was happy because you were unapologetically you, no matter how much it hurt me. You probably never knew that hating me would make me fall in love with you."

It was the stupidest thing he'd ever felt. The absolute greatest mistake he would ever make. There was no defending it. And by the aching sincerity in his eyes, I knew he wouldn't try.

I felt it too. I was in love with him. In love like fireworks and lightning and drunken desire. In love like windows and Ferris wheels. In love with the obligation to want love. In love with the beautiful futility of humanness.

But above it all, I was in love with the idea that I was the only one he ever needed. The only one he ever would.

"I'm not the first girl you've said that to, Snake," I whispered. The sun was fully shining, reflecting off the hood of the cars. "I'm not the first girl you've loved, and I won't be the last."

"Carla? That's what you were talking about yesterday on the ride, wasn't it?" He shook his head in frustration. "Yes, I told her I loved her. Yes, at the time I thought that maybe I meant it. I wanted to mean it. I wanted her to be the one I felt this way about. She's having my baby, the least I could do is try to fall in love with her. But I couldn't. I can't. Is that what you need to hear? I don't love Carla."

"You don't love her now," I said, knowing that I needed to end this before I broke down. Before he did. Before the wreckage was unsalvageable. "But she's your family, whether you like that or not. And you're going to have a baby to take care of. Together. You could easily fall in love with her, and where would that leave me? Where is any of this going to get us? I can't be with you, Snake. I'm sorry. I just can't. The truth is, we have too much on our plates. And we're too young. And we're too depressed to hurt each other any further. So why don't we leave it at that, all right?" I took a step away from him, succeeding in creating a world of distance in the asphalt between us.

He stared at me, all of the needing and wanting and Snakeisms I'd come to love crushed and tarnished behind his eyes. He nodded like he was giving up, like he'd done everything in his power to repair the damage and was being forced to leave it unfixed. I wished I could have told him. Not everything was meant to be mended.

He ducked into his car, fumbling for his keys with shaking hands. He turned the ignition key, revving the engine. I backed up, unable to watch him drive away knowing it was the last time, knowing this absence was the permanent kind. I hated a world where absence was permanent and nothing else.

"Reggie," he called. I glanced over my shoulder as I was heading back to the building. He was preparing to drive off, one hand on the wheel. "I think I finally have a trigger."

CHAPTER twenty-one

I DIDN'T GO TO SCHOOL THAT week. By the time Wednesday rolled around, I'd missed two tests, one Spanish project, and a horrendous choir sing-off that proved to be the sole benefit of being hospital-bound. Work wasn't much of an obligation, either. I called Peyton to tell her I wouldn't be able to make it in that week. She grieved my unthinkable situation, promising to help via <u>praying and fruit baskets</u> (see: phony concern).

My days were rubber spaghetti platters in the cafeteria, my drooling nephew spitting milk gunk on my lap, and afternoon talks with a dad who couldn't hear me. It almost made the stages of depression seem like warm-ups for the real depression, the overpowering sense of being wholly, inescapably alone.

I hadn't talked to Snake since our rom com–style

breakup in the parking lot. That's not to say it wasn't the only thing I thought about, even when I tried to imagine happier unhappy memories. It was always his eyes. His pained eyes, half sparkling in the sun, half hidden in the shadow of his hair. His eyes were all I saw when I looked at Killian's chubby cheeks or stirred the gross hospital coffee in my Styrofoam cup, or listened to my mom read Bible passages aloud to my dad as the bars on his machine arched and fell.

I saw Snake's eyes and imagined rain. It should have rained. There should've been a drenching downpour and begging pleas and a sappy goodbye kiss that left the audience inside our minds weeping at what could have been, grasping at hope for that notorious happy ending.

But it was a cool day. It was cool and sunny, and the weather was pleasant. The birds still sang in grating pitches, and the cars still drove by, paying our slow deaths no mind. It was like every other day. It was no respecter of its victims, of the nonliteral hells we suffered in and the very literal pain of being nothing. Nothing to anyone but ourselves.

Therapy was rescheduled for Friday. The start of the weekend. The day nondepressed teenagers hung out with their friends at the movies or threw sketchy parties that ended in police visits and wasted vomiting. Friday wasn't the ideal day for my version of vomit, for rehashing old feelings on a green couch while a woman with two PhDs scribbled *self-destructive* and *emotionally unavailable* in my evaluation file.

When I got there, I sprawled out on the couch like I did every week. She started with the simple questions. How did my week go? Where was I on the theoretical emotion scale? What was I doing to bridge the communication gap between myself and others?

Then it got tough. And uncomfortable. And we talked about my mom. And dad. And hearts. And how unfair it was to be alive.

The way she looked at me in that particular session was so different from what I'd grown used to. Her eyes were heavier, her breaths slow and carefully drawn. Maybe her dad had a sucky heart. Maybe she could relate. Or maybe it was just me needing someone. I probably needed someone to understand so badly that I convinced myself she did. I guess there was no way to know.

She laid her glasses on the floor beside her, leaning forward to generate an environment of welcoming, or whatever it was the doctors called it. And then she didn't say anything for a minute. No inspirational speeches or exaggerated psychotherapy terms or pretend reassurances. It was just her eyes, which I had never noticed were brown, and her careful inhales that sounded sharper than most, and silver-painted nails tucked under her chin.

"Let me tell you something I wish someone had told me

when I was your age," she said, her tone peaceful and honest. Genuine to a fault. She reached for a piece of paper and a pen on the table next to her and drew a mark. "This is life. We exist on a straight line. There's point A, the beginning. Point C, the end. And point B, all the crap in between. And this tiny line, a drop of ink on paper, this is our line. This is all we get. It's our one shot. And it's terrifying, isn't it? Because it ends. It's not a circle that will loop us back around for another chance. We get stuck in point B, where we grieve and cry and get scared and fall in love and get left and wish that we could outlive our line or draw a better one." She pointed to the center of the mark, her finger lingering on the page. "But that's the beauty of point B. No one's is exactly the same. This is the only line you've been drawn, Reggie. And it's unfair that one line is all you get, but it's all any of us get. The only way to waste it would be to not live it. And to not love the people who walk their own."

"Like a tightrope," I said.

She stared at the page, her expression puzzled. "Huh. I guess it is."

Monday, I returned to the gossip-fueled bane of my existence (see: school). Karen had suggested getting back into my usual monotonous routine to help me cope with what she called this "spiritual hurdle" I was jumping over. It was funny, because it felt more like a crushing boulder the size of a very familiar house by the pond. But I wouldn't dare insinuate that my "spiritual hurdles" were linked to more than physical forms of dying.

A girl named Taylor in my U.S. history class told me her family was praying for my dad. My chemistry teacher gave me an article to read that felt a lot like *Coma Facts for Dummies.* Here and there, someone who knew a guy who knew a guy told me how sorry they were and promised to do anything they could to help. I wanted to tack a banner to my locker that said LEAVE ME THE [non-Karen-approved expletive] ALONE. I wanted to scream and beat the desks with baseball bats and kick the walls because my dad was dying, and the guy I hated in the best way was having a baby soon, and my chosen hobby was quickly becoming staring at the cracks between hospital tiles and hating the mere act of inhale-exhale. But people needed to feel like they were helping, I guess.

Carla didn't show up to school that day. It kind of made sense. I wouldn't have gone to school either if my friends abandoned me the way hers did, and my baby's dad didn't want to be with me, and my stomach was heavy enough to sink me to the bottom of the pond. The more pity glances I got, the more I wondered how Carla had done it all this time. I hated to consider it, but maybe she was stronger than I'd ever given her credit for.

Polka sat with me at my house that night while my mom

and Frankie stayed at the hospital. Karen made me take the home-alone teenager oath that I wouldn't party it up with my extensive group of friends (see: Polka), and that I would finally get around to typing my paper. I could hardly argue. It was due Friday and the only words I'd typed were my name.

And I did work on it. Sort of. I typed random thoughts that kept me up at night, random thoughts that wouldn't shut up. English enthusiasts like myself called it "brain-storming."

- Not everything leaves
- Point B
- The only life we've got
- Wild hearts
- Twizzlers

"How's your paper coming?" I asked Polka. After I typed *Twizzlers*, I knew I was getting nowhere.

"Done," Polka said, smiling behind his MacBook. He sat in my dad's recliner, propped so far back he was practically lying down.

"Did you go with *freedom*?"

"Yeah."

"I bet that was hard to define."

"Not really," he said, wrinkles appearing on his forehead

as he studied the screen. "It make sense to me. Easy to write when it make sense to you."

"I still don't know what to write about," I said, clicking my fingernail against the mousepad.

"Well, what make sense to you?"

I leaned my head back, watching the cursor blink on the page.

Nothing made sense to me. I had so many thoughts I could have drowned in them, but they all felt betrayed when I tried to force them into words. I didn't know how to grab ahold of one and define it so simply. All of my thoughts felt vast and infinite, like the thousands of stars shining above the Ferris wheel. That night, the only thing that had made sense to me was that I was holding Snake's hand. And that I was scared of dying. But more than that, I was terrified of being alive.

"Polka, can I ask you something?"

He sat up and looked at me sideways. My mother's shag rug separated us, and it seemed weirdly coincidental that something always did. Whether it was a picnic table, a desk, or a rug, we were always close enough to reach out and touch each other, and distanced enough not to. I didn't want to upset the delicate system we'd created, but I wanted to know why Polka was so content with being less than a friend and more than an acquaintance. It was strange that he didn't demand more the way most people did.

"Why don't you sit with your friends at lunch?" I asked.

"I don't have friends at lunch."

"Yeah you do. The other exchange guys who eat in the cafeteria. I've heard them invite you, and you never go."

Only briefly did he look up, and just as briefly did his dark eyes reveal a sort of unusual softness. "Because I want to sit with you," he said.

"Why?"

"Because if I don't, you sit alone."

"It's just lunch."

The corner of his lips quivered, but didn't move. It was the closest to smiling he'd ever come. "Then why it matter if I sit with friends or sit with you? It just matter that I sit somewhere."

I looked out the window and thought about pills and letters and lunch tables and things I could never define. But it might not have been about defining anything. It was about recognizing that pain existed and deserved to. That everything I felt, from loneliness to hatred to fear, existed and deserved to. What I tried to understand wasn't the point. The point was that I tried to understand it.

"You can sit with your friends," I told him, after typing *The Definition of Depression* across the page.

He shot me a rare Polka smile. An extraordinarily comforting sight. "Who said I don't?"

CHAPTER twenty-two

CATFISH WERE THE UGLIEST CREATURES TO ever move on the
earth. It was like God made them as a joke just to say,
*Hey, I can make really beautiful things like flowers and Ryan
Gosling, but I can also make the ugliest possible creature any
mind could ever have the displeasure of imagining.* I watched
the slimy excuses for marine life blow bubbles on the surface of the pond, ignorant of their own hideous misfortune.
The dock was wobbly underneath me, like the <u>hundred
pounds of ugly</u> (see: catfish) were forming an anarchy to
take me down. If I'd still been talking to Snake, I would
have demanded that the elusive pond committee fund a res-
toration project immediately.

Carla had texted that Tuesday morning to ask me if I
would meet her on the dock after I left the hospital. Once
again, she'd been a Hawkesbury no-show. Like the Snake

standard, she'd better have been dying, dead, or having a baby for her absence to be permissible. If I had to suffer through seven hours of busywork, social drama, and hardly edible grilled cheese, so should she. But she was Carla Banks. She had money, an intimidating dad, and a giant ginger squash stuffed in her womb, so she could pretty much get out of anything.

I didn't want to talk to her. I didn't want to see her. And I sure as hell didn't want to brave the pond knowing that Snake could come down at any minute and confuse me. I didn't want to hear his voice, and see his much-too-pretty eyes, and listen to one of his arrogant speeches that was actually kind of endearing, and forget why I left him in the first place.

However, there was always the grand *but*. And that particular one was that there wasn't much left to lose. The afternoon could turn out to be a hormonal tearfest or plot for revenge or battle of the ex- and sorta-ex-girlfriend, and it would amount to nothing. I couldn't get hurt any worse.

She made it to the pond only five minutes after I did, her red hair tied back in a curly ponytail. She wore a pink sundress that swelled her up like a pregnant peach. Her stomach was abnormally huge, so much so that I worried about her getting near any sharp objects for fear of popping. That would have been a mess I wasn't willing to clean up.

When she saw me, she grinned like we were old friends

who hadn't seen each other for a stretch. I thought it best not to mention that we were in no way friends and that not seeing her for a stretch would have been what got me grinning. She waddled to the dock and wasted a minute attempting to sit down gracefully beside me. There was nothing graceful about it.

"Thanks for coming," she said, straining to catch her breath from the grueling sit. "I didn't think you would. I know you have a lot on your plate, with your dad and every-thing—"

"I thought if you saw my disinterest in person, you'd get the hint that I'm not your BFF."

"I got the hint when you didn't answer my first fifteen calls." She smiled. "Thanks for that."

"Anytime. And for the record, calling someone fifteen times in thirty minutes could be considered harassment. It's unethical."

"So is stealing a pregnant girl's boyfriend, but I didn't fault you for it." She smirked at how well she was keeping pace.

"Touché. But I didn't steal him. We were never dating. I'm sure he made it sound that way, though."

"Don't worry. I know he's very skilled in embellish-ment." She caressed her stomach with her hands. There was a solemnity in her eyes that seemed like too deep a feeling for her. She didn't look like picture-perfect Little

Miss Flashburn. "How come all of our conversations end in Snake?"

"He's the only thing we have in common." I shrugged and tore off a splintered piece of wood from the dock and tossed it in the water.

"Is he? Because we knew each other years before we met him."

"Yeah, but we weren't friends. You were captain of the prissy posse, remember?"

She smiled, embarrassed at the reminder of her seventh-grade self. "That lasted one month. Tops." She gazed across the lake, the water bobbing in her eyes. "We should have been friends."

"Me and you? Friends?" I faked a laugh. "That would have never worked."

"Why not?"

"Because you're you. You're beauty-pageant, mansion-by-the-pond material, and I'm the one who quietly mocks your kind from across town. It's a delicate balance. It would have been detrimental to our health to upset it."

She looked at me with amusement and curiosity, but also a hint of grief. Grief for herself, or me, or her baby. It was hard to tell. It was oddly not Carla. Truthfully, it was a familiar despondency. Like looking in a mirror.

"I don't think that's me anymore," she whispered, her voice floating through the crisp air. "Something changed when I got pregnant. I can't explain it. It's like, all the things I cared about before seem so ridiculous now."

"Like what?"

"Like prom. Before I got pregnant, I would have gone dress shopping with my friends and taken pictures and danced with my boyfriend, and it would have been the most exciting thing to happen to me all year. But it wasn't like that. I wore a maternity dress I had to buy online, and my friends didn't even talk to me, and I didn't want to take pictures because I looked bloated. And Snake, well . . . let's just say the evening was a far cry from 'Ohmigod, this is so romantic.' I mean, we danced and everything, but none of it felt the way it was supposed to." She sighed, staring down at her stomach.

New Carla was having quite the uncomfortable effect on me. It was similar to compassion. Sympathy, maybe? Whatever it was, I didn't like it. Carla and I couldn't . . . get along. A bearable Carla who was potentially half friend material defied the laws of sanity. But I was understanding her in ways I hadn't before. And her life was almost as twisted and senseless as mine. And I just . . .

I couldn't hate her the way I wanted to.

"What did it feel like?" I asked.

She glanced at me, chewing on her bottom lip. A guilty expression took over and she drew nervous circles on her belly. "That's actually why I wanted to meet you here. I wanted to talk to you about that night." She took a breath, readying herself for what I anticipated was something I really didn't want to hear. If it dealt with Snake, it would be too much for me. I would care, and I couldn't. I couldn't let myself. She spoke anyway. "I kissed Snake after prom."

She looked away instantly, watching the catfish fight over a piece of food. A sensation of jealousy rushed over me, but I forced myself to repress it. Dr. Rachelle wouldn't have advised the burial of emotion, but it seemed like the right thing to do. And though I was hardly in the business of doing the right thing, Carla's guilt made me want to try. It made me want to try, because she shouldn't have felt guilt for wanting to be happy. Hurting others to survive was a Flashburn epidemic. God knew we were all infected.

"Did it change the way you feel about him?" I asked. The second I said it, I realized that I had been so caught up in Snake, so caught up in me, that I had never stopped to ask Carla how she felt about any of it. My depression-centered selfishness had struck again.

"Yes." She said it boldly, as if discovering her voice for the first time. "He didn't kiss me back the way he used to. He just kind of looked at me like I was an obligation, or something. And it hurt my feelings at the time, but looking back, I get it. We've been forcing something that's just . . . not there. I've been trying to love him for Little Man, but I don't. And he doesn't. It's not that consuming, passionate, can't-breathe-without-each-other intensity that love is supposed to be. I'd rather us be apart and okay than together and not. Except that, right now, he's not okay. And I think you might have something to do with that."

"Me?" I asked, wondering how much Snake had told her. There was an air of freedom to being known, but it was a staggering freedom. Being known made me vulnerable, and I didn't want the shame that came with it. But if anyone besides Snake were to know me, I was starting to be glad it was Carla.

"He's depressed," she whispered, as if it were a scandalous revelation.

"Really?"

I played it cool, but deep down was in sidesplitting laughter at the notion of Snake's depression being news.

"He won't leave his room for anything other than school. He even called out of work this week. When he came over to my house to pick up his paycheck, he said all of two words the entire time he was there." She shook her head. "I went to his house and demanded that he tell me what was going on, and he said you guys aren't talking anymore. That he doesn't feel like himself. I thought it was pathetic at first, but now I think it's sad. He's so blatantly in love with you, Reggie. He's miserable."

I could picture Snake buried beneath his covers, countless packages of Twizzlers emptied on his floor. I bet he drew the blinds. I bet he lay in darkness and listened to the disturbing lameness of the Renegade Dystopia until his body got too heavy to bother keeping him awake. If Carla was right, he was in full Disconnect mode. He was frozen. Unreachable. He was broken because I was scared. I thought I had mastered the art of hating, but knowing that I was the reason for Snake's Disconnect was an entirely new kind.

"He'll get over it," I muttered, brushing away the image.

"I don't think he will. I've never seen him this upset."

"I can't be with him, Carla," I snapped. "We would never work. He's having a hard time seeing it, but the sooner he realizes it, the better. If you want, I'll text him and tell him to stop acting like a wimp and start paying more attention to you."

"I don't want him paying more attention to me. That's not the point I'm trying to make. What I'm trying to say is, he's better when you're around. He's happy. Believe it or not, as mean as you are, you can change someone for the better. That's no small feat, especially when that someone is Snake." She rubbed her stomach, a calmness in her hands. In her eyes. She was at peace about the way things had turned out. The girl with the most to fear, and she wasn't scared. Unfortunately for me, it was an admirable bravery. "I don't know what's holding you back. I don't know if it's me, or Little Man, or your dad, or yourself. What I do know is, our lives are messy and weird and won't work out perfectly for any of us. We're all entirely screwed no matter what, so we might as well do what makes us happy. Snake loves you. It's as simple as that. And if you love him, then love him. You two are miserable enough together. Without each other, you're nightmares."

I laughed, and she laughed, and amid the madness of being us, it didn't feel so out of place. The catfish bumped the dock underneath our feet, water splashing onto our skin as we soaked in the insanity of being young. And terrified. And depressed and pregnant and erratic and alive.

"Is this your official blessing?" I joked, tossing a pebble into the water.

"No. You still stole my boyfriend, whore," she quipped, smiling while she attempted to fake a glare. "This is my 'I won't write dirty things about you on bathroom mirrors' speech."

"If that courtesy is expected to go both ways, I'm going to need a washcloth and some cleaning solution."

She smiled, her golden eyes fixated on me like she was glad I was there. Like she was glad our messes collided. "Are we friends now?"

"No."

"How about now?"

"No. We can be friendly acquaintances, but that's all you get."

"I'll take it."

We sat side by side, and no one said a word. It was frustratingly pleasant.

"By the way," she said, the sun striking gold in her eyes, "if you do end up dating Snake, don't have sex. You'll get pregnant and die."

"*Mean Girls*?"

"That movie is remarkably educational."

I didn't know if I would open up to Snake again. I wasn't sure if I would take the hurt and the love and wait for the impact to kill me. But it didn't matter. What mattered was that the sun was still the sun. What mattered was that I was breathing swampy, humid air that smelled like nature and piss, and I hated Carla in the good way, and I wasn't alone.

CHAPTER twenty-three

"REGGIE?" CARLA SHOUTED INTO THE PHONE, her voice nervous and panicked. I could hear low rumblings in the background. "I need to ask you a huge favor!"

It was Saturday morning. I was resting in the window seat in my dad's hospital room, my journal perched in my lap. He was still comatose, his machines beeping and clicking like they had been for two weeks. His heart hadn't given up on him yet.

The moment Carla's name had flashed across my screen, I'd considered not answering. One afternoon at the pond and a few semikind sentiments, and suddenly I was her go-to person. She'd texted me on Wednesday to "make sure I was doing okay" and left me a message on Thursday to "see how I was holding up." She needed to get a life. Then again, I needed to be meaner.

I answered the phone anyway, because I didn't want to hurt her feelings or be roped into another waterside heart-to-heart. I rued the day I became a <u>good person</u> (see: worst kinds of people).

"I'm a little busy," I replied, adding a sentence to my entry. "Call one of your friends. Olivia, or someone."

"You know we aren't talking anymore." Her voice quivered like she had been crying all morning. "I want it to be you."

"Want what to be me?"

"I'm at the hospital," she said, as a man's voice demanded a glass of water in the background. "I started having contractions during the night. I need you to come be my coach like you did in birthing class."

"You can't be serious." My disbelieving laugh echoed into the speaker. I paused and waited for her to say that she was kidding. She didn't. "You're serious?"

"My stepmom can't get off work in time, my dad is no help, and pigs would have to fly over a frozen hell before I would let Snake watch me give birth." She yelled something to her dad away from the phone before bringing it back to her lips. "I just need someone to hold my hand and give encouragements. You did it once before."

"That was pretend, Carla," I said. My mom raised a brow at me as she walked into the room with a bag of McDonald's. She handed me a hot chocolate and mouthed something indecipherable when she noticed my journal.

"Please," Carla pleaded. I didn't have to see her to know that she was crying. "I can't do this by myself."

She blubbered into the phone, a nurse spewing information behind her. I heard the words *dilated* and *pushing*. The reality of giving birth was already making me queasy, and I wasn't even the one who had to do it.

"Is Snake there?"

"He's on his way. Please, come."

Good deeds were the absolute worst. Worse than depression. Worse than waiting rooms. Worse than the worst kinds of people. They were the worst because they were compulsive. And as much as I'd never intended to yell *push* while a girl I barely tolerated gave birth to the spawn of the guy who made me care, good deeds and pesky compassion trumped my aversions.

"Are you at Central?" I asked.

It was like I could hear her smile. "Yeah. Second floor."

"I'm on the third floor with my dad. I'll come down."

"Thank you!" she yelled. "Thank you so much! You don't even know."

"Don't thank me yet. I haven't decided how encouraging my encouragements will be."

"I'm sure you'll say the right thing. You're not as bad as you think you are."

The call clicked out.

My mom was digging into a bacon and cheese bagel, highlighting passages in her devotional book. "Who was that?" she asked.

"Carla." I closed my journal and slid it under the cushion. "She's having her baby."

She glanced at me, and where there should have been self-righteous judgment, there was an unbelievable lack of disapproval. Her hand glided along a verse as she painted it neon yellow. "She wants you to be there? I didn't realize the two of you were friends."

"We're not," I said, though I was starting to lose my footing. If I kept up with these Carla-inspired good deeds, I was going to have to ditch my friendless image. That might not have been such a bad thing. "She doesn't have anyone else. It's not right that she should have to go through that alone."

"Will Snake be there?" she asked.

"Yeah."

"Good."

I wondered if I'd heard her correctly.

"Good?"

"Yes. He's taking responsibility for himself." She looked at me, the glare from the window making it difficult to see her eyes behind her glasses. "I still don't like him. But I've been doing a lot of praying, and I've discussed the situation with Frankie, and you know what they say—God is the giver of second chances. Who knows? Maybe there's a good boy underneath all that rebellion."

"There is," I whispered.

She smiled. "There better be."

If it weren't for the shrill beep of the machines and the sunlight casting heat against my back and my palms sweaty with shock and nerves, I wouldn't have believed that the woman speaking was my mother. My mother who always kept her distance. My mother who never tried to understand anyone. And she was giving Snake, possibly the hardest heart to learn, a second chance. Maybe I wasn't the only one getting better.

"He's not a bad guy," I said as I moved to the door. She was watching me leave and not trying to stop me. And I think she understood, or at least was trying to. It was all I could ask for. "He's no more flawed than the rest of us."

"Maybe not," she said quietly, glancing at the clock across the room.

"Mom?" I looked into her eyes, and for once I felt like they were really seeing me. "You quit your job for me, didn't you? To take care of me?"

She didn't look surprised. I think she knew I'd figure it out eventually, even if it took longer than we both would have liked. "Everything I do is for you, sweetheart."

Against myself, against reason, I felt the urge to hug her.

She didn't know how to take it when I dove and wrapped my arms around her body, burying my head in her wiry hair. I felt her tremble, but I knew she wouldn't cry. Like me, she was sick of crying.

"You should go," she whispered against my neck. "I think Little Carla could use a friend right about now."

I nodded before running out the door. And for once, I didn't feel shame in what I was leaving behind.

When I made it to Carla's room on the second floor, her dad was seated in a chair against the wall. He was clad in a flashy three-piece suit that made him look like a secret service man avowed to protect Carla's royal baby. His graying hair was combed over with so much force I didn't question that he was balding and <u>insecure</u> (see: pond people).

Carla perked up when she noticed me in the doorway, her hair plastered to her face with sweat. There was a lump of needles jabbing into her arms. She waved me over. "You don't know how happy I am to see you," she said, her makeup-less eyes puffy and bulging. In the past two months, I had come to know many versions of Carla I didn't know before. Angry Carla. Strong Carla. Independent Woman Carla. But none was as pitiable as Crybaby Carla. Even that version wasn't too intolerable, though. "They said I'm going to start pushing soon."

"Can't wait," I muttered.

Her phone buzzed on the table. "Will you get that

for me?" I handed it to her, and she read the screen, relief washing over her. "Snake's here. He's in the lobby down the hall."

Her dad got to his feet, towering over me—my head was at his stomach. No wonder Carla blindly obeyed everything he said. He was a real-life giant. "He's not going to be in here for the birth," he reiterated, as if to remind Carla he was in charge of her child and her life and her ex-boyfriend and anything related to her at all.

"I know, Dad," she groaned, making a shoot-me motion where only I could see. "Neither are you, so you can go wait with him now."

"But I—"

"Go, Dad. Seriously."

He scowled, eyeing Carla as if he were about to pitch a rebuttal like he was at one of his business meetings. Then he huffed and stormed out of the room toward the waiting area.

Carla sighed exaggeratedly. "I can't believe he listened. I thought I was going to have to call my stepmom and have her threaten him."

"He doesn't seem easily intimidated."

"He's not. When it comes to my stepmom, however, he's as easily manipulated as a five-year-old boy."

She rested her head against the pillow and closed her eyes, both arms wrapped around her stomach as her forehead crinkled into a bunch of little lines. "This hurts so bad," she moaned. "Finals are next week. He couldn't have waited to come until after then? He's been in there nine months; what's another week?"

"I don't think it works like that," I said, leaning against the armrest. "And you might as well get used to having him around at finals, because he'll be here for all your finals to come."

"I asked you here to be encouraging, not to scare me to death."

"I told you not to trust me."

"Well, I do trust you." She opened her eyes and looked at me, completely unguarded. "In spite of the whole Snake fiasco, you're one of the few people I trust. Don't go acting like we're not sort of friends."

I opened my mouth to counter with some sarcastic remark that would delay the inevitable truth that maybe she was right. But I never got the chance.

Two nurses appeared with the doctor, informing us that it was time to start the miracle process that was hardly a miracle when you considered the fact that an entire floor of the hospital was dedicated to women all doing the exact same thing and rearing the exact same result. But, whatever, we would go with miracle.

I sat beside her head and stared at nothing but the wall. I was sure that if I even thought about rotating at any sort of angle that would land me a glimpse of the unspeakable, I would turn into a pillar of salt like that lady from the Bible. Stuff started happening, and I mental-blocked every last bit of it. The only thing I didn't forget was the way Carla looked at me and said, "I can't do this. I'm scared to be alone."

I smiled. She probably didn't know how to handle a Reggie smile. I took her hand, and a tear slid down her cheek. She looked bewildered. And disoriented. And strangely okay.

"You're not alone," I told her.

The infamous miracle process lasted an extensive period of time, filled with tears and abnormal shrieking and scarring sounds I all but burned from my memory. One minute I was staring at a wall and wanting it to collapse on top of me to spare me the experience, and the next I'm hearing another shrieking, bloodcurdling cry. Except that time, it wasn't Carla.

I looked at her face and had never seen her so tired and sweaty and worn out. She was wrecked, but her eyes were something else entirely. You would have thought someone had just handed her the key to happiness and the lock was attached to this gross, bloody baby the doctor placed in her arms.

I'd never believed in the maternal, love-at-first-sight propaganda people always tried to sell. Like, you see this underdeveloped mutant thing for the first time and it steals your love in an instant. But as it cried, and Carla cried, and it pressed its hand to her chest, I thought that maybe there was a chance it existed.

The doctor cleaned the baby off, wrapped him in a blanket, and put a tiny blue beanie on him. Carla held him in her arms, brushing his cheek with her fingertip.

"He's beautiful," she whispered, pressing her cheek to his forehead. "Ohmigod, I love him."

"Someone's here to see his little boy," the nurse announced, stepping aside and motioning him in.

Snake stood in the doorway, dressed in his THE RENEGADE DYSTOPIA T-shirt that he had worn the first time I met him. This time, coupled with frayed jeans and dirty sneakers. He glanced at me and then at Carla, like he didn't know how to process everything at once. His hair was messier than usual, his blue eyes drifting and overwhelmed. Carla looked at him and smiled, and he smiled back at her. A beaming Snake smile. Seeing it almost made the separation worth it.

He walked to the edge of the bed and caught a glimpse of the baby.

To that day, I had seen Snake at what I thought were his best moments. When he talked about the snake and the mouse with wonder and admiration. When he filmed the sky with pride in his ability to capture uselessness. When he sang like he didn't care how terrible it sounded. When he stared at me, not wanting to waste his opportunities, not knowing why he couldn't stop. All of those moments were happy and easy and as alive as either of us ever thought we would be.

But those fleeting pleasures paled in comparison to the Snake who looked at his shriveled little baby for the first time. He didn't need a pill or me or Carla to give him a feeling. He wasn't wanting too much. He wasn't needing. He was fearless in his disposition, no matter how pointless it could be. He was as messy as the way he chose to love, but through it he was finding the greatest privilege of being alive.

Fearing nothing.

"You want to hold him?" Carla asked.

He nodded. Carla gently placed the baby in the nook he made with his folded arms. He couldn't keep the dorky grin off his face when the baby opened his eyes and looked at him. "Bad news, Carla," he said. It was the first time I'd heard his voice in nearly two weeks. It was also the first time I'd heard him call her anything other than babe. "He's got blue eyes."

"So?"

"So I have blue eyes. And you don't." He looked at her

and smirked. "I think he's going to look like me."

"All babies have blue eyes when they're first born. Give them time to darken."

He lifted up on the hat. "Bad news part two. He has some hair, and it's not red."

"Shut up." She smiled. "I'll deal with his uncanny resemblance to you later."

He kissed the baby's forehead. "Consider yourself lucky, Little Man," he whispered. He glanced over at me for a moment. And it was like I'd never left him. He wasn't mad or distant or craving something to fill the void.

We were surviving. But more than that, we were okay. Only okay and nothing more.

"I'm glad you guys are here. I pictured this going a lot differently," Carla said, her eyes scanning from Snake to me. "I like the way it went."

"Do you have a name picked out?" I asked her.

"Preston," she answered. "Preston Henry Banks."

That name was one of <u>God's great jokes</u> (see: catfish) (also see: my life). And by Snake's subtle grimace, I knew he agreed. But he didn't say anything because he wanted to keep her happy. It was a small price to pay in the long run.

"It's perfect," he said. "Preston Henry Eliot."

"Banks," she corrected with a glare. "Someone has to carry on my family legacy."

"Your family legacy of unreasonably priced soft serve?" I taunted.

Snake laughed, but didn't look up from the baby's tiny blue eyes.

Mr. Banks came in only minutes later, followed by Snake's moms. There was excessive cooing and balloons and family pictures and talk of how beautiful a baby Preston was. I stayed for most of it, because every time I tried to sneak out, Carla called me back in and ordered me to stay. Snake's complaints about her bossiness were not the slightest bit unfounded.

An hour later, I received a text from my mom telling me to rush upstairs immediately. My stomach dropped when I read the words, knowing that what awaited me could change my life forever. My point B could be my dad's point C. It could be his end and my middle. My pain to endure.

I said goodbye to Carla and ran out of the room without giving her a chance to stop me. When I was halfway to the elevators, I heard a familiar voice call from behind.

"Wait!"

I turned around and saw Snake standing in the hallway, his arms dangling at his sides.

"I just wanted to say thanks for helping Carla. I can imagine it was quite the challenge for you."

"She's not completely insufferable," I replied. "Good

luck with the fatherhood thing. I'm sure that's quite the challenge for you."

"It's not completely insufferable. Where you headed?"

"Third floor. My mom said to come as soon as I can. I don't know why."

He looked concerned for me, like he wanted to help but knew he couldn't. He wanted to be with me and not. He had his own point B.

"I'm here if you need anything."

"I know," I said, hitting the elevator button.

"I guess I'll see you around."

The doors opened. I glanced at him over my shoulder, and knew that I wasn't walking away. This absence wasn't the permanent kind. We were only as temporary as we chose to be.

"See you around."

CHAPTER twenty-four

SOME POINT C'S WERE REACHED UNFAIRLY. When a person felt too young to let go of their line, but knew they were too old to mourn the length of the line they were given. Many hit point C with dread and regret and a resentment for the beautiful messes they had left in their wake. And maybe one day my dad would reach point C and he would determine his line too short and insufficient and plain unfair. But as I sat beside his bed and saw his eyes—open, awake, clutching point B for as long as it would allow him—I knew today wasn't one day. Eventually, "one day" would screw us all. But in the present we were alive. Temporarily and chaotically alive.

"We prayed for you every day," my mother cried, her hand holding tightly to my dad's. His glasses were back where they belonged, lopsided on the edge of his nose. His eyes were as lifeless as they'd ever been, but they weren't dead. Not yet. "Frankie read you some of your favorite verses. Even Reggie prayed."

My dad's eyes gradually shifted from Mom to Frankie to me, lingering on me the longest. "Is that true?" he whispered, his voice hoarse.

"Yes," I answered. "I didn't think it would work."

Despite his weariness, his lips moved upward into a lazy smile. "It doesn't always. That's the great thing about prayer. We don't get everything we ask for."

"Well, we got what we asked for," my mom said.

Frankie, who was standing by Blondie on the opposite side of the bed, bent down and touched my dad's arm gently. "How do you feel?" he asked.

My dad looked thrown for a moment. The skin around his eyes crinkled, and he concentrated on the wall as if the perfect answer was scribbled on the surface. Then he relaxed, and his eyes were tremendously still. He wasn't looking at Frankie, but at me. And he was pleased. Pleased with himself like the day in the basement when he promised me that nothing ever died. Maybe it didn't.

"I'm just happy to be alive," he said, releasing my mother's hand and reaching for mine. I wrapped my fingers around his palm without hesitating. I had wanted to hold his hand from the moment I had walked through the door. It was cold, but like his eyes, it wasn't dead.

Neither was I.

"Me too," I said.

My mother glanced at me, unable to conceal her contented smile. Her eyes watered and her lip quivered so badly she had to bite it to keep it still. She reached for my other hand, and I let her take it. I wasn't the only one who deserved to be understood.

"Love you," she mouthed. She was crying as her lips moved. She meant it like a prayer. I nodded so she would know that I loved her too.

It had taken me too long to realize that, but I did. I was capable of caring, and that didn't make me weak. It hurt more than it didn't. It hurt too much, sometimes. But if love didn't hurt, I might not have felt it at all. Accepting the pain of it made the <u>good parts</u> (see: answered prayer) easier to see.

CHAPTER twenty-five

A WEEK LATER, MY DAD WAS released.

I went to see Dr. Rachelle while my parents visited Pastor James. She sat in her usual spot when I arrived, holding her clipboard loosely in her lap. When she spotted the journal in my hands, she looked so nontherapist I wondered if she was even the same woman. I took a seat on the couch knocking the journal against my leg as I waited for her to start with her basic, pre-heavy-stuff checklist.

But she never said a word.

I looked up to find her watching me, a subtle smile pulling on her lips. She pointed to the journal.

"I see you've finally done your homework," she said. It wasn't an accusation, but a weird sort of appreciation.

"Yeah," I muttered, playing with the binding. "I screwed up, though."

"Oh?"

"I didn't exactly follow directions."

I extended the journal to her.

She took it slowly, opening to the first page. Her lips drew back into a full smile when she read the heading scribbled sloppily across the top.

"'What depression means to me,'" she read. She looked up, her eyes glued to mine. "No, you certainly didn't."

"I couldn't define *crazy*, because there's too many interpretations. And I couldn't define *lonely*, because it's too big an emptiness. I don't understand all the things I am, and I sure as hell don't know how to explain them to you." I leaned forward, mentally rebuking myself for stealing her spotlight. "But *depression*. Depression is only as complex as the person who's defining it. It's whatever I choose to make it."

She rubbed her fingers along the words. "And what have you chosen to make it?"

"Simple. I think the more you try to convince yourself that you don't need something, the more you need it. And I've only recently realized that needing is something I can survive. Like pain. It's surprisingly bearable."

She stared at the page, a familiar hope in her eyes. "So, where's the line?" she asked. "Between what's bearable and what isn't?"

I shrugged, staring back at her. Unafraid. "I guess the line is wherever you draw it."

She almost looked teary, which made me uncomfortable, because despite the fact I'd grown used to dealing with <u>criers</u> (see: Carla), other people's emotions still weren't my strong suit. I watched her mark something on the clipboard, and I had a pretty good feeling it wasn't "emotionally unavailable."

Before I left that day, I made her promise to read the entry when I wasn't still around. I wasn't big on hearing my feelings repeated back to me once I'd already felt them. And I was afraid she'd tell me how proud she was of my progress, which could have gone <u>south</u> (see: hugging).

I stopped in the doorway on my way out, suddenly remembering that needs weren't specific to me. "By the way, I have an answer for you," I said.

She spun her chair around, still grasping my book tightly. "Answer for what?"

"What to do when you're alone on a street corner." I smiled and pulled my bag onto my shoulder. "Look up."

Later, I visited the pharmacy to pick up my prescription. This time sans my mother, who after much coaxing had reapplied for a position at the daycare. Initially, she tried to use my dad as a cop-out, saying that someone needed to keep an eye on him in case his condition took a bad turn. But I knew she wasn't worried about my dad so much as she was doing what she'd always secretly done — taking care of me. After promising her that I would be okay as long as she was happy, or at least some version of it, she begrudgingly agreed to follow her passion right to the <u>kiddie kennel</u> (see: daycare).

I stood in the back of the store, rocking on my heels while I waited for my name to be called over the intercom. The pharmacists scurried around from shelf to shelf, checking labels and dealing with ornery customers shouting demands from the drive-thru window. As an old man yelled about how long he'd been waiting in line, I heard another loud voice behind me. A voice I knew. A voice like home. I turned around, letting life in its pitiful and never-ending cycle bring me full circle.

The first thing I noticed was his hair, not hanging scruffily in his face, but clean-cut, to the top of his brows. His blue eyes were unconcealed, sparkling as they stared at me, not afraid of being seen. Of course, the weirdness of his haircut was in competition with his blue T-shirt that bore the phrase ALLERGIC TO STUPIDITY. In his hand was a basket filled with diapers, baby wipes, and a stick of deodorant.

He took a step closer, smirking with all the Snake-ish presumptuousness he could possibly attain in one grin. "Well, whaddya know? I see you're still popping pills."

"I could say the same about you." I motioned to his basket. "You know, lavender-scented Dove is for women."

"It's for Carla. I'm heading over there later."

I laughed. "She's got you buying her toiletries now? Your back must be sore from that whip."

He hung his head with a smile, but his hair didn't cover his eyes like it used to. There was something about him that seemed so different. Not necessarily his haircut or his clothes or his basket full of diapers, but a vague change. It was like he'd aged five years in just a matter of weeks, growing out of Snake the rebellious, charming boy into Snake the man. I wondered if he saw the same when he looked at me.

"How's your dad?" he asked, looking up again.

"Got released two weeks ago. The doctors said he'll be fine."

"That's good. And you?" He moved closer, switching his basket to the other hand. I spotted a new tattoo blazed into his wrist that said PHB. "Are you doing fine?"

No one but Snake could have eyes as dull as they were bright, as numb as they were vibrant and inconceivable. He was the emotion between two slim spaces, the line drawn between contentment and devastation. I wasn't sure which one he was in the expanse of time he waited for my answer. I only knew that I was both, and neither one was worth fearing anymore.

I pointed at his wrist to avoid the subject. "Another crappy tattoo, huh?"

A smile spread across his lips, and he rubbed the mark

with his index finger. "Yep. Preston's initials. Got it a few days after he was born."

"Did your moms never teach you that tattoos are irreversible?"

"Well, my love for him is irreversible, so it's fitting."

I slapped my hand across my face. "Oh my God, you're becoming one of *those* dads."

"What?" He laughed, half self-consciously.

"Please tell me you don't carry a three-by-two photo of him in your wallet."

His reached into his pocket and grabbed his wallet, flipping it open to a professionally shot photograph of Preston lying naked on a fur rug. "You caught me."

"If I ever see you wearing socks with sandals, we're never speaking again."

He tucked the wallet away and watched me with a pretty, weirdly mature expression. "So that means we're speaking again?"

My name echoed across the intercom, cutting me off before I could say something I would regret. Before I could tell Snake that I was more miserable without him than with him. That I wasn't scared of getting hurt anymore. That being close to him at all, whether as a girlfriend or friend or just some girl, was enough for me. The medicine aisle wasn't the ideal place to finally admit what I'd always known he wanted to hear:

We were worth it.

I nabbed my prescription from the counter and told him goodbye. And just as I was about to leave, he called, "Reggie!"

I spun around, and his eyes were dripping with every existing feeling. One look, and I knew I'd been wrong when I said we only had a scrap of useful passion. He felt it all, and found ways to keep feeling more.

"Can I come over sometime?" he asked.

I didn't answer.

He must have taken that as a yes because he showed up at my house a few days later with Preston in tow. He walked straight into my living room like he'd received a formal invite (plot twist: he didn't), plopping down on the couch and setting Preston's car seat on the floor beside him.

"This is the first time I've sat on your couch," he said, hitting the cushion. "Better not tell your mother the heathen's been here. She'll burn it."

My shoulder brushed his as I sat beside him. It was the first time I'd touched him in nearly a month. It was the first time being next to him, huddled close, didn't feel any more wrong than it felt right.

"Doubtful," I said, watching Preston's little blanket move up and down as he breathed. He really was Snake's Mini Me, cute enough to make even a baby hater like me soften just a little. "She's on this new kick where she's all understanding and kind. It's disgusting."

"I don't believe you. That doesn't sound like the Karen we know and barely put up with."

"I guess you're not the only one who's allowed to change."

"You think I've changed?"

"I think we both have."

He glanced at his hands. "I don't feel the way I used to. I don't know why. I'm not sure if it's Preston, or finally being in a good place with Carla, but I haven't eaten a Twizzler in three weeks. Three weeks. I've never done that before."

"So you think you're not depressed anymore because you cut licorice from your diet?"

"No," he said. "I think I've lost the urge to need. And I think I've already been as depressed as I'll ever be."

I thought about my dad and how empty the world seemed when I tried to imagine it without him. How everything reminded me of despair — real, hollowing, pit-in-your-stomach despair. It was nothing more than fearing my own darkness.

"You were afraid," I said, sinking closer to him. He smelled like baby powder and not like strawberry. "Without me, there was nothing to distract you from the pain."

He placed his hand in mine, and I slid my fingers through his. We sat like that for only a fraction of an instant, but an instant was enough. I didn't dread the temporariness of us.

"When you stopped talking to me, I was in the worst place I'd ever been in. I couldn't eat or get out of bed or do anything, really. It was horrible. I thought I wouldn't survive it. But seeing you at the hospital changed something. I realized it wasn't your job to make me better. Only I could do that. And I can. I can survive without you. I can survive without needing you to fix me. And maybe I'll never be completely okay, but I know I'll never be completely broken, either. And that's life, I guess. Survival. That's the tightrope." He ran his thumb along my wrist.

"It gets better," I said. I'd never believed it more than I did then.

He glanced at his sleeping baby, his face lighting up. "Life is a hell of a lot more generous than I was giving it credit for."

Our eyes met, we both smiled, and inevitably it happened. I don't know if it was his will or my own, but our lips fell together, and his hand clutched my neck, and we were a tangled mess of recklessness and hurt and depression and existence. It didn't matter if I loved him. It didn't matter if I didn't. It mattered that I could feel him, feel everything, and not need to hate it.

He and I would never last. Even the happiness of now

couldn't delude us into believing that. But as long as there was a *now*, there was no use in worrying about a later.

"I have something you need to see," he whispered against my lips.

I glanced from him to Preston. "Now is not the time."

"Reggie Mason, what a dirty mind you have. That is not the something I'm talking about." He grabbed my hand and held Preston's car seat with the other, dragging us both up the stairs. Once we reached the top, he nodded down the hallway. "Point me to your room, will you?"

I led him into my bedroom, pausing to let him laugh at the bareness of it. The white bed, the empty walls, the uncluttered desk. Not all of us could be grunge band poster enthusiasts (see: emo narcissistic dicks).

"It's . . . yellow," he tried to say through the laughter. "Like, the happiest color in the rainbow."

"Karen's tried every trick in the book." I sat down on the bed, moving toward the wall to make room.

He unstrapped Preston from his car seat and cradled the baby's head to his chest, leaning back against the headboard. Using his free hand, he reached into his back pocket and retrieved a DVD case with a white label reading THE SHEER USELESSNESS OF OUR CONDITION. I finally knew what this little setup was. A makeshift movie premiere.

He noticed the twitch in my mouth as I tried desperately

not to smile, and his smirk grew to full width. "And without further ado," he announced, waving the disc at me, "I present to you *The Sheer Uselessness of Our Condition*. Directed by the brilliant Snake Eliot. Starring that girl with resting bitch face, Reggie Mason, and Carla Banks, the mother of my awesome child—who would kill me if she knew I didn't show it to her first."

I balled up my fist to punch him, but released it when I realized punching a dude who was holding a baby was probably illegal in Ohio.

I stuck the movie in and let it play. It was everything I didn't know I wanted it to be, and everything I hadn't realized we were until that very instant. Shots of sun rays and lightning and dumpsters and collapsing buildings and bottles of pills. Sped-up shots of Carla holding all her sonograms, of her crying and smiling and talking about all the possible good things that were to come. Of me being miserable and cynical and brutally aware of it all. Of me in the Hawkesbury parking lot theorizing that nothing we do matters, that nothing makes a difference. Voice-overs of Maks and Margaret, all the same as from the sneak peek I'd watched that night in Snake's room. Sad piano pieces, and *The Onslaught* soundtrack lady, and the Renegade Dystopia. Preston lying in his hospital bed blinking wide-eyed at the camera. Carla laughing. Snake and his moms holding Preston, kissing his forehead. Sunshine. Warm colors. Spring spilling into summer.

Nothing gelled perfectly. It was choppy and rough, and didn't fit together no matter how stunning the score, or how seamlessly edited the footage. But it was as real as the people who lived it all. It was our lives on catastrophic display. It was *our* uselessness. And it really, really mattered.

As the screen cut to black, all that was left were Margaret's words.

It's a strange occurrence, walking a tightrope into the night. I once believed that opening my eyes would be scary, a dreadful awareness that my journey would inevitably reach a close. Never did I realize that looking forward was only frightful when I refused to also look to the side, to observe not only the abyss that surrounded me, but the people walking their tightropes alongside my own. And now I know why they say it's better to open your eyes than to blind yourself. If we are all destined to fall into the darkness, at least we'll fall together.

CHAPTER twenty-six

THAT AFTERNOON, WE MET CARLA AT the park. The moment we arrived, she scooped Preston up in her arms and kissed his forehead. Snake leaned against the metal bar, a burp cloth slung over one shoulder and a diaper bag on the other. I took the swing beside Carla, digging my shoes into the mulch.

"Snake, does this onesie really say LADIES' MAN?" Carla asked, rocking Preston back and forth. He was awake and flashing red gums, his Snake-blue eyes taking it all in.

Snake smiled at me from the corner of his eye. "I may have put that on him after I changed his diaper."

"How about you leave his fashion choices to me."

He glanced at me and frowned.

"And you better be coming over tonight," she added, doing a complete 180 from Mommy Carla to Nagging Carla. After all this time, the different Carlas still popped up so quickly they made me do a double-take. "My stepmom's insisting on some big family dinner so you can bond with my dad. You can come too, Reggie."

"I'm not family," I reminded her.

She laughed. "You're my best friend, who's also dating my son's dad. If that's not family, I don't know what is."

"On what planet am I your best friend?" I motioned to Snake. "And since when am I dating this jackass?"

"Oh, we're totally dating," Snake said, his smirk growing into a full-on smile. "And you two are definitely best friends. Just embrace it."

He slid to the ground, his back against the swing set. I watched him unfasten his camera, the familiar light blinking red. I opened my mouth to protest, but realized the lens wasn't aimed at me.

"Again with this?" Carla said, exasperated. "You filmed me breastfeeding last week."

"How was I supposed to know you were breastfeeding?"

"I don't know. Maybe because my boob was out of my shirt?"

"Please tell me I got footage of that."

I cut him a knowing look I knew he'd recognize. "*The Sheer Uselessness of Our Condition: Part 2*?"

He moved the camera away from his face and stared up at me. I didn't want to look away. The only thing more useless than our condition was pretending that it didn't have extraordinary possibilities.

"I guess we'll have to see," he said.

Smiling, I closed my eyes and kicked my legs in fast propelling motions. All that remained was the air, and my desperate need to breathe it. I opened my mouth and let the warmth fill my lungs. There was a time when I would have done this alone. When I would have lifted, torn, clawed my way to the sky inside a bubble. I could return to that life if I thought it was worth it. If feeling pain, even the good kind, proved too frightening. But as I climbed higher, the vibrations of laughter and distorted voices and wind circling my body, nothing had ever been as terrifying as it was necessary. Suddenly, I wasn't tethered to the blackness. I wasn't being thrashed about by the earth. Nothing slowed me down, and nothing stopped me.

I was completely <u>alive</u> (see: happy) and completely aware of it.

WHAT DEPRESSION MEANS TO ME

For: Dr. Rachelle

By Reggie Mason

It's been said that humanity exists in what is called the circle of life, a continuum of time that is characterized by the give and take of a phenomenon that never ceases to exist. However, I choose to liken our experiences to a line. A tightrope, if you will. Humans tread this fine strand, always one misstep away from tumbling into the darkness. This darkness indeed is death, but not merely death of the body. It is death of spirit. Death of hope. Death of heart. Death of wishing to escape the temporariness of time. Whether a person walks alone or alongside another, they are unsuccessful in their attempts to be more than what they are. We are all decay. We are all chaotic. We are all hopelessly flawed. We are all incurably human. And we, all of us, have monstrous hearts.

Some choose to numb their realities with medication or seclusion. We call these people depressed. But what is depression if not an extension of human fatality? What is depression if not a painful awareness of the imminent abyss? What is depression if not a mode of self-preservation?

Nothing on the tightrope can be explained, much less wholly defined. But every indefinable thing has a beginning, and the beginning of understanding depression is simply this:

You're never as alone as you think you are.

ACKNOWLEDGMENTS

Thank you to Houghton Mifflin Harcourt and Margaret Raymo for believing in this story and giving me the incredible opportunity to share my words with the world.

Thank you to my agent, Maria Vicente, and the entire team at P.S. Literary for being champions of my work and seeing this novel through every step of the process.

Thank you to my Pitch Wars mentor, Erica Chapman, for being the first person in the writing community to take me under her wing. I can't express how much your wisdom, support, and kindness have touched my heart and given me the confidence to keep writing.

Thank you to Brenda Drake and the Pitch Wars family for welcoming me with open arms. I would have given up on this story years ago had it not been for you all.

A million thanks to my big sisters—Haley, who just may be my soulmate; Kasey, who takes unparalleled pride in my accomplishments; and Jamie, who calms me down when I'm convinced my antidepressants are sending me into anaphylactic shock. I hate you all in the best way.

To my parents, Buster and Danilynn, who keep me sane, spoil me like a queen, and love me for no reason. Thanks for never trying to tame my wild imagination.

Thanks to everyone who read the manuscript for this story in its early drafts—Natalie Cook, Natalie Williamson, Kayla and Michael Humphreys, and Maureen Lovell—you all are the reason I'm holding this book in my hands.

And to Betty Phelps and Jessica Phelps, my second mother and my adopted sister, thank you for your unconditional love. Without your warmth and snuggles, I would have never survived the path to publication.